Forever Warriors

Forever Warriors

M.J. Sewall

ALSO BY M J SEWALL

Contents

To my daughter, Chelsea.
You're a big reason I'm like this.
Thanks for that.

2004 - SRI LANKA

The sound of David's chains broke the silence.

The two brothers pulled David up the steep hill. The early morning sun was already hot, few people were out to notice the strangers.

"Why couldn't we use handcuffs?" asked Derek.

Earnhardt spoke in his heavy German accent, "I don't trust flimsy, modern handcuffs. Chains are better."

Earnhardt chained David to a tree at the top of the hill, overlooking a vast expanse of ocean. David didn't resist. His back to the tree, facing the sea, he felt the weight of the heavy chains. The burden of the necklace they made him wear was worse. The cold, evil charm chaffed against his skin.

David looked out to the Indian Ocean, marveling at the expanse of blue on blue. He forced his attention to the danger. *I will never help them,* he thought. *At least she's safe.* He caught his own thought and buried it deep. Even stray thoughts were dangerous now.

"Will it be high enough? Can we get out in time?" said Derek, combing fingers through his short blond hair. "So hot already. I think I'm sweating out my breakfast."

"I've told you to stop eating meat, it's bad for you," said Ehrhardt, wiping his sweaty hands on a handkerchief. He surveyed the area, "Yes, this will be high enough."

Derek rattled the chains, "You ready for this, Davy?"

David winced at the nickname, *as though we're friends*, he thought. David said, "You can hold me prisoner, but you can't make me help you."

Ehrhardt said, "Wrong. You will help us. You forced this day by your defiance."

David leaned back harder against the tree, having no idea what would happen next. The tree offered little shade from the sun as David squinted his eyes at the spectacular view.

Derek's slender chest was still breathing heavily. He looked to his older brother, "How old is that body of yours this time? 35? How do you keep fit with just curry and rice?"

Ehrhardt shook his head. "How old is your body? 23? You are panting like a dog because you don't take care of yourself, meat eater."

"I'm a carnivore, I won't apologize." said Derek.

"Barbarian." spat his older brother.

"Vegetarian!" Derek fired back.

Ehrhardt went to the edge of the hill, scanning for the prime spot to begin.

Derek came close to his brother, and whispered, "You sure you're up to this brother? There are other ways to punish him. This is going to put you in bed for a week. There are less extreme ways."

"This will solve several problems, brother," said Ehrhardt. He called to David, "Last chance."

David refused to meet his gaze. Ehrhardt shook his head, then peered out at the expanse. Directly in front of them was the wide Indian Ocean, to their left was the Sri Lankan coast. It was early, and only a few fishing boats were out on the water.

Along the coast there was a mix of huts and luxury buildings. The modern was a backdrop to the past; crude, shanty structures stood at the foot of tall hotels and resorts. An elevated train track snaked along the coastline.

David tried to ignore them, but Derek kept talking, "I'll never get used to the new name Sri Lanka. I liked when they called it Ceylon. It had a pleasant flow on the tongue. They don't even spell the name of their own country right. It should be spelled with an s-h sound. Shri Lanka, not Sri Lanka. What does it mean anyway?"

Ehrhardt said, "It's complicated, but 'venerable island' is about the closest..."

"I really didn't want to know that." Derek shook his head. "How can you not get the hang of rhetorical questions by now? Hey, didn't you have a battle here once?"

"Yes. A few lifetimes ago. In the 1840s I battled an ancient in a sapphire mine. That Viking. I'm sure you remember him."

"Oh, yes." Derek changed the subject back to the matter at hand, "This will be hard on you."

Ehrhardt was resolute. "I'll pay the price. He must know the extent of what we can do. He's the best finder we've ever had. He will obey us."

Derek nodded. They looked at David chained to the tree. He was watching the waves.

Ehrhardt shouted. "I'm taking away your name. From now on we call you the Witness."

"Oooooh. Witness. I like that." Derek said, "I think you may be growing an imagination after all these lifetimes, brother."

The Witness kept looking out, no emotion, his face a mask. But cold sweat ran down his back.

Ehrhardt went to the edge of the hill, dropped to his knees and dug his hands into the grassy earth at his feet. He said some words that David didn't understand, perhaps a mix of several languages. Ehrhardt kept repeating the same words over and over again, digging his fingers deeper into the warm earth.

They all felt something. It seemed to come from all around, but the feeling hit David in the pit of his stomach. It was like they were on a train, used to the vibration on the tracks, then violently lurched to a stop. To compliment the feeling, an image of a train flashed into his mind. David shifted his body to look at the elevated train track.

Ehrhardt repeated himself, getting louder with each word. David looked out to sea, then back to land, but nothing seemed different. Only a moment had passed since the first lurching sensation began. Then the feeling came again. David realized this was no hollow threat. Something terrible was coming.

It was quiet. Deafeningly quiet. Ehrhardt had stopped speaking. He was holding his head as he sat on the ground.

David looked at the brothers, then saw the fish. There were fish everywhere, jumping out of the water by the shore. As David stared, he realized they were not jumping out of the sea. Instead, the water had left them. The ocean had receded back into itself hundreds of feet, leaving the fish flopping, dying.

Derek went to David and grabbed the back of his neck. He forced him to look. "You've earned this, Witness."

David watched the excited children running for the fish, laughing and cheering. But adults were running for the children, yelling at them, clearly terrified. Derek snapped David's head back toward the ocean. It was returning.

A lot of ocean.

A real tsunami is not like a Hollywood special effect. It does not look like a high cresting wave that a surfer would ride. What David witnessed was as though the ocean had multiplied in its brief absence from the shore. Now it was returning at three, four, five times its former size. It was like the land had shrunk, gone flatter, and a huge surge of water was now an invading army.

The voluminous sea swept deeply onto the land, covering trees, buildings. And people, so many people. It rushed in, pushing those on the beach deep into land. The helpless people were swallowed, or smashed against the strange mix of small structures and tall, modern buildings.

"No!" the Witness yelled, but no one could hear him. The earlier silence had surrendered to the shattering destruction below.

Derek pointed. "Uh oh. Train's coming."

A long train on an elevated track, maybe a dozen feet over the streets was approaching. It was barreling right into the former coastline that was now part of the sea.

It came to a slow stop, the elevated track now engulfed in swift, rushing water. People climbed out, to scramble onto the roofs of the train, or nearby structures jutting out of the water.

Then the next surge hit, larger than the first.

The new swell of ocean swallowed the train. Train cars were knocked off the track like they were toys. David could not look away no matter how much he wanted to. He realized he was sobbing.

Ehrhardt rubbed his head while he watched his work.

Derek said. "We had to destroy this breakout instead of using it. Instead of three warriors for us, you get this destruction."

The Witness looked at the brothers, great sobs rocking his body. The tears poured, unable to stop. He didn't even hear the helicopter landing a few dozen feet away.

Derek pursed his lips as though he understood the Witness' pain, showing compassion for the first time since they'd taken him prisoner. Derek came to the Witness and slid his finger under the man's eye, catching his tears. Derek put the wet finger in his own mouth. "Hmmm, despair. Tastes sweet."

They unlocked the chains and had to pry the arms of the Witness from the tree. As they all loaded into the helicopter, Ehrhardt shook his head. "Look what you've done."

PART 1

"Great secrets lurk in unlikely places."
~ Demonis Codex

PRESENT DAY
SEA VALLEY, CALIFORNIA

CHAPTER ONE
ZACKE

Zacke Penna took a deep breath and pushed open the shiny glass doors, stenciled with palm trees flanking a cartoon hamburger. He stood in line behind a boy about sixteen, his own age, but didn't know him. The boy ordered and stepped aside.

"Hello. Welcome to Ocean burgers. How may I help you?" asked the girl at the register.

Zacke gave a shy smile, "Hi. I'm looking for Ted, the manager. I'm supposed to start today."

"Oh. Cool. I'll go get him." The girl smiled back.

The slightly overweight general manager Ted, came to the counter, "Hey. Zacke, right?" *I wonder if his mom is black, or his dad?*

Zacke thought, *oh no, not today*, as he tried pushing the manager's thoughts out of his mind. He realized he'd paused for too long before answering and responded, "Yeah, I'm Zacke. I hope these shoes are okay. They say they're non-slip."

"They'll be fine until we order the right shoe; part of the uniform. Come on around that counter there," Ted gestured. "We'll get your paperwork done."

Zacke went around the counter and through the light-weight swinging door. There were several other people working as he and Ted made their way to the office behind the kitchen. Following him through the maze of tables and cooking equipment, Zacke did his best to focus. Luckily, what Zacke was picking up were only fragments of thoughts today.

Black? I'm not sure...

...kind of cute...

Nice eyes...

...Tall

Zacke avoided eye contact. It seemed to help keep out the thoughts. Zacke imagined two halves of a great metal sphere. In his mind, he made the two halves screw tightly together. That usually worked, but it was getting harder lately. Taking this job was a big gamble. But, with his dad still drinking, it was a good way to get out of the house and make his own way.

Ted sat Zacke at a small desk, "Go ahead and look over the rules here. There's an I-9 and W-4 to fill out. I can help you with those, or you can take them home to your parents."

"Just my dad." corrected Zacke.

"Oh, okay." Ted said professionally, "Your dad can help and you can bring it back." *Divorced?* "But you can't get your first paycheck until I get all your paperwork." *Dead, I hope his mom's not...*

Zacke imagined two big hands screwing the sphere together even tighter. Ted's thoughts went quiet, "Thanks. I think I can handle this without my dad. Thanks, Ted."

"After that, you'll watch a few training videos on the computer here." The manager explained what else he'd have to do. Zacke understood, and left him alone in the back room. The paperwork was easy. He wasn't sure how many dependents to claim, so he put down himself as one. *Just me. That's how it feels these days.*

Zacke would handle his first job all on his own. He was half way through the first fifteen-minute training video when a girl walked in. She looked to be a year or two older than himself. Her long black hair was in a tidy pony tail, and her pale skin made her hair seem darker. Zacke tried not to stare at her backside. He failed, but he didn't think she noticed.

"Oh. Hi. You're the new guy?" she said as she breezed past him to the set of lockers on the far wall.

"Yeah. I'm Zacke." He concentrated on keeping the sphere sealed. But the orange-dyed tips of her dark hair loosened his concentration.

"I'm Victoria." she said, turning her back and opening her locker. "What's your last name?" She removed her shirt, revealing bare shoulders and a bra strap. She quickly put on her work shirt. Zacke couldn't believe she'd casually changed in front of another employee. He realized he was staring, and had taken too long to answer.

"Um. Um, Penna. Zacke Penna," Zacke finally got out.

Victoria cocked her head, "Italian name? Or something else?"

"Yeah. I mean, yes," Zacke fumbled, "my dad's side is Italian, mostly."

She swiveled around, having buttoned up her shirt. Tucking her uniform shirt into her pants she said, "Oh," she motioned to her shirt, "Sorry, I'm not shy. I did a lot of theater in high school. Quick changes off stage strip you of all modesty. Pun intended."

Zacke looked back to his paperwork to avoid staring, "Oh. No, it's cool."

"Zacke Penna. I like it. Nice to meet you Zacke Penna." She walked toward him, adjusting her nametag, "So, what are you?"

Zacke smiled. *Blunt. I like that.* Without hesitation, he replied, "I'm mixed. My dad's white. Mom's black."

"Cool. Those are pretty green eyes," she put her hand out to shake, "Nice to meet you..." She glanced down at his paperwork, "Zacke with an 'e'. I'll be your trainer for the next two weeks."

Zacke listened closely for any stray thought, unscrewing the steel sphere just a little. He heard nothing. *Good. Maybe it's finally gone,* he thought. *Or maybe it's her.*

Victoria still held out her hand, "Zacke, it is customary for us humans to shake hands when we meet."

"Oh. Sorry." He realized he'd paused too long again. Zacke shook her hand.

"Come see me when you're done with the videos." she smiled.

She walked out, but turned back to flash another smile. He loosened his mental sphere a bit more, but heard none of her thoughts.

I think I'm going to like it here.

* * *

A few days later, Zacke still couldn't get used to how busy it was. The lines of people never seemed to stop. It was just now 7:00 p.m., three hours into his shift, and he couldn't keep the tables bussed fast enough.

He saw lots of kids from Sea Valley High. SVH was only a few blocks from Ocean Burgers, so he knew they got slammed for lunch. He'd even stopped by a few times between classes himself, but he didn't realize the rest of the night would be so busy.

Zacke still couldn't get used to the open campuses in California. He still felt new at SVH, and the fact that you walked out into the sunshine to your locker, or your next class, still seemed surreal.

He recalled being jammed together in the noisy multi-leveled school halls during the cold, wet winters in Michigan. The slippery floors, the constant echoing sound of lockers slamming shut. Being able to walk off campus to go get lunch was an awesome idea, but Zacke usually stuck to campus. It was cheaper that way, and he was determined to keep his eyes on his future. Looking ahead kept him from thinking about his mom.

His trainer Victoria flung him a smile. He thought the name Victoria was an old lady name, but she made it hot. Zacke still hadn't been able to hear any of her thoughts, which somehow made him like her more. He needed to concentrate. *Stay focused. Keep the lid shut tight.*

With all the people around, it made it hard to shut out the random thoughts, which was one of the reasons he took this job. *I must control this.* Zacke took a tray full of crumpled burger wrappers and dumped them in the trash, headed for the next dirty table.

He had gotten better every day, keeping the thoughts out. Zacke let himself experiment, letting specific thoughts come into his mind. His control was getting better, and the thoughts were also clearer to understand, stronger.

The blonde with her boyfriend thought, *...I'll just ask to use his phone, he knows mine's broken. It's not snooping...*

The mom with her little boy off to one side thought, *I hate all these crowds. I'll get it to go next time...*

A group of jocks were just coming through the door, into the long line. Zacke recognized one of them. It was Cody Nichols. He was so far undefeated on the Varsity team. The first game of the new school year was a blowout at 47-6, and Cody was the youngest quarterback in history at SVH, to hear the locals tell it.

He had noticed Cody around before, mostly because of his bike. It was an old beat up green bike a little too small for him. Zacke had noticed it because many of the older jocks had cars. Being younger than most of them, Cody couldn't drive yet. But he thought it strange that the quarterback rode a beat up old bike to school.

Zacke must have focused on them too long. A thought came, *...she's hot, I wonder what...* Then he focused on Cody, who was joking with his friend, and a strange image came to his mind. It was a treasure chest with a large old-fashioned lock on it; a lock you'd see in movies with knights and castles. He let his mind drift toward it, then Cody looked at him.

Zacke saw the confusion on Cody's face, and Zacke quickly looked away. High school guys knew the secret code; you never keep eye contact for long. But Cody looked back anyway, with confusion and maybe some fear written across his face. Zacke looked down again and went to the trash can, out of view of the jocks.

It was only half full, but he emptied it anyway, tied it and put a new plastic bag in quickly. He rushed around the counter and went through to the back room. His mind would not leave Cody. His green bike kept flashing in Zacke's mind. He figured maybe Cody's parents couldn't afford anything better.

Trash emptied, hands washed, Zacke came back into the main dining room. The treasure chest with the old lock popped back into his mind and he looked up to see Cody and his friends leaving with their to-go bags. Cody stared at Zacke. A thought popped into Zacke's head that felt foreign, not his own.

Get out of my head.

It was as clear as any thought he'd ever had. When Cody saw the expression on Zacke's face, the look that Zacke had heard his thought, Cody looked shocked. Cody quickly left with his friends.

Did that just happen? thought Zacke. *I've definitely gotta talk to that guy.*

CHAPTER TWO

KATIE

Katie Moran stood in the small grove of eucalyptus trees. She had changed her clothes, and pulled her boots up. She carefully slid the short skirt and tank top into her backpack. Her auburn hair hung to her shoulders. She examined herself to make sure the clothes she had worn to school were all safely in her bag. *Sammy seemed to like my outfit today.* Leaving the trees, she was surprised by a voice.

"Hi Katie."

"Megan! I told you not to scare me. How long were you standing there?"

"Long enough," said Megan, smiling.

Katie breezed past her, "I'm not walking home with you."

Megan replied, "Mom said you have to."

"Walk behind me then." Katie sighed, adjusting her long sleeve shirt. "Come on then, little monster."

Megan scowled. "Mom said not to call me names."

Katie shook her head. "My mom. She's not your mom. She's my mom, little step-sister."

Megan shrugged, and followed Katie down the packed earth trail along the edge of their field. They passed cabbage heads, lined up in neat rows as they made the last leg from the bus stop to their ranch style farm house.

Megan asked, "Do you have a tissue, or something?" She walked four paces behind Katie.

Katie kept walking. "Wipe your nose on your sleeve."

"I meant for you," Megan said, "You probably want to wipe off your make-up before Mom and Dad see it."

Katie stopped, shot a "why didn't you tell me" look at Megan and un-slung the backpack from her shoulder. She took a well-used washcloth out of the front pouch, wiped her face. "Thanks. You can't tell them."

"I won't." said Megan, "Do you wanna watch a movie after chores?"

"I don't know. I have a lot of homework." Katie continued wiping. "Did I get all of it?"

"Yeah. Can you show me how to put on make-up?" Megan asked. "Jason and Mom freak out about me wearing make-up and I'm fifteen. But they like you better, so they probably would let you try it at eleven."

Megan cocked her head, smiled widely and extending her arms out dramatically, "It's true! Everyone knows they like me better." She giggled and ran toward the house.

"You are a little monster!" Katie said as she ran after her, but she was smiling too. They raced the last hundred feet to the ranch style house, nestled on three sides by farm land. They stopped, panting. Then Megan screamed.

"Megan, don't move!" Katie whispered. As if the rattlesnake responded to her voice, it raised its head and noticed the girls. The rattler's body was coiled, less than a foot from Megan's leg. Megan breathed heavily, frozen.

The coiled snake flicked its forked tongue out, deciding when to strike. Megan screamed again.

Katie's hands shot out in front of her. The snake leapt into the air at the same moment, but whipped in the opposite direction from the girls. It landed ten feet away, and laid still.

Megan stopped screaming. She turned to Katie. "Did you...?"

Katie put her hands down. "No!" said Katie. "Maybe... you can't tell anyone."

Jason burst out the front door, "What happened? Are you girls okay?"

Megan looked to Katie, shaking her head.

"There was a rattler." Megan pointed over to the snake. It still hadn't moved.

"What happened?" asked Jason.

Katie pointed. "The rattler. I... I picked it up and threw it."

"You what? Do you know how dangerous...?"

Katie answered, "I wasn't thinking! It was right next to Megan's leg, and ...."

"Megan, honey, are you okay?" He grabbed his daughter gently by her shoulders. Then he looked over and noticed the condition of the snake. Blood poured from its head. "Katie... what happened to it?"

Katie hesitated. "I don't know. Must have landed on a sharp rock or something." she looked to Megan, warned her with a sharp stare. Megan didn't say anything.

"I'm just glad you're both okay. Katie, you should have gotten me. Rattlers are..."

"I'm sorry I saved your daughter's life, Jason!" Katie exploded. "Next time I'll let it bite the little monster!" she ran into the house, slamming the screen door.

Jason sighed. He asked Megan, "You sure you're okay, sweetie?"

"Yeah, Dad. It wasn't Katie's fault."

Jason smiled at his daughter. "I know. Go on in the house. I'll take care of the snake." He went to the dead snake. The head looked like it had smashed into a brick wall.

* * *

Later that night, Katie loaded her plate and headed for her room. Mom had given up eating together as a family. She was tired of fighting moody teen syndrome. Katie went to her room with her dinner plate and Megan ate in the living room with her dad and step-mom.

It wasn't long before her mom knocked on Katie's door. The laptop screen was facing away from her mother, but Katie clicked her favorite band's fan site tab closed anyway, leaving only her history research on the screen. "Hey."

"Hey, came for your dirty dishes." Mom looked at the days-old pile. "I should have brought a push cart."

"Ha, ha." Katie answered sarcastically.

Mom sat next to her desk, "I heard what happened."

Katie sighed. "Of course you did. Didn't even bother to get my side."

"That's why I'm here, Katie." Mom moved to the edge of her bed.

Katie said quietly, "Please don't call me that, Mom."

"Kaitlyn, sorry. I get it, that you want to go by a grown-up name. But that also means you can't throw tantrums. That snake scared Jason. It could've hurt you both."

Katie closed her laptop. "Did you tell him?"

Her mom checked to make sure she had closed the door all the way, "No, Kati... Kaitlyn. I've always told him you're special, that's all."

Katie said, "Special. Great, so he probably thinks I'm a retard."

"Hey! We do not use words like that in this house. Do you call your friend Jeanie that?"

Katie felt immediate shame at the thought of her developmentally disabled school friend. "No. Of course not. It just slipped out. Why does Jason hate me?"

"Jason? Honey, he thinks you hate him!" Her mom inched closer on the bed.

Katie rolled her eyes. Mom pressed, "Do you hate him? Is that what's happening?"

"No. No, I don't hate him. I just..." she changed the subject. "Can I go see Dad?"

Her mother tensed. "No. Not during the school year. He said he'd try to bring you out before Christmas. You were just there this summer."

"Yeah, for like a week," Katie moaned. "He worked the whole time."

"You'll have to talk to him about that. I can't control what he does. Let's get back to the snake, Kaitlyn."

She hesitated. "I didn't mean to kill it. I just, it just scared me and I... I can't control it."

"I know, honey. But I thought this, whatever this is, had gone away. This is a lot more than closing doors from across the room."

"It was kinda gone for a while. It just..." Katie struggled. "I don't know how to explain it. It just happened."

"Well I'm glad your talent was able to help your sister." Mom rubbed Katie's back.

"Step-sister."

Mom conceded, "Fine. Step-sister. But she looks up to you, Katie. Especially after today."

"Yeah, she's alright. She's not as annoying as she used to be." Katie smiled, until an image flashed into Katie's mind, like an explosion. Her smile faltered.

"Honey. Honey, are you okay?"

Katie nodded to her mom, and cleared the awful image. Out of habit, she threw the thought into her mental suitcase, the shiny metal one she imagined when certain thoughts needed to be packed away. She smiled and lied, "No. I'm fine. Just have a little headache."

"Your face went white." Mom looked into her daughter's eyes, "I know when you're lying. You're terrible at it. What's going on?"

She burst into tears, "I just... I don't want to be a freak, Mom. I'm scared."

Her mother hugged her, "Oh, honey. You're not a freak. I don't know what's happening. There's no doctor to tell us what this is."

Katie broke the embrace, "I know," she wiped her eyes, "I wouldn't want them to lock me up or anything."

"That won't happen." Mom said. A knock sounded at the door. It opened slowly.

"Sorry, your phone's going off honey. It's your boss. She texted three times. Everything okay in here?" asked Jason, Mom's phone in hand.

"Probably wants me to do a double tomorrow. Flu season, gotta love it."

Instead of asking if her daughter was okay in front of her husband, she put her hand on Katie's wrist and asked with her eyes. Katie nodded that she was okay, and her mom walked out.

Her stepfather turned to Katie, "I really appreciate how you protected Megan today. Thank you, Kaitlyn."

Katie nodded and offered a smile. Jason smiled back. He closed the door. New tears formed. How could she tell her mother that she wasn't scared for herself? The flash in her mind was Megan, face down and covered in blood.

CHAPTER THREE

CODY

Cody Nichols lifted the pads off his aching shoulders and let them drop to the floor. He thought briefly of putting them in his closet, but let them rest on the pile of dirty clothes instead, promising himself to do it later.

He combed his hands through his short brown hair and stretched. *Hard practice*, thought Cody. He stripped off his shirt, drenched with sweat. He thought of getting a beer from the hidden mini-fridge in his closet, but Mom was still home. He didn't want her to worry. The bedroom door was ajar. From the hall, he heard a whistle.

"Looking good, son," said his mom, smiling as she nudged the door open.

Cody smiled, "Don't be weird, mom."

She entered his boy cave. "I mean it, kid. Look at those muscles. The coach making you work out that much? Or are you doing it for the ladies?"

"Mom," he protested, but smiled anyway. "No girls yet."

"That's from your own self-image. Son, look in the mirror." She stood next to him facing the full-length mirror, "You are not the scrawny kid you were on that soccer field a few years ago. Newly sixteen, with all those manly muscles. You just need to see yourself as you are right now. Girls like confidence."

"I guess," Cody shrugged.

"Fair warning, I will automatically hate your first girlfriend. My only son is too good for those hoochy mamas."

"Mom..." They both laughed.

Mom said, "Your dad never had muscles like that." Cody lost his smile. "Sorry. I haven't brought him up in a while. Anytime you want to talk about..."

"No, thanks. I know all I need to," Cody said. "I have to shower."

She took an exaggerated whiff, "Yes, young man. Yes, you do. Girls don't like stinky boys."

Cody changed the subject, "Do you work tonight?"

"Yeah, that's what I came to tell you. I'll probably be late," she continued, "Two girls called in sick. You'll have to make dinner yourself. I could bring you something, but it may be after midnight."

"That's ok. I'm going to the gym later. I'll probably get a burger or something."

His mom shook her head. "You just got back from practice. The gym? You're ridiculous, number one son."

"I'm your only son."

"Got me there. Love ya, kiddo," she said, closing the door on the way out.

"Love you too, Mom."

Cody rubbed his shoulder, checking for new bruises. The coach announced loudly that no one would be left out of the fun, and had made them use the blocking sleds repeatedly at practice. He knew Coach was trying to make sure no one thought he was being treated special. Some of the guys resented Cody's new position as quarterback, and the coach was trying to help with the heat. Maybe his mom was right, maybe confidence was the way forward. *Fake it 'til you make it*, he thought.

He looked at his chest and arms in the mirror. The gym and football practice had helped slowly add muscle. He was getting bigger. Cody naturally compared himself to the biggest guys on the team, who were huge compared to Cody. He would just have to work harder.

In the driveway, mom tried to start the car. Cody listened to the engine try to turn over, and fail twice. He clenched his fist, and said quietly, "Come on Mom, try one more time." The twenty-year-old Ford Focus tried to start again. Cody felt the tingle pass through him. He clenched his fist and the car roared to life.

Cody imagined his mom's sigh of relief as the ancient car got her to work one more day. He didn't know how much longer his weird little talent would help her. But it had worked for the last few months. That wasn't the only weird thing that had happened of course, but he tried to push those thoughts from his mind.

Just about to head for the shower, he thought of that cold beer again. He didn't like hiding stuff from his mom, but the beer did help after a hard practice. He knew a lot of the guys drank on occasion.

He stripped out of his soggy pants.

Cody glanced back at the mirror. But it wasn't his room he saw. He froze. In the mirror, he saw a bookcase. He held his hand up to the mirror, but he did not see a reflection. The books, stacked in a haphazard way made him think of a shop from the Harry Potter films. *Ok, I am going crazy.* He swallowed and came closer to the mirror, changing his angle to try and see around the bookcase.

A small table was there, and a very old man. He was sitting, hunched over a large, ancient looking book. There was a laptop behind him and a painting that looked like a modern art piece. The man's lips were moving, but Cody couldn't hear anything.

With a start, the man looked right at him.

He seemed just as surprised as Cody. A chill went through him as the old man stared with pale blue eyes. Cody couldn't look away. The man was on his feet quickly, moving faster than any old man should, coming up to the other side of the mirror. Cody blinked, *is this really happening?*

The old man smiled. Ice ran through Cody's spine.

Cody picked up his shoulder pads and hurled them at the mirror. The image disappeared and it was just a pile of broken shards, reflecting his own room from a million angles.

He stood there for a moment, breathing heavily. A fresh layer of sweat covered him. He was glad his mother had driven away, not heard the breaking glass. He didn't know how he would explain another broken mirror. *But, I've never seen anything like that.*

Cody couldn't tell her what he'd seen, of course. In the past, there were strange images that shouldn't have been there, easy to dismiss even though they scared him. Sometimes a landscape from somewhere else, sometimes a pitch-black void where his mirror should have been. That was bad enough, and had led to two other broken mirrors in the past year. But this was very different.

Cody shook off his fear. *Fake it 'til you make it.* Careful not to step on any glass, he went to the smashed mirror, picking up a large shard. No old man, just his own face staring back. He would clean it up after the shower. Cody wouldn't get a new mirror for his room. He didn't need to see weird old men staring back.

He shook his head, trying to physically remove the image of the old man, wishing once again there was someone he could talk to. The other guys on the team wouldn't understand. He thought of his dad for some reason, but angrily shut out the thought. *This is probably his fault.*

"I know one thing that will help," he said aloud. He gave into his recently acquired habit and went into his closet. The can of beer was ice cold from his small, hidden fridge. Cody took two long gulps, putting the can down on the counter, before he showered. Feeling a small buzz begin, he let the fear of the old man fall from his mind.

As he stepped out of the shower and reached for the sweating can of beer, a small black spider skittered across the counter. A jolt of childhood fear knocked out his beer buzz. He grabbed the hand towel and smashed the spider. Cody wasn't sure why, but the image of the old man popped into his head again.

CHAPTER FOUR

ARIANA

Ariana surveyed her backyard filled with family.

"Ariana, you look so pretty," exclaimed Mary, her first cousin, "Have you lost weight? You're too thin already."

"Maybe a little." Ariana smiled. She stood in a pale red dress, her long black hair flowed down to the small of her back.

"Too bad," her cousin teased, "my Mami brought her famous tres leches cupcakes."

Ariana eyes widened. "Oh no, why did I start a new diet two days before your birthday?" They both laughed.

Mariachi music blared from the large speakers in the corner of the backyard. Mary had moved on to see other relatives in the crowded space. Ariana made her way to the food tables.

Her mother Josie asked, "Mija, could you help me with another table?"

Ariana looked at the two eight foot tables filled with food, already surrounded by a dozen people. "Where will we put it?"

Josie rolled her eyes. "I have no idea. But people keep bringing more food," her mother said, "We'll make room, even if we have to push some of your cousins into the pool."

Ariana smiled. Her Tia Helen stood nearby. She heard her mother's remark and scowled.

Tia Helen said, "I know a way we could make more room." Helen rubbed her own stomach and looked at Josie. At over 300 pounds, Ariana's mother had gotten used to being teased by her sister Helen. Ariana never liked her Aunt Helen, especially when making fun of her mother's weight. Ariana frowned at her aunt.

Josie knew not taking the bait would make Helen fume. "You'll be the first one in the pool, Helen!"

Ariana knew she wasn't really joking where her mean Aunt Helen was concerned. Ariana smiled at the small victory. Tia Helen stalked off indignantly.

"You want me to get Jorge for the third table?" asked Ariana.

"No mija, he's probably out front with Marco and Florio. We can manage."

They got the table, setting it up at the end of the first two, having to herd family members out of the way. It was just in time, as more people and food arrived. They found a way to make it fit.

Luckily, the distraction of the arriving clown had cleared the small ones from around the tables. There was a flock of kids around the man in the rainbow wig. His hands were furiously making balloon animals of all types.

Josie whispered to her daughter, "Don't tell anyone, but I hate clowns." Josie left, to try and manage the children. She said loudly to the horde, "The clown is here! Yay! Now let's line up."

Ariana noticed her sister's son was sitting by himself in the far corner of the yard, next to the pool. She made her way over and sat next to him. "Hey Celio. The clown just got here."

The boy shrugged. "I don't like clowns."

"Me neither," she looked to the clown and the circle of kids around him, "reminds me of a scary book I read. Clowns are creepy."

The boy smiled, but not for long. She didn't need to ask what was wrong. An image of a girl flashed into her mind, sitting behind her young nephew in a classroom. She was eight years old, like Celio, but she towered over him.

Ariana *was* Celio for a moment, and she could feel the sharp pencil lead poking him in the back. There was no sound in her flash, but it was clear the girl was taunting and picking on her small nephew. The flash ended, and she was Ariana again, back in the present.

Ariana consoled him. "I'm guessing someone is picking on you in school."

Celio looked at her a little surprised, then nodded.

"Why don't you tell the teacher?" but she already knew that he had.

"Teacher doesn't believe me," said Celio. "Well, maybe she believes me. But nothing changes."

"My brothers could stop it," but she already knew that he wouldn't tell them. He was small for his age, and felt like he had to keep up with his older cousins; it was a matter of young pride.

He shook his head and stared at the shimmering water of the pool.

Ariana gave him the bad news, "You know, when I was your age, I would do mean things to a boy if I liked him."

Celio snapped his head to look at her. "I know. She wants to be my girlfriend!" he exclaimed a little too loudly, and looked around to make sure no one else could hear.

Ariana smiled. "I'm fifteen and don't have a boyfriend. You have a girl fighting over you at eight?"

She put her hand on his side and tickled him. He squealed with delight and bucked to get away from her fearsome tickling.

Celio's shoulder hit a pedestal supporting a heavy clay flower pot. Her mother had put it in the corner of the yard to avoid this exact kind of accident, but it tumbled over anyway.

Ariana extended her hands. A few inches from the pool water, the flower pot and pedestal stopped in mid-air. The stand was tipped horizontal to the pool, frozen.

Ariana leapt to her feet, pretending she had caught it before it hit the ground. Righting the pedestal, she placed the heavy pot back on top.

Celio's mouth was open. He stared, clearly un-fooled by her maneuver. She looked to the crowded yard, and hoped no one else had seen what happened.

Ariana got on her haunches in front of the boy. "Little man, I promise not to tell anyone about the girl, if you keep quiet about this." She manually closed his gaping mouth.

He looked at her hands and said, "Deal. I don't want to mess with you."

CHAPTER FIVE

LUCAS

Lucas T. Sandler sat by the long table, and pushed the glasses back up his nose. He concentrated his bright green eyes on his work. The wooden keel and main body of the model ship were done, and the sails and mast were laid out carefully, ready for the next step.

"We only have about fifteen minutes left. You could at least tell me how school is going," said the psychologist in the overstuffed chair. The forty five year old doctor shifted his large frame in his seat. He had a round face and kind eyes. The small office was painted in pastel blue, that had a soothing effect on most of his clients. For Lucas, it seemed to inspire silence.

"School's fine." Lucas knew not to say more than that; his clever ship-building partner only needed a small foothold to pry things out of that Lucas. That was his job, after all.

"That's all I get, huh? That forces me to go right for the red meat, Lucas." The doctor leaned closer, writing pad in hand, "It's been almost a year since..."

"I don't want to talk about that." Lucas said as he assembled the main mast of the wooden ship.

"I get that. You know I've been very patient. But your parents are still worried you might... well, try again. The thing is, I like building model ships, but these kits come out of my pocket." The man waved his hands around to the shelves on his office wall, all filled with model ships of different sizes.

Lucas smiled. "Sorry, doc. I've told you and my parents I'll never do anything like that again. And I won't. I don't need to talk to anyone. I wish they'd spend their money on something else besides a psychologist."

You wouldn't believe what's going on anyway, Lucas thought.

"So I should just pronounce you cured, then? It doesn't work that way, my friend. Therapy is about talking through your troubles. I know your grades are back up at school, and you are getting stronger. But I can't take credit for any of that, since all we do is *not talk*, and build models together."

Lucas looked at the clock, two minutes until five.

"Any more dreams?" asked the psychologist.

"Nope," Lucas lied.

"I've brought this up several times, but I am trained in hypnotherapy. Your parents have okayed the use. In fact, it's my most direct tool..."

"No."

"Why not, Lucas?"

Lucas imagined letting the doctor ask him what he'd been dreaming about. *They'd lock me up for sure.* "Sorry doc, I've told you I don't want that."

"Any more bullying? That boy, Billy, moved away two years ago, right?"

"Right. No issues there, doc. I can take care of myself now. The Kenpo helps a lot."

"Martial arts classes going well? Good." The doctor made a note. "I'm glad it's helping."

The clock hit five, but Lucas was already slinging his backpack over his shoulder as the alarm went off. He was going to leave in silence like always, allowing no hints. But Doctor Mason had been kind and patient. He turned to his psychologist. A gleam of hope flashed in the doctor's eyes.

"Doc, I love my parents. But, I was named after George Lucas, I have the same middle name as Captain Kirk, and my last name matches a movie star. All of that makes me bully bait. Am I messed up? Probably. I'm 15. I'm supposed to be a little messed up. Right, doc?" Lucas smiled.

Dr. Mason smiled back. "I'll see you next week."

"Last session, right?"

"Yep," the psychologist said with a sigh, "then we go on permanent hiatus."

He turned away from his frustrated doctor and left for home. Walking the eight blocks, he allocated time for what he wanted to get done with the rest of the day. The self-imposed structure is what had gotten him through the last year. He went through his mental list:

Homework – forty-five minutes. Just get it done. Training – two hours. Push harder, but don't lose control. Dinner with Mom and Dad. Reward – Binge watch three hours of Heroes, even though season two wasn't so good. And season three is going off the rails...

His thoughts were cut off by a vision from the past. Billy. Billy Miller. *No, it can't be.* But he was real, and standing in his path. Billy was taller than Lucas by six inches. Handsome, trim and athletic, Billy radiated an over- confidence reserved for the shiny gods of high school.

"Hey Tiberius," said a voice he thought he'd never hear again.

No, no, no. Suddenly Lucas was thirteen, ten; a small shaking kid in the clutches of Billy. *Should I pretend I don't hear him?*

"Captain Kirk, I'm talking to you," said Billy.

Lucas fought the old feeling of panic. *Too late, here he comes. You're a different guy now. Don't let him get to you. What is he doing here?*

"Why you ignoring me, Captain? I missed you, pal." Next to him, his friend Jonesy smiled his weird, crooked smile; right back in loyal henchmen mode.

Lucas looked at his former bully, "Hey, Billy."

Billy matched his stride and put his arm around Lucas. "Oohh. Getting some muscles, Captain. You working out?"

Lucas said nothing as they walked down the street, looking like old buddies with Billy's arm around him.

Billy seemed cheerful. "Been gone two years. But Dad got stationed back at Camp Cooke. I've only missed a few weeks of school. Maybe we'll have some classes together. I go back to 'SVH' tomorrow."

Lucas concentrated. *Keep your cool. Don't lose it.* He thought of a few Kenpo moves to incapacity his "old bully," but didn't want to tip his hand. The shock of Billy being back made Lucas wonder if he could control his anger.

Billy continued, "Hey, is your mom still hot?" Jonesy laughed like Igor at Dr. Frankenstein's witty joke. Billy kept going, "She sure was a MILF..."

Lucas stopped and shrugged off Billy's arm.

Billy stared. "Oh. Jonesy, maybe the Captain here wants to try his new muscles out. Come on Lucas Tiberius, I know you've always been gay for me. You want to kiss me, or fight?"

Jonesy had already puffed out his chest, ready to hold Lucas down, or flank him when Billy made his move. Just like old times.

Lucas fought every impulse to show Billy what he could do. Two flashes came quickly. Billy was either going to hit him in the stomach, or try to pants him. Lucas stared into Billy's eyes. He focused on the second flash, ready to stop him. Lucas smiled knowingly.

Billy caught the glint in Lucas' eye and saw it as a challenge. But Jonesy got nervous at something new about Lucas. Just then, a car pulled up behind the two bullies.

Billy's demeanor changed when he saw the car, "Oh, Hey, Officer Jack."

"Hey boys," said the police officer from his car window, "I saw the moving truck around the corner. Why don't you go help your parents unload? You too, Jonesy."

Billy smirked. "I was just catching up with my old buddy here."

"You being the son of an Army Major doesn't make you any less of an ass, Billy. Any new trouble starts; I'll assume it was you."

Billy stopped smiling; his usual charm did no good on this particular adult. *Maybe he's losing his touch*, thought Lucas. Billy nodded, glanced back at Lucas, and he stalked off with Jonesy trailing behind him.

The blood that pumped just behind Lucas's ears started to recede.

Officer Jack said, "I'm proud of you, Lucas. Billy's been gone a while; he doesn't know how hard you've trained. I'm glad I didn't have to call an ambulance for that little stain. Good control."

Lucas allowed a smile, "Thanks Sensei."

Police Officer Jack Tanner replied, "Just don't go to juvie for those two. I'll see you at the dojo on Thursday."

They said goodbye and Lucas got home, slipped into the side door of the converted garage that was his bedroom.

"Okay. Billy's back. New agenda," he said to himself.

He locked the door that led into the house, for his dad's protection. His dad was home, and Lucas couldn't chance anyone seeing a real training session. Lucas set up the five wooden opponents. He'd made them with scrap wood. They all stood much like the cardboard cutouts of sports stars, but these were made with plywood and two by fours. He set them in the widest circle he could, using the small sandbags on the bases to keep them upright.

Lucas couldn't remember how long he'd thought of the door in his mind. Maybe just after he started martial arts classes? The door in his mind, when opened, made a lot of things possible. He'd only opened it a few times before, scared of what it meant: Especially since it required his blood.

But today was not a day for control. He needed to be unleashed.

He got his phone and put it in his iHome, turning the music up to cover the noise he was about to make. Lucas took the small pocket knife and stood in the center of the circle of wooden foes. He took his shirt off and decided under his arm was the best place to cut. Lucas sliced, a small line of blood appeared. He closed the knife and tossed it onto his nightstand. Putting a finger on the blood, he then touched his tongue.

He closed his eyes and the blood rose back behind his ears; surging, pulsing. The door flew open in his mind and he wasn't Lucas anymore. In his mind, he was awash in red power. He opened his eyes and stared at his wooden opponents. For Lucas, they all had Billy's face.

Three minutes later, he stood in the room, surrounded by splinters of wood, none bigger than his fist. Sawdust hung in the air, but Lucas continued breathing heavily until all the red tint faded from his vision. He brushed himself off and dropped to one knee, exhausted.

This was the worst part, the coming down, the closing the door to this other thing. His body ached and shivered as the effect wore off. He closed the mental door tight. Sweat made sawdust stick to him. His body drained, Lucas laid among the splintered wood, and sobs racked his body until he fell asleep.

CHAPTER SIX

THE ELDER

The old man put down his cell phone on the antique table. An image came of a battle long ago, of an old foe tearing into ten men with his blood rage. It was an odd thought, but as he got older, random thoughts came often. Sometimes they meant nothing. Sometimes they meant everything.

The elderly man looked out at the view from his palatial estate on the Amalfi Italian coast. The expansive view showed a wide harbor with ships of all sizes dotting out to the horizon. The sanctuary, his office was decorated in an eclectic mix of antique furniture and modern office equipment. He absent-mindedly rubbed his temple and went back to the mirror. He ran his finger over the small crack, when there was a knock at the door.

Derek Sommers breezed in before the old man could respond. He was wearing a form-fitting designer jacket. The elder demanded his agents be well dressed when summoned. "I'm here. What you said on the phone didn't make any sense. Why would a naked teenager be in your mirror?"

"He wasn't just in my mirror, he was able to crack it when he broke his own," said the old man, with an edge to his voice. "Have you lost all respect for me, Sazzo?"

"Uh oh, using my ancient name. Must be trouble." quipped Derek.

The elder stared with his unblinking, pale blue eyes, "I may be trapped in this old body, but I am still your Elder."

"Of course. Forgive me," Derek put his hands together and bowed. "Due respect, Elder Zamma. But what you described isn't possible. The talent for mirror viewing has been lost, except for your own power. Are you sure you're not just tired?"

"This body is 92," said the elder, impatiently, "Of course I'm tired. But I know what I saw. More disturbing still, I had a flash of a warrior I know had a true death. The two things at once are no coincidence."

"What are you suggesting?" asked Derek.

The elder spoke, almost to himself, "It may be a breakout."

Derek smiled, and stretched out on the antique sofa, "Elder Zamma. With respect, you say that three times a year. Isn't Ehrhardt in Mozambique right now investigating a possible breakout? We haven't seen a real one for quite a while."

"Get your feet off my couch. It belonged to Charles the fourth." Zamma shook a finger at Derek. "There are only four elders left. I'm stuck in this body and will not move on. We must remedy this imbalance by new recruits."

"Their numbers have dwindled too, we suspect, but the Amartus have been quiet for so long." Derek added, "They have their small natural talents, but we are stronger with our magic. Why chase after every new possible recruit? We have the numbers, we will win."

Zamma sat, "Your overconfidence is tiresome. We've survived this long by rooting out even a possibility of a breakout. We only build our numbers by recruiting. We must work harder. This wiping out civilians tactic has made me enemies. Remember 2004? We need recruits, not mass extinction. Keep your brother in check this time."

"That wasn't my idea..." Derek had a thought. A flash of a man on a train. It was on the coast of some country. The ocean. Then the thought was gone. "I just had a flash."

"I'm not alone, then. What did you see?"

Derek's phone rang in his pocket with a snippet of Mozart. He looked at the screen, "Now that's interesting," he mused before answering. "Hello? Yes, brother. I did have a flash just now. We were just discussing... wait, I'll put you on speaker. I'm here at the palazzo with Zamma now."

Elder Zamma came closer to the phone. A rough voice with a German accent broke through the phone's speaker, "Elder Zamma? Is something happening? I just had a flash. Derek tells me he did too."

"Your brother thinks it's old age, but this feels like a breakout. Are you done there in Mozambique?" asked the elder.

"Yes, I am flying back tonight," said Ehrhardt through the speakerphone, "It was a girl who could start small fires. The girl wouldn't join us. She had a swimming 'accident,' I'm afraid. No witnesses, but she's the only one. No breakout here."

Derek gave his elder a knowing glance. The elder glared. "What about this flash?"

"It was a flash of that berserker Viking. But I gave him a true death long ago. Does that make any sense?"

"Yes. I had a flash of him too." Zamma smiled, "Await instructions. I think I know where to start looking."

"Let me know." Ehrhardt hung up.

"I guess I don't get a goodbye." Derek put his phone back in his jacket pocket. "Where do you think it is?"

"California," answered the elder.

Derek was dubious. "Well, that narrows it down. But that's a huge state. I know, this body was born there. How did you get California?"

"The boy had a California license plate on his wall. One of those plastic types you get with your name on it. It may have said Corey or Cody. But there was another detail. I think he threw some sports equipment when he broke the mirror. The uniform near him was blue and white."

"Very observant."

The elder smiled thinly. "I've lived a great many lives. Elders have to be observant."

Derek sighed. "So, a teenage boy who plays a sport, somewhere in a huge state that is bigger than Germany? What if he got that trinket when he visited California?"

Zamma wasn't amused with the challenge. "What did your flash show?"

"Someone on a train. Looked like it was by the ocean." Derek rubbed his chin. "Okay. Ocean, California. Makes sense. I guess I'm going to Google every high school sports team in California with blue and white colors. I'll set up the trip. No fun for me tonight."

Zamma added, "I want you to take the Witness."

Derek shook his head. "I don't think that's a good idea. He hasn't been reliable in over two years. We used him up."

"He's the best finder we've ever had. If it's a breakout, he's our best chance. Start at San Diego. Drive up to every town and city with a matching sports team. If it's a breakout, the Witness will sniff them out. You and your brother can recruit them."

Derek said, "Sounds like a fun road trip."

The elder caught the sarcasm, but didn't comment. He turned his back on his underling. Derek knew he was dismissed.

* * *

In San Diego, Derek waited in the rented convertible. Montgomery Field was smaller than the international airport in San Diego, catering mostly to private jets. He tapped his fingers on the console between the front seats, doing the calculations out loud.

"Mozambique and San Diego are 10,000 miles apart. The elder's Bombardier 850 jet goes about 450 miles per hour, tops. That means with refueling, Ehrhardt had been on the plane for over 24 hours. And he is being summoned here for what surely is a waste of time. He'll be in such a great mood. Road trip ruined."

"Could you please stop that?" said the Witness from the back seat.

Derek checked the rear view and continued tapping his fingers. "Sorry, does that bother you, Witness?"

The Witness didn't respond, but asked instead, "Why now? You haven't used me for years. Why don't you just let me die in my cell?"

Derek scoffed, "We make the rules, old buddy. You failed us last time. I told my elder we should kill you. My brother volunteered to do it. Thank our elder you're still alive."

"I did everything you asked," said the Witness quietly. He was grateful to finally be out in the open, cleaned up with fresh clothes. They made sure his necklace had stayed around his neck, of course. He would never get used to the evil metal thing that kept him a prisoner.

"Yes, but you didn't do it fast enough.' Derek continued tapping his fingers, "Oh, here he is."

The car door opened. "Open the boot," said Ehrhardt.

"We're in America," Derek said lightheartedly.

"Open the trunk then!" Ehrhardt slammed the door, taking his traveling bag to the trunk.

"I used to love road trips," said Derek. The witness ignored him.

The trunk slammed as well, and Ehrhardt got in the passenger seat, fastening the seatbelt. He slammed his door shut.

Derek offered, "Nice to see you brother."

Ehrhardt looked in the back seat. "We're using the Witness? He's unreliable."

"Not my call, brother," said Derek, "Our loving master thought it best."

"Stop calling him that. He does not own us. Why did I have to make this flight right now? I've been on a plane for over 24 hours."

"It's a breakout." said the Witness from the backseat.

"No flies on you," said Derek, "Who told you that, witness?"

The Witness said, "Lucky guess."

Ehrhardt turned to look at the man in the back seat. "Listen very closely, Witness. If this is a breakout, you will help us find them. California hasn't had 'the big one' yet. With the mood I'm in, I will make the entire state fall into the sea."

The Witness began to bow his head, but raised it instead, "How much did Sri Lanka hurt? You must have slept for a week. Don't forget the other costs of evil acts. I can't wait to see what horrible life you'll lead next time around."

Ehrhardt yanked the Witness by the hair. "I don't know where you find any strength to resist. But I am done with you, after this. Either way, this will be your last trip." He turned to Derek, "Let's go."

The Witness said softly, "I know I'm dead already."

Derek put the car in drive, and checked his mirrors. As he eased out onto the surface street, he sighed under his breath, "Best road trip ever."

CHAPTER SEVEN
BULLY

Ariana walked with her two closest friends toward Sea Valley High. It was mid-September, and in Central California that meant the summer was fighting its last battle with autumn. That day, summer was still winning, and even at 7:45 in the morning, it was hot.

In her small city, at least a third of her high school class walked to school. At barely three miles by three miles square, holding nearly 50,000 people including outlying suburbs, it was a town made for walking.

Dora continued, "...so hot. He came with my cousin Alberto last night and was like..."

Ariana was barely listening. She was worried about the strange things that were happening, and Ariana had no one she could talk to. Weirdness had happened in the past, even a few incidents that she was sure her mother had seen. A few years earlier, she had tried to talk about them, but her mother got strange and kept changing the subject. She realized even though she had a large, strong family around her, she was on her own.

Lately, things had gotten worse. During the summer, more things started happening, even scary dreams of people chasing her. Random flashes kept coming into her mind for no reason. Two men with no faces, a mirror that she couldn't see herself in, and weird symbols that she couldn't decipher. But these flashes lasted only a fraction of a second. She imagined the silver jewelry box in her mind and tried to keep it locked, but it was getting harder lately. She wondered for the millionth time if she was going crazy.

"Are you even listening to us, Arry?" asked her other friend Sylvia. "We are discussing seriously hot guys here."

"Sorry, I'm a little out of it today," Ariana admitted. Her gaze had been drawn to a scene in the parking lot.

"Oh, I think Arry is into skinny white boys now," teased Dora.

Sylvia said, "Shut up. That's the Sandler kid. Is that Billy Miller?"

"Oh wow. I think it is," Dora exclaimed, "Didn't he move away, like, years ago?"

"Yeah. I guess he's back," Ariana said.

Dora said, "Okay, if you are staring at Billy, he is hot; I don't care if he's white."

Ariana frowned. "And a total jerk. Especially to that kid."

"I heard the Sandler kid tried to kill himself last year," Sylvia added.

Dora agreed, "I heard that too. Do you have any classes with him?"

"I think he's in my Algebra 2 class," Ariana said, "That's sad. I'm not really sure. I'm such a bad person."

"He's kind of weird." Sylvia offered.

Ariana said, "You're kind of weird, chica. I feel bad for him."

They were too far away to hear, walking parallel to the scene in the parking lot. A few other kids were watching from a distance. Billy and two friends were laughing at the kid's expense. That was obvious at any distance.

As they got closer, Ariana kept looking at Lucas. *Yes, Lucas is his name,* she thought. Right when she thought of his name, he flinched and looked around. She looked away, unsettled. She'd tried hard to keep other people's fragmented thoughts out of her head. *Can I broadcast them too? Did Lucas just hear my thoughts? What is going on?*

She imagined her mental jewelry box shut tight. Panic rose, but Ariana tried to act casual in front of her friends. She felt compelled to look back to the scene.

Lucas was staring at his tormentor; but Lucas' face was like stone. It was as though he was patiently waiting for a child to stop speaking. Ariana was sure he saw just the hint of a smile on Lucas. It made her sick how boys like Lucas were treated. He wore glasses, and was a little short and too thin. Then Ariana realized that he had some muscles she'd never noticed. They must have been going to the same schools for years, even shared classrooms, but they'd never even spoken. She doubted Lucas even knew her name.

His tormentors laughed again, and now she was close enough to hear Billy was talking about the size of a certain body part. That made her feel angrier. She felt sick to her stomach. His henchmen were laughing. Ariana stared at the one called Jonesy. Then something happened. Billy's friend held his stomach, and the next second, the lewd joke was silenced by Jonesy launching projectile vomit all over Billy. The other henchman laughed until he too was soaked in a stream of puke coming from Jonesy.

Lucas looked stunned, his calm mask breaking. The girls passed the scene. Ariana's friends, and the other kids gathered around, all howling with laughter. Billy could only repeat an angry, "What the f...!"

Then Lucas stared at Ariana.

She thought, *Did I just do that? Does he know I just did that?*

Her friends just led her away, laughing. Lucas walked in the opposite direction. The first bell rang out through the campus. Ariana was in a daze as the three girls broke apart to go to their separate classes.

As she stepped into her classroom, she clearly heard a word whispered in her mind.

Thanks.

CHAPTER EIGHT
TARZANA

Derek asked wearily, "Who knew blue and white were such popular colors for high school sports?" He put down the soft top on their rented convertible. They left the greater Los Angeles area, headed north on the 101 freeway.

Ehrhardt consulted the GPS. "Westlake Village is next. We're finally getting to the prettier places in this state. When were we here last? 1999?"

Derek corrected, "2000. The boy who could breathe under water. We gave him a true death."

"That's right. It was that ancient called Paxix, right? That little *scheisse* escaped us forever. Remember when we almost caught him in Berlin?" asked Ehrhardt.

Derek remembered. "Yeah. Couldn't have been worse timing. 1945. The Russians took over East Berlin the day we had him cornered."

"Oh, I remember. You were in the body of that blonde woman." Ehrhardt said, "I like it better when my brother is in a man's body."

Derek laughed, "The River decides where our ancient goes. Sometimes a male body, sometimes a female. But we always are true to our core. We always find each other again, brother."

Ehrhardt nodded. "Being an ancient warrior means we get to see the world over the expanse of time. Too bad the inferiors are determined to destroy it all."

"I remember last time in California you hooked up with one of those 'inferiors'. You had a boy together, didn't you?"

Ehrhardt sniffed. "We all have weak moments. She claims he was mine. I have no way to know. I only used her for her body. I've no time for anything else."

"You're too hard on regular humans. Not everyone gets chosen by The River," mused Derek, feeling philosophical. "Look around. I think they keep getting better at this civilization stuff. I don't miss the days before toilets."

The Witness in the backseat shifted uncomfortably. They allowed him a shower and new clothes, but denied him sunglasses. Having hands chained was uncomfortable in any car, especially in convertibles which are not generally known for their comfy back seats. His long, sandy brown hair wiped in his face.

"How you doing back there, Witness?" asked Derek over the wind.

He didn't want to talk. He had to concentrate until they passed Tarzana. Any stray thought could betray her.

"Not speaking to us? We have treated you with some kindness this time. Don't be rude," added Ehrhardt.

The Witness got an idea. They had just passed Encino, and Tarzana would be the next city off the 101. He couldn't afford to let even the smallest thought escape.

"Treated well?" shouted the Witness, "You've kept me prisoner for over ten years! You make me root out our kind so you can kill them. Screw your so-called kindness."

Ehrhardt slowly turned his head to see the man, "Did you just grow a new spine, Witness? What is wrong with you?"

"Wrong?" the Witness shouted over the wind. "Besides the fact that you punish me by killing thousands if I don't comply? I hate you and your pathetic master!" The Witness started kicking the back of Erhardt's passenger seat.

44

They had just passed Tarzana. The next city was Woodland Hills, then Calabasas. He had to focus them on something else besides his worry for her. He continued kicking, keeping his mind blank.

Ehrhardt grabbed the legs of the Witness to get him to stop. Derek engaged, "Whoa there, partner. Calm down. You know we had no idea some of those punishments would get out of hand. We didn't mean to kill, well, *all* those people. When you wouldn't help us put down that breakout, we had to be sure, but Ehrhardt just outdid himself that day in Sri Lanka. Didn't you brother?"

"And I paid for that," Ehrhardt said, still staring at the Witness in the back seat.

The witness said, "And you'll pay for it again. I hope next life you're born starving in some third world country."

Ehrhardt took off his glasses, suspicion dancing across his face.

The Witness finally looked away, to *seem* ashamed of what he'd said. He glanced up long enough to see the green highway sign that read "Pkwy Calabasas Exit Only." The danger had passed.

"I am sorry. Forgive me." The Witness bowed his head and closed his eyes, letting his long hair fall over his face. *She's safe, at least. I haven't betrayed her again.*

Ehrhardt stared at the Witness, deciding if he was hiding something. He shook his head and looked forward again. "I think the boredom of captivity has begun some actual madness. Witness, if you help us, with none of your tricks, we can try to take you on more missions. You are a good finder when you want to be."

"Yes, sir." The Witness' eyes were still closed. Being this close to the sight of his betrayal hurt.

Derek tried to lighten the mood. He pondered, "Do you think this is a true breakout? We haven't had one in living memory. Since, what, the 1870s?"

"I don't know why you focus on dates so much." replied Ehrhardt, "Why not just enjoy each life as we are born into them?"

"This is body number 27 for me. How can you not remember where you came from?" asked Derek.

"Oh, I remember that, brother," Ehrhardt said, "I just try to remember the good things like epic fights and beautiful women. Even the good deaths are nostalgic to me. We've both had a few spectacular deaths."

"We have," Derek agreed, "But I don't want to remember how the city smelled in say, the London streets of Shakespeare. Or the leeches by so-called doctors. Look around, brother, this life is amazing."

Ehrhardt shook his head. "Why? The inferiors are still disgusting. Raping this planet, killing animals for food. Barbarians. Idiots in any era! Take climate..."

"Oh no, let's not talk about global warming again," said Derek.

"Climate change, actually. It's science!" Ehrhardt exclaimed.

Derek disagreed, "Nonsense. Do you honestly think that these humans can kill this planet? It shrugged off the dinosaurs. The climate is changing, yes; it's called weather!"

"I don't know how you have the accumulated knowledge of dozens of lives, but you can ignore what 97% of scientists know." Ehrhardt said.

Derek argued, "Take our master..."

Ehrhardt screamed. "He's not our master!"

"Ok. Sorry, our boss, our elder," Derek clarified, "Our elder can do magic. So can we. Your precious 'scientists' don't believe magic exists. And you put your faith in inferior human kooks? The ones that said the earth was flat? The ones that once believed in 'spontaneous generation'; that mice could just wink into existence?"

"You're an idiot," said Ehrhardt, staring forward.

They were silent for a while. The Witness smiled. He loved when they fought. Which was often. It was the only small joy he got out of life.

Derek gave up the argument. "I really just want to relax, watch a movie. We work too hard."

Ehrhardt was glad to be onto another subject. "I would kill for a long shower. What movie will you watch?"

Derek laughed. "Strange. I wish you could still just go rent a movie, just stop at a rental store like years ago. I have the strangest desire to watch an old movie."

"Which one?" the elder brother asked.

Derek shook his head at his own silly impulse, "Tarzan."

CHAPTER NINE

JOHN

John Billings got off the train in Santa Helena. Like most train stations nowadays, it was in a rundown part of town, even in the affluent seaside town. Seeing the glittering city from the coast side, it was stunning at any time of day. The multi-million dollar estates climbed up the mountains, the entire city resembling a large half-circle, nestled between the tall mountains and the ocean.

Despite the city's splendor, the trains were deeply unreliable. He had arrived at the station a full two hours late. The train was supposed to continue to the next stop, Sea Valley, within the half hour, but John was dubious.

He stretched his legs, walking off the train to the smell of fresh air mixed with salty sea. He rubbed his dark, shaved head. He looked around at the fellow passengers milling about, most of them white. He wondered what the black population was in this area. Not being noticed was his best talent, so he promised himself to look it up on his phone. He couldn't afford to stand out as he searched for the teens.

The flashes were getting more frequent now, but their meaning was still unclear. He feared stretching out his mind too far. Anyone could be catching flashes. He only hoped they were correct. *A true break-out,* thought John. So many false leads these days, and no one left to interpret them. The Amartus numbers had grown so small, fewer re-births each cycle. And John feared the same was not happening to the other side, the Rageto. Their elders always seemed so much stronger, always recruiting, cycle after cycle.

In the small train station waiting room, John glanced over the wall display of tourist brochures to help allay his worries. 'Santa Helena, The American Riviera' caught his eye. He smiled to himself. Naming yourself America's Riviera seemed overly pretentious. But he was headed north, away from this *Riviera* by the sea. The place he was drawn to was fifty miles north, and divorced from the ocean a few miles inland. Sea Valley was a quiet workman's town. Probably no glitz there, and hopefully he would find the teens quickly.

John opened his own mental cabinet, just a touch. It was dangerous, with the Rageto surely on the same trail. Plus, John was not the best finder. All the real finders were gone. Both his Amartus side and their Rageto side were just fumbling around in the dark now, hoping for the great River to deposit gifts.

He would have to find a connection outside the struggle, confer with the Sect. His last contact in the City of Commerce had told him of a small shop in Sea Valley. The Sect's old habit of keeping agents in smaller towns continued. John glanced toward the horizon of the north. It was full dark now, the electrical haze lighting just the outlines of the hills and small mountains ahead.

He had no flashes. John opened his cabinet wider and looked to the north again. The breath caught in his throat at the bright green glow that hovered over his destination. John thought, *what's coming is big.*

This was not just one or two teens he was looking for. This was the biggest breakout that John had ever been close to.

I can't be the only one that will see that. A new birth? Even one could change everything.

John rushed onto the train, hoping for no delays. Mostly, he hoped he was not too late.

An hour later, John walked off the train into the night just as it was finally cooling off. He had his checked bag in his hand. The train left, and he was alone. The small unmanned train kiosk stood silent in the dark, lit only with a few lights.

He could hear the ocean, but could barely see it; this part of California was ruled by fog and a thick marine layer. He kept his back to the water, letting the power of the sea crash into his ears. It helped steel him for the dangerous work ahead. He bent down and retrieved his sheathed short sword from the bag, strapping it to his back. He ditched the empty bag in the nearby trash can. John breathed the sea air, then abandoned the ocean and walked toward the city.

John passed miles of farm land, nestled between the ocean and Sea Valley. The rows of cabbages and flower fields made the walk pleasant. From this close, the glow over the city was stunning. John wondered if anyone from the Rageto had shown up yet. He locked his mental closet, and the glow disappeared. It was too dangerous to leave his thoughts wide open. John would find these teens with stealth.

The route from the ocean was not the main way into the city. Highway 1 ran through Sea Valley, the older main highway of California. It was the first major auto vein, during the time of 'kicks on route 66' elsewhere in the country. Tucked away, some twenty miles from the main California Highway 101, Sea Valley was a very unlikely spot for a breakout. But John understood there was no second guessing the great River.

Using his smart phone, he found the address for the small shop. Sea Valley was laid out on a grid pattern like most cities built after the 1880s. Urban planning was the norm, so it was very easy to find his way around. John thought back through many lifetimes, remembering cobbled streets and winding roads. He allowed himself a little smile at the wonders of the modern world.

John's main talent was his ability to hide from other finders, to be invisible. He needed help to search for the warriors, especially if one or more was a new birth. *The Sect is my best shot.*

The small building had only one old, yellow exterior light illuminating the entry way. A one story structure, with decayed California stucco, the faded painted sign read "Bird's Eye Television Repair." Old junk and ancient televisions were stacked haphazardly in dusty piles along the wall leading to the door.

John smiled, knowing that the residents must drive by every day and either not notice the business, or wonder how they could still be in business at all. There were rusty bars on the windows, all the glass blacked out. He knocked on the plain door.

No one came, so John knocked louder. There were rustling noises inside the small shop before a muffled voice said, "It's nine o'clock. We're closed. Especially to strangers in hoodies."

John put down the hood of his sweatshirt and used a phone app to draw a symbol with his finger.

He held the image up to the peep hole in the door. He heard more shuffling sounds and the door swung open. A large man filled the doorway, peeking around John. Sure that no one else was with John, the giant man with the bushy beard ushered him inside. Both inside, the man replaced the heavy wood bar across the door.

The man shook hands. John felt like his hand was being swallowed by the man's enormous paw. "Name's Pete."

"John."

"Sorry I was leery. We've got a drug and homeless problem in this part of town. Never a good knock after dark, you know?"

John smiled, "I thought it was a black man in a hoodie kind of thing."

"Never that," said Pete, "This is a very diverse part of California. Who has time for racial nonsense? It's the twenty first century. I just wasn't expecting anyone so soon."

"What made you expect anyone at all? Does the Sect know what's happening here?"

Pete said, "We're still outside the struggle, playing referee between the Amartus and the Rageto. The Sect is made up of us ordinary folk, what one side calls 'inferiors.' I won't say which side."

John laughed at the jab toward the Rageto.

Pete scratched his head. "We monitor a lot of activity with the Rageto Elders and their agents. Two agents are headed this direction right now. Makes sense you Amartus are in these parts too. We don't know what they're looking for yet. My bet is on a relic. Can you enlighten us?"

John nodded. "I'm here because I felt a breakout was happening. Maybe they got the same idea."

"You mean somewhere on the Central Coast?" asked Pete.

John shook his head. "No, I mean right here, in this city. I'm sure of that."

"That's a troubling coincidence," said Pete, "Come with me."

John followed the man to a set of stairs leading down. He noted how Pete's head barely missed the ceiling. "I didn't know you had any cellars in California."

"Cellars? That dates you a bit. We call them basements, and you're right, no one has basements in California. Earthquakes and basements don't go together. This one was built special. The walls and floor are lined with lead, nearly a foot thick, and two feet of concrete around that."

"Lead?" John looked closely at the walls, "Is this a station?"

"Yep," They arrived at a metal door. "What's your warrior name, John?" Pete asked, unlocking three separate locks.

"Pentoss," replied John.

Pete stopped, "The legendary Pentoss in my place? I've read some Sect histories about your exploits. You've been around a long time."

"In one body or another," said John, "Happily, no one's given me a true death. But the Rageto keep trying."

"The Sect is neutral." Pete whispered, "but off the record, I hate those Rageto jerks."

The lights came on automatically. They walked down a staircase into a large room. In one corner, Pete pulled a thick blanket to reveal a clear plastic bookcase full of ancient books. The bookcase was enclosed in its own thick plastic case.

Pete said, "It's locked and temperature controlled. What you're looking at are many important spell books the Rageto elders would love to get their hands on again."

John smiled, "Glad you're leaning a bit toward us good guys."

"I speak only for myself. Your side has done things we've disagreed with. But it's clear to see who has the better intent. The Amartus don't want to enslave anyone, at least."

"No," John said grimly, "But it's very troubling that these books are in this area at the same time a major breakout is happening."

"I take it you don't believe in coincidence."

John asked, "Do you? Sometimes it feels like the River has some crazy plans. Other times it feels like it's screwing with us for fun. Is that Egyptian papyrus?"

"Yes. An early Egyptian Book of the Dead." Pete pointed, "that scroll contains a part of Lord Joland's Thirteen Principles, with hand written spells. There is the Demonis Codex. We also have both volumes of the Xemaricon Journal."

"Why not just destroy them? I've never understood why the Sect keeps them."

"Balance. You've been around a while, Pentoss. The same awareness of the River that brought you here is shared in some way by all the ancients, warriors, and elders on both sides. To destroy these works would release this knowledge back into the consciousness of the River. Imagine a renaissance of books being written like these. A new flood of dark knowledge being rediscovered, flowing through the imaginations of Rageto elders. No one would consciously know why these ideas were coming to them, but they would slowly make it back into the world all the same. We keep these secrets safely out of play."

An icy hand touched John's spine at the idea. "But the Sect is made of, no offense, regular humans. You don't feel the connection to the river."

"Yes and no," said Pete, "'Normal' minds are less in tune with the River. The Sect learns what it knows from traditional methods. We read books, do the leg work, pass down knowledge. The Sect might not have the mastery of instinct that you Amartus have, or the ability to use magic like the Rageto, but many can tap into the continuum of the River. Nostradamus was human, Einstein was human. Stephen Hawking is human. They all have understanding, a connection to the River."

John said, "I see your point. I suppose all humanity is touched by the River somehow. Sorry, I was never much of a theologian. How long do these books stay in each station?"

"Well, I could tell you that, but then I'd have to kill you," John noticed Pete's giant size again. Pete smiled, "Just kidding... well, kind of. The length of stay varies at each station. It's the only way to keep the knowledge safe. The number and location of the stations will remain the Sect's secret, Pentoss. Do you prefer I call you John?"

"John is fine. I've had this current life a while now."

Pete said, "John it is. Amartus numbers aren't what they used to be. Too many true deaths in recent years."

John knew firsthand how right Pete was about their dwindling numbers. He changed the subject, "Have you added to your collection recently?"

"Not for a few years," Pete said, looking back at the books, "We found the nest of the people suspected for some bad disasters. The Sect stole fifteen books from that elder in Italy. I don't think he's very happy with us. But our crown jewel is this."

He handed John lead lined gloves. "You'll want to wear these. One of your kind touching this could open a window. Someone might get a flash of where these books are."

John took the gloves, "They're that sensitive?"

Pete said, "Yep. Since the elder owned some of these books, touched them, used them, he has a pretty strong bond. We've removed most of the connection, but if he sees a flash of you handling the book. Well, I have enough problems, thanks." Pete opened the case and put on his own gloves before bringing out the book.

John stared, "Is that really a copy of..."

"Yes, it's a "Vitaeizicon. The legend of this book was what inspired Lovecraft to invent his Necronomicon. This book has many spells, and many tricks. Most of them concern death. There is also a spell to make relics."

The book was clearly centuries old, with a thick animal hide binding. An intricate silver metalwork covered the book, and the back was more elaborate than the front, almost like a metal sculpture woven into the binding. John guessed it was a dark puzzle that no one should ever solve. He did not want to touch it. Pete put the book away and locked the case.

"Why did you show me that book?" John asked.

Pete took off his special gloves. "To show you what's at stake. If this is a true breakout, they will be coming for the young warriors. When will the rest of your team arrive?"

John shook his head.

"Just you? I assume you're not kidding." Pete paused a moment, "Let's just hope the young ones will be on your side. I say that as an objective observer, or course. I'll ask my Sect brothers if we can speed up the station transfer. The books must stay at least three more days, no matter what. The Sect isn't as big as it used to be, either."

John understood. "Then I guess I'll have to fight whoever is coming on my own and activate the warriors as fast as I can."

Pete shook his head, "I've gotta get an easier job."

* * *

The Witness shifted again in the back seat, but no position was comfortable. He stared out the window as they headed further north on the 101 freeway. They had driven through Saint Helena, and were now driving parallel with the dark coastline. To their left, the sea. Ahead, a series of cities further north that made up the Central Coast of California.

Don't they see that? Even they can't be that blind, thought the Witness. He stared at the intense green glow over the tall hills. At that moment, a flash came into his mind.

"What is it?" asked Ehrhardt, who was now driving. "You felt something, didn't you?"

"No," he instinctively lied, "Maybe. A flash of an old book." He ignored the glow coming from the horizon, and hoped the book would be enough of a distraction for them.

"What book?" asked Derek.

This time the Witness told the truth, "I don't know. It was only a fragment. A metal binding. A word. Vitz... nomicon, something like that."

"The Necronomicon?" asked Derek, excited.

Ehrhardt said, "I keep telling you that book doesn't exist. It was made up."

Derek protested, "But, I've seen..."

Ehrhardt cut him off, "You've seen silly books of pretend spells in shiny new book stores, people who created a hoax. You will find no actual spell books in a Barnes & Noble. Which way, Witness?"

He wanted to lie. But the last three times they had punished too many innocent people. "There, turn there."

The highway sign read "Hwy 1, Sea Valley 17, Camp Cooke Army Base 23."

Ehrhardt asked, "Brother, is Sea Valley on the blue and white sports list?"

Derek consulted his notes, "Why, yes brother. Yes, it is. I think we found them."

They left the 101 and took the exit. The winding road headed west, leading straight into Sea Valley. The Witness kept his head down, but his eyes on the bright glow. *It is a true breakout. Please let them find this book instead of the warriors.*

CHAPTER TEN

LAST SHIFT

It was 9:50, ten minutes to closing time at Ocean Burgers. Their training had told them when customers walk in near closing, even one minute before, they were to be treated like any other customers of the day.

The girl behind the counter smiled as three men entered, secretly hoping it was a takeout order. Her smile wavered when the man spoke. It wasn't his German accent, but something else about him that unnerved her.

Zacke was in the back room, filling the mop bucket. He'd gotten better at keeping his random flashes in check. His mental sphere was nearly welded shut when he was at work. A strong flash came anyway.

He wondered if it was that Cody kid again. He'd wanted to approach him at school, but still couldn't figure out how to do it. *Hey, you hear other people's thoughts, too? Hey, are you a weirdo like me?* There was just no easy way to handle it. No, this flash was of three men.

Zacke wheeled the mop bucket out, along with the bright yellow sign with the falling stick man, demonstrating what could happen if you slipped.

There were only three employees left to close the restaurant. His shift manager Victoria had left a few minutes earlier. Wes was on the grill, and Jody was taking orders. He paused when he saw Jody's expression. It was the three men from his flash, alright. They had ordered and were taking a seat. Jody came to him, and whispered, "There, like, aren't any more Nazis, right? One of those guys gives me the creeps."

The Nazi question made Zacke smile, but her expression made it flicker. He didn't need a flash of her thoughts to know she was freaked out.

"No more Nazis." He saw the three men huddled in the corner table. "But I'll take their tray over when the food's ready." She smiled her thanks.

Zacke mopped the area behind the yellow floor sign until their food was ready. Jody gave a signal, and Zacke took the three burgers and fries to the men. One man reached for the food quickly, but the other man caught his hand.

"I'll take it." said the younger, blond guy.

Zacke noticed the chains on the man who had reached for the tray first. *He's a prisoner being transferred,* thought Zacke.

He'd seen a few of those already, although the chains looked like no handcuffs he'd seen. Being close to a federal prison, it happened. But most of the time, the guards were in uniform and drove a prison bus. They rarely brought the prisoners inside for anything more than the bathroom.

The blond man smiled and took the tray before Zacke put it on the table. He did a strange thing, his finger brushed under Zacke's wrist. He almost dropped the tray, but the blond man steadied it and said, "Oh, sorry. We're just really hungry after our awesome road trip."

Normally, Zacke would have engaged them. Maybe asked them where they were from, what brought them to Sea Valley. But not tonight. He smiled thinly, left the table and went to wash his hands and wrists in the kitchen hand-wash sink. They still didn't feel clean. He hoped they would eat and leave quickly. Not only were they creepy, he had a ton of homework to finish when he got home.

He certainly didn't want to get into the business of these three, but his sub-conscious must have wanted to know more. A few fragments came. No images, just words.

Mixed race I think
But power?
Yes. Strong mental lock...
hidden power
New Birth?
Activated?

Are they talking about me? Zacke wondered. He looked out to the dining room. They were eating their burgers and fries. The doors had been locked to new customers, the open sign turned off. The other two employees were doing their side work in the kitchen. Zacke had no choice but to go back in the dining room with his mop. He finished the far side of the dining room, and spied two of the men going to the bathroom.

One of the men was standing outside the door. *Definitely a prisoner.* That was the same procedure he'd seen before. The guard had nothing to worry about, since there were no windows in their bathrooms.

The chained man came out and the guard escorted him back to the table. *Good*, thought Zacke, *the bathrooms are the last things to clean.* He put the sign in front of the men's room door, just as the guard tried to come back in.

"Oh, sorry sir. This bathroom is closed. You can use the ladies room. No one's in there." Zacke smiled, and the blond man returned the smile, but seemed to be sizing him up.

He said "Thank you," but didn't enter the ladies. The blond guard walked back to his table. Zacke locked the men's door behind him, then saw the mirror. In rough streaky pink soap, the message read:

Zacke Run

A chill went through him, but he forced himself to stay calm. *No one spells my name like that. Name tag is in my locker. How'd they know my name at all? Who are these people?*

A knock came at the door.

It was his co-worker, "Zacke? Those guys just left. I'm done. Can you use the buddy system and leave with Jody?"

Trying to slow his heartbeat he replied, "Yeah dude, I got it."

"Thanks, Zacke," said Wes, his footfalls fading.

He finished the bathroom and checked the ladies just to make sure no one was hiding there. *You're being dumb*, he told himself, but that message on the mirror was not a hallucination. Jody finished and they both left together out the back door, setting the alarm as they went.

Jody's boyfriend picked her up, and Zacke looked around, unnerved by the thought of the three block walk home.

Ehrhardt stepped out from around a corner, "Hello there. I wanted to thank you for the good service."

Zacke's heart sped up. The man was shorter than him, probably in his thirties or forties. His confident manner made Zacke think that he could handle himself, and Zacke himself had never been in a real fight. "Thanks. You can leave feedback online if you want. There's a survey at the bottom of your receipt."

"We wanted to thank you in person," an American accent came from the other direction, "you seem like a very special kid."

Zacke briefly wondered where the third man was, but clearly, these were the dangerous ones. Just about to take the message's advice and run, the German man spoke, "Don't you feel special, Zacke? Maybe you can do things no one else can do? Can you tell what I'm thinking?"

Zacke didn't answer, but felt an unpleasant sensation, like something foreign in his head. He clamped his metal sphere tight, and saw the blond guy wince, then smile, "My boy, you are special. We can help you understand what's happening to you."

"Stay right there," Zacke said, trying to sound formidable.

The men were about a dozen feet from him, both coming closer. Zacke put his hands on either side of him, outstretched to each man, as though a gesture alone could stop them. He knew of one way he could get away. He thought of his mother and knew he promised himself he'd never do it again. A warm tingle danced through him, warming his entire body. Both men paused, sensing something might happen. The German looked angry, the blond man smiled.

Zacke jumped when he heard the honking. He noticed the German reach under his suit jacket. A small white rusty Toyota sped toward him. The honking continued as it pulled up. He looked inside, then pulled on the handle and jumped in.

As they sped out of the parking lot, Zacke looked in the side mirror. Both men just stood there, not moving. They disappeared out of sight as the small getaway car zoomed around a corner.

Zacke asked, "What are you doing here? You left like a half hour ago."

Victoria replied, "I was in the parking lot trying to figure out how to ask you out. Looks like I'm saving your cute butt instead," she smiled. "Who were those guys? Should I call the cops?"

"I have no idea. Some Nazi and a surfer dude," said Zacke, looking back.

"That's a weird combo. What did they want with you?" asked Victoria, "Were you about to take on both of those guys?"

"No way." Zacke let his heart slow down. He felt the special tingly heat drain from him. "Guess I was hoping for a knight on a white horse." He indicated the car.

Victoria laughed. "Ha! I like that. Here I thought that I was being a stupid girl, all afraid to ask a guy to coffee. Now I'm the hero."

Zacke smiled, "I could use some coffee. Can we get it to go? I don't want Hitler and Joe Surfer ruining our first date at Starbucks."

Victoria smiled, and looked sideways at Zacke, "Starbucks date, takeout. Deal. No Nazis allowed."

CHAPTER ELEVEN

NIGHT WALK

A text went off in Katie's dark room. She'd only been asleep for a half hour, after finishing season four of the British show *Misfits*. Sammy hadn't texted her all week, but now a one appeared at 12:52 am.

Hey girl. You still awake? Take a walk with me.

She stood up, and went to the window. There he was, standing just outside the fence by the gravel driveway. He smiled. She smiled back, and texted a reply.

You're so bad! Gimme 2 minutes.

She sniffed two piles of clothes until she found pants and a shirt that were mostly clean. She put on a light jacket to hide the fact that she was too lazy to put on a bra, and climbed out her window. Her mom and stepdad's window was across the house on the other side, but her step-sister's was right next to Katie. She'd have to be careful.

Katie inwardly cursed their loud gravel driveway as she landed, and jumped onto the strip of cool grass as soon as she could. Instead of going down to the squeaky gate, she jumped the fence and Sammy helped her over, his hands firmly on either side of her waist.

A tingle went up her back as she landed next to him. The moonlight lit his light brown hair from behind as she looked up to him. A full foot taller than her, she imagined him lifting her against the fence and kissing her by moonlight.

Instead he smiled. "Come on, let's go to the park."

Katie knew which one he meant. The run-down park was just a hundred feet of grass in a narrow strip, with a small merry-go-round and an ancient swing set. It was nestled next to the hill that marked the end of their town. No one went there, especially this late.

It was perfect.

"Sammy, I thought we were gonna hang last Sunday," Katie said, trying to sound casual.

Sammy replied, "Sorry Katie Kate, I had to stay with the fam. Mom has this new thing about Sunday dinners. My brothers bolted right after dinner, but I had to watch *The Notebook* with her."

Sammy said, "I hate that movie..."

At the same time, Katie said, "I love that movie." They both laughed.

Sammy rolled his eyes, "Ugh. The only good part is when they finally have sex."

"Ugg. Boys," said Katie, "Of course that's the part you like. Kissing in the rain? Them staying together? No romance in this town, I tell ya."

He turned quickly and presented a white daisy. She hadn't even seen him pick it. He smiled, she smiled. He presented his hand. She put the small flower in her hair, and took it gently. They walked like that for the next block. *Why does he even like me? He's a senior and all the girls love him.* But she silenced the thought as she felt the warmth of his hand. *But those girls aren't here, are they?*

They got to the park. He broke the hand holding and sprinted for the swings. Katie ran too. He got there first, but she pretended like she'd won and insisted on taking his swing. He wouldn't budge.

"We can swing together." He gently pulled her onto his lap. She wanted to resist, but part of her didn't want to resist. They swung together, their body heat making her a little dizzy.

"This is nice," he said. Then the flashes came.

His body on top of her...
The cool wind on her bare skin...
His hands pushing her down...

She jumped off the swing.

Sammy stopped swinging, "Whoa. Katie, I'm sorry. Did I do something wrong? I just... I really like you."

Katie stood, facing the swing.

He stood, his hand slowly rising up the chain, He looked down, and said, "I've just... never felt like this about anyone."

Her heart skipped. Sammy looked like a lost little boy. She took a step closer, his face shadowed by the bright moonlight. Then slowly, her lips were on his. He didn't fight it. Her first real kiss had taken much too long, and she would enjoy it.

They broke, then their arms were around each other again, kissing deeply. Before she knew it, they were laying on the cool grass, his weight pressed down on her. It felt nice, at first. Then something changed.

It wasn't a flash, he was actually starting to hurt her, pushing her hands down. Katie struggled, "Sammy, stop."

"Oh, come on Katie. I want this. I know you want this too. It's too late to stop now. Come on," he grabbed her hands and pulled them roughly up over her head with one hand. *He's so strong.* His other hand was on her stomach, moving up.

She said, "NO!"

In a flash, his weight lifted, and Sammy was flying. He vaulted five feet in the air, flailing his arms. She scrambled to her feet as he landed just short of the rusty merry-go-round.

The look of shock on his face was like a cartoon. His hand shot to the back of his head. Sammy realized his head was less than an inch from the hard metal edge of the merry-go-round. He scrambled on shaky legs, enraged, "How the hell...?"

For a split second she felt shame. Then anger flared in her. He faltered at the look on her face. Sammy regained his swagger and stepped toward Katie, "What the f..."

"Now, now, my boy. No reason for vulgarity." said Ehrhardt.

The brothers appeared. Parked by the curb was a red convertible, its top up.

Derek said, "We saw what happened. You were trying to take advantage of this girl."

The boy looked from man to man, his eyes wide. "Wait, I didn't..." then he found his arrogance. "You're not a cop. I didn't do anything. Mind your own business."

The bravado leaked away as Ehrhardt stepped toward Sammy. "Boy, listen to me. You will go home. Erase her number from your little cell phone there. Ignore her at school. Never speak her name again. Don't even think of her." Ehrhardt was in the boy's face, his breath hot, "If you come near her again I will rip off those little bits that boys your age value so dearly, and feed them to you one spoonful at a time."

Sammy's brave persona cracked. He stumbled, then sprinted away. Sammy didn't look back.

Derek looked to Katie, "Are you okay, miss?"

Katie had wrapped her arms across her chest, her thin jacket not stopping the chills from rocking her, "Yes, yes I think so." she worried about how much they had seen. She'd never flung a person into the air before.

"Would you like us to call anyone?" Derek asked tenderly.

"NO! I mean, no. Thank you," stammered Katie, "I have to go home now."

Derek soothed, "I understand. I'm sure you would not accept a ride from strangers after what just happened, but maybe we could walk you home? We only want to make sure you're okay."

She didn't want anyone around her now, but how could she refuse? She wasn't sure how much her talents would have protected her from an angry Sammy. They may have just saved her. Also, there was something vaguely familiar about them.

"I'm Derek, and this is Ehrhardt."

"Hi, I'm Rebecca," she lied.

"Hello 'Rebecca,'" Derek smiled, "I wonder if we might discuss that little trick you just did."

They did see me, "What? Umm... Oh, I don't know. I guess it was one of those emergencies. You know, a mom can lift a car when their kid's in danger. Like that."

Ehrhardt shook his head, "That was not an accident. My brother and I are special, too. On the way to your home we'd like to discuss how we can help you bring out some of your powers."

"Powers?" Katie said, "I'm not, like, a superhero or anything."

"Neither am I," Derek moved his hand and whispered some words she didn't understand. A giant barn owl appeared on his arm, "I'm no magician either. There are more of us than you know. We can help each other." The owl looked at her, made the questioning noise owls do, then flew off into the darkness.

She released a little of her mental control and a few images floated in, a small glimpse of some things these men could do. The images were amazing, even though she sensed they were not showing her everything. But somehow, in some strange way, she felt stronger around these men. Safe. They walked to her house and Katie was told amazing things.

* * *

Outside the park, from the deep shadows among some trees, John looked on. He was about to rush in when he saw the boy on top of the terrified girl. A car pulled up before he could act. When the boy went flying off the girl, the two men were too fast, and made contact first. Two men. *Please don't be the brothers.*

John looked for the license plate, but it was a rental car. No help there. Then he saw movement in the back seat. Just then, a man with long hair spun around and looked right at John.

John thought, *Impossible. A real finder?*

The man looked at John and held up his hands to show that he was chained. By then the brothers were walking off with the girl. They rounded the corner and were gone.

John went to the door, but it was locked. The man said "Driver's side."

John opened the door and flipped up the front seat to get to the back. "Who are you?"

The Witness spoke quickly, "My name is not important. Everyone in this town is in danger. Those are very dangerous men. How many are you?"

John said, "Just me. How did you know I was here? Not even the best finder can see me."

"I *am* the best finder," said the Witness.

John replied, "Then let's get you out of there."

"You can't. They have the keys and I'm chained to this..."

John thrust his short sword in and up, breaking the chain. The Witness was free. John replaced his sword into the scabbard strapped across his back. "Let's go."

"You have to remove my necklace. It's a binding charm," said the Witness.

"Is it safe for me to touch?"

"Yes. It was charmed to bind me alone."

John carefully removed the charm. The Witness shrugged like he'd shed a thousand pounds. The necklace fell to the floor of the car.

Out of bondage, the Witness thought of using his old talent to disable the car for good. But it would bring the brothers running back. He said, "We need to hurry. You alone are no match for those monsters."

John led the way, hurrying on foot away from the captors. "I need to know everything, but first I need to know who those men really are."

The Witness kept up the fast pace, "Their true warrior names are Caron and Sazzo."

"The brothers. Damn," remarked John, "It is them."

"Who are you, really? How can I trust you?"

"My warrior name is Pentoss," replied John.

The Witness showed a true smile for the first time in many years.

CHAPTER TWELVE
LAST BELL

Ariana was going to be late. She had already texted her friends to go ahead without her as she rushed out the door in the morning sun. She finished her text and looked up, nearly running into Lucas.

She stopped, surprised. "What... what are you doing here?"

He put out his hand, "Hi. I'm Lucas. You know why I'm here."

"Ariana." she shook hands awkwardly, then she lied, "I have no idea why you're here. I don't even know you. I do know we're going to miss the first bell."

"We better hurry then," he stepped off the sidewalk to let her pass. "We have to talk about yesterday."

Ariana side-stepped the question, "Umm, Lucas, right? I don't even know you, so what is there to talk about?"

"We've been going to the same school since like third grade," said Lucas.

"Yeah, I've seen you, I guess." she dodged. "But I really have to get to class."

He appeared in front of her again, "Come on... stop for a sec. How did you do that yesterday? How did you make Jonesy throw up? What else can you do?"

"I don't know what you're talking about," she said, "Get out of my way, please."

He let her pass; something like a bow with a wave of the hand, which should have made him seem weirder. For some reason, she thought it was nice. Ariana focused again. "I don't want to talk about it."

"Well, sorry Ariana, but you have to. Do you know how crazy I used to think I was? Now I find someone else in my own school can do stuff."

Ariana whispered, "Listen Lucas. I don't want to talk about any of this, and neither should you. These weird things are not something you, like, want to draw attention to. A lot of people already think you're... well, no offense..."

"I know what people think of me, Ariana," she smiled inwardly when he got the subtle accent of her name right. Lucas continued "But I need to know I'm not alone."

"Hello." Zacke was standing on the corner, right where they were about to cross.

"Umm, hello," said Lucas. They continued walking, but the look in Zacke's eyes made them pause.

"Wait," said Zacke, "This is going to sound really weird, but I had a dream last night. You were both in it."

They stopped. "What?" Ariana asked.

Zacke said, "And not just you. There were two other kids from our school."

Lucas asked, "Your name is Zacke, right?"

"Yeah."

"Okay." Lucas said, "this is getting awesome."

"Awesome? I don't want any part of this." Ariana denied her own curiosity. "I have to get to class."

Zacke blurted out, "I can hear people's thoughts sometimes, well, a lot of the times, lately. I think we're supposed to meet."

"That's enough! I'm leaving..." Ariana stepped into the street and didn't see the car approaching. She whipped her head and saw the car was only a few inches away. She gasped, and instinctively put her hands out in front of her.

The car came to an immediate stop, but not because of the brakes. It stopped cold, like time was frozen around it. Lucas looked closer and saw the front of the car was low to the pavement from slamming on the brakes. The look on the driver's face was stuck in an expression of shock.

Zacke scanned the scene, but no one else was around. They all crossed in front of the car, shooting amazed looks at Ariana, and each other. Ariana made sure they were all clear of the car and flicked her hand. The car unfroze and the sound of skidding tires sounded. The vehicle ended up a few feet passed where Ariana had been standing. She would have been hit.

The driver's head whipped around, scanning for the girl he was sure he had hit. He spotted the three teens a few feet away. Ariana rushed over to the driver's door, which was just opening. She closed his door back on him before he could say anything. Her words were a blur. "I'm so sorry. I didn't see you. But I'm okay and I have to get to school. I'm fine. But I, like, really gotta go. Thanks."

She bolted from the scene as the befuddled man tried to speak. Lucas looked at the driver and wondered what a few seconds of missing time felt like. It must have been like cutting a few seconds out of a movie. He pondered how the man's mind would adjust to that missing moment.

Ariana was halfway down the block before Zacke and Lucas could catch up with her. They heard the car drive away. The boys found her sitting on a concrete bench, just in front of a small store that hadn't opened yet. She wiped her eyes as the they approached. "Just leave me alone!"

"Did you just freeze time? That was amazing! Can you freeze me?" asked Lucas, but Zacke shook his head. Lucas shut down his excitement. Ariana was sobbing. Zacke touched her arm, but she shrugged it off.

"Don't!" she yelled, "Sorry, I've... I've never done that, nothing so big."

Lucas said, "So you *can* do stuff!"

"Cool it, dude," said Zacke, "she's scared."

Ariana yelled, "That's right, I am scared! I don't want any of this. Why is this happening?"

Zacke touched her shoulder and this time she let him, "I have no idea, but it is happening. That wasn't our imagination. Something is going on and we have to figure out what it all means."

Ariana stared, "How? Call the doctor? Talk to a priest? They would throw us in crazy jail."

"Crazy jail?" Lucas smiled.

That changed the tone. Ariana attempted a smile while she wiped her tears. "You know what I mean."

"Then we should help each other," said Lucas, "It can't be a coincidence. Three of us in a town this size? Maybe more, able to do weird stuff?"

Zacke agreed, "I don't know about you, but for me it's getting stronger."

"Yeah, me too," confirmed Lucas.

"Well, obviously, me too," Ariana said, pointing back to where the car had been, "I just froze a stupid car."

They all laughed nervously. Only two blocks from school, they heard the bell sound; school was about to start.

"Crap, that's second bell. We're already late," said Ariana.

Lucas said, "Guys, this is more important than school. We have powers."

"Calm down. We're not X-men," said Ariana. "Whatever this is, we should at least act normal, right?"

Zacke nodded, "You're right. But we need to meet. Can you all come to the game tonight? We can meet under the home team bleachers."

"Isn't that where the pot heads go to smoke and drink?" asked Ariana.

"Good point. We'll meet behind the east side visiting team bleachers. No one should bother us there." Zacke elaborated, "It's usually deserted over there when the game starts."

They all agreed, Ariana reluctantly. But she promised to be there.

Zacke added, "And I'll try to find the others from my dream."

Ariana walked off on her own, but the two boys walked together onto the campus. They compared a few notes just before they broke to go to their separate classes.

Lucas asked, "Really? Ambushed you outside your work?"

"Yeah. They said they could help me," said Zacke, "but something wasn't right."

"They could show up anytime, anywhere. How did they find you in the first place?" asked Lucas.

Zacke just shrugged as they walked to class. It was the beginning of a very eventful day.

CHAPTER THIRTEEN

DAVID

John took another sip. "Thank you. Good coffee."

Pete sighed, "You should thank me for more than the coffee. I told you the Sect doesn't like to get directly involved. I shouldn't have let you two in."

"I'm glad you did. I never thought I'd get away," said the Witness.

"You were really a prisoner for more than ten years?" asked John.

The Witness said, "Yes, they grabbed me out of the train station in Chicago. I wasn't paying attention, letting my mind wander. I was so relieved to be away from my family, at first."

Pete gave a quizzical look.

The Witness clarified, "I know that sounds cruel. But, I had to leave to protect them. I was getting flashes of things that terrified me. I was a late bloomer, my powers only surfaced after my kid was born. Then I had a bad accident with my main power. Almost killed us all. I thought I couldn't tell my wife. I thought I was protecting her."

John said, "All the women I've known, I doubt your wife would have felt that way."

The Witness nodded. "You're right, of course. That's the horrible irony; I had decided to go back to Tarzana, to my family. In that huge train station in Chicago, I realized that I couldn't live without them, no matter what. But then the brothers cornered me in that bathroom, and they've made me work for them ever since."

"I don't mean to pass judgment," said John, "But didn't you try to resist?"

"Of course I did. Their elder has some finding talent of his own that he augments with his foul magic. That's how they found me. They knew I would be a strong natural finder, so they put that charm on me. It doesn't interfere with my finding ability, but it knocks out my other power."

"You'll have to join us in the Amartus. We think of them as talents, not powers."

The Witness continued, "Then they started punishing me when I refused to help them. There was a potential breakout in Russia. They found two teens, talented kids. I refused to find them. They beat me first, but I still refused. Then they made me watch as they brought two passenger planes down. One exploded in mid-air right in front of me."

"Monsters," said Pete, "Crap, I keep forgetting to be neutral."

"Yes they are, but that time there were two teams. They found the teens anyway. They tried to recruit them, but they couldn't and killed them instead. They started to put the numbers on the wall of my cell; all the deaths they claimed I caused. Then came December 2004."

"The Sect believed the 2004 earthquake and tsunami was one of the Rageto, but they couldn't prove it," said Pete.

John added, "I've lived through a few Caron-made earthquakes. But he'd never managed anything like that before. Just horrible."

"Not as horrible as watching." said the Witness, "I saw that tsunami sweep onto the land. I was there as they killed all those people because I wouldn't help them find new recruits. They were trying to find four teens in Sri Lanka; three ancients and one possible new birth. Because I wouldn't help them, they killed over 200,000 innocent people that day. They made me watch news reports night and day for the next month."

"Now, these two ancient warriors are in my town, looking for you. Great. I've got to call my boss again." Pete left the room.

John put his hand on the shoulder of the Witness, "They made you Witness horrors, but that's over now. Time to reclaim your real name, David."

David accepted his name back. "Feels good to be a person again."

John knew there was no lasting comfort for David. He had seen too much. John focused on the present. "Now there are five more hidden warriors, here in this place. You'll have to help me find them before they do."

"Five? Strange. I can only feel four. But this town is small; there's only one high school. They contacted two last night. You saw the girl; she talked with them willingly. They've probably already poisoned her mind and recruited her. The other one, a boy, got away. You are just one warrior against two ancients, John. You said you encountered the brothers before."

"I have," John said grimly, "and I've fought their elder. Now, we are two. We have four, possibly five, very powerful warriors to activate. The girl we saw last night was already half way there. I just have to reach the rest of them first."

David countered, "That doesn't mean you can activate their warrior selves and convince them to join your side. The Rageto don't try recruiting for long. They give a choice, join or die. They will kill these kids if they have to, no hesitation."

John nodded, "I know. We must find them quickly."

David said, "The brothers were talking about the high school. They could be there already. But they mentioned that this high school has over 1000 students. It will be hard for the brothers to find them without me."

John glanced at his watch, "It's Friday. In a small city in September, that means football. It will be our best shot to find most of them, maybe all of them."

David agreed. "Makes sense. The elder was convinced one of them played sports. Are you sure you can activate them?"

"Maybe. My best talents are fighting and stealth. Very few can detect me if I don't want to be found. I only have a small talent as a finder."

David said, "I'm the best."

John nodded. "That's why I was so shocked you spotted me. David, you know I have to ask..."

"You want me to go with you."

"Yes." John said, "But I will keep you safe."

"No, John. I can't. I'm sorry, I won't be responsible for any more deaths. If they see me there, they'll kill this entire city just to punish me."

Pete walked back in, fresh from conferring with the Sect. "Okay, I've talked to my people and they have moved up the timeline. We'll transfer these nasty books to the next station in two days. That's about all I can do for you."

"Funny you should say that," said John, "I must ask one more favor."

Pete stared at John. "I just said..."

"I know, but it's just a ride I need," said John.

"You are bad mojo, John. I'm putting another layer of security around the books tonight."

David asked, "What books?"

Pete answered, "Books that needn't concern you, sir."

"I had a flash about a book coming in to the city. These aren't books taken from Elder Zamma, are they?" asked David.

"Maybe." Pete eyed their new visitor. "That's why they're being transferred to the next station."

"What are the odds that those books are here while all this is going on?" asked David.

"The River never makes anything easy," lamented John.

* * *

In the small rented house, Ehrhardt's cell phone rang, an ominous ring tone resounding. "Guess who." Derek saw the name of his cell phone screen and handed the phone to Ehrhardt.

The German paused before speaking, "Yes, Elder Zamma?"

"Say hello for me," Derek said in a whisper, smiling.

Ehrhardt made a sour face and shook his head, trying to focus on the call. "Yes... I see... but, it is only a matter of time..."

Ehrhardt did everything except roll his eyes. Derek whispered again, "Say hello."

Ehrhardt hit the end call button.

"You didn't say hello for me." said Derek, fake hurt in his voice.

"He wanted to remind us to hurry, before they become activated and remember how dangerous they really are." Ehrhardt put the phone back on the table.

"Thank you, Elder Obvious," said Derek, stretching out on the bed.

"Also, little brother, he wanted to remind us not to use overt force that would cause undue attention," said Ehrhardt, sitting on the other bed.

"Like 2004."

"He'll never let me live it down. Fires to cover our tracks, fine. Building collapsing to hide a kill, no problem. He's a micro-managing pain in my *arsch*." Ehrhardt slipped into German cuss words.

"A tsunami that killed a quarter million people and he just won't let it pass," Derek remarked, sarcasm dripping, "Gotta break some eggs to make omelets, after all."

Ehrhardt looked at his brother, "Do you think you're being funny?"

He ignored the question. "I noticed you didn't tell him about the girl we contacted. Or that we lost the Witness."

"I will tell him when our mission is done here," said Ehrhardt, "When we have five new disciples for him."

"Aren't we the confident one. We don't even know who's lurking inside these kids. There are lots of ancients unaccounted for. They could all be un-swayable ancient adversaries hiding in teenage bodies. We've made a lot of enemies over the ages."

Ehrhardt made sure his gun was loaded. "We can handle it. Do you think the girl will be of help?"

"Hard to say. Don't think she's one of the new births. Hopefully she has no awkward history to worry about. She's fifteen and seemed convinced by my smooth talking last night. I think she'll help, and our elder will have his first disciple. Not that we'll get any credit for it. Zamma's been in a bad mood lately."

"He's old. He knows this is his last body. His inner sanctorum was raided by thieves, valuable books stolen. He still blames us for that too, like we are his personal body guards," said Ehrhardt, "His fear is showing as anger. I'm tired of him taking it out on us."

"I'm with you, brother," Derek agreed. "Let's get going then. I want to get a hot dog before the game starts."

Ehrhardt shook his head. "More meat. Disgusting."

CHAPTER FOURTEEN

THE BIG GAME

Cody laced up his cleats, tying the special lucky loop just like always.

"Good game, man. Go waves!" said a teammate as he passed.

"Yeah, good game," Cody replied, but his head was anywhere but in the game. He was getting so many flashes tonight. It had never been this strong before. He always relied on his mental gift to know what the other players were about to do. No one could understand that's what made him so fast, so able to know what everyone would do next on the field.

Another teammate called over, "Good game, Cody. Let's smash those Jack Sparrow little bitches!"

Cody laughed. They were playing the Pirates from a rival school, and they would never live down the Johnny Depp film-inspired nickname. Cody closed his eyes and concentrated on putting his random thoughts away. He had to focus, let just enough of the glimpses in to win the game. He kept flashing on random people from his school. Four other people he'd seen around, but didn't know, including that black kid from the restaurant. *Weird.*

Cody went to his locker, and popped in his mouth guard. He checked his face in the small mirror attached to the locker door. But it wasn't his face.

The old man was back. He seemed startled at first too, but recovered and started saying strange words, gibberish. Cody shook his head, feeling the old man trying to get inside his head. He grabbed his helmet and smashed the small mirror. The shards fell to the floor and each one contained an eye of the old man.

The whispering continued in his head until he stomped on the shards with his cleats. The old man receded from his mind, the broken mirror just ordinary glass again.

The coach yelled, "Cody, you ok? What happened?"

"Oh, Coach, hey... no, I'm good. Broke my mirror. I'm starting a new pre-game ritual."

The coach scowled, "You're cleaning that up after the game. Alright, on the field. Head in the game, Cody."

Cody's mind felt unclean, like it was streaked with ancient dust. He slapped his own face to snap out of it. *Focus. Game time.*

* * *

The football stadium was an open field, with bleachers rising fifty feet high on either side of the field; one side for the home team, the other side for the visiting team. The stadium had been built in the early 1960s, and the wood planking and metal cross-beam supports were due for an overhaul. California had been working slowly to make old structures earthquake resistant, but funds were tight and progress was slow. The tall, powerful lights illuminated the field and bleachers, leaving the back side in shadow.

The teens stood behind the opposing team's old bleachers, under the shadow of the metal cross beam support structure. The heavy planks shook as the crowds above cheered.

Katie finished her text, then slipped her phone into her back pocket. She crossed her arms. "So, this is it? The white girl, the Mexican girl, the geek, and what are you?"

Zacke smiled. "The token black guy, I guess. Or token mixed-race kid. Take your pick."

That broke the tension. The four of them stood in a rough circle behind the bleachers. The game was under way, so it was tough to hear through the shouting and the pounding of feet on the bleachers. Except for a few random kids milling around the far end of the bleachers, they were alone behind the crowd.

"I really don't want to be here. One of my cousins will see us," said Ariana, "How am I going to explain?"

Lucas spoke up, "I think this is a little more important than teenage politics, or whatever. We can all do stuff; like supernatural stuff."

Katie looked skeptical, or maybe just bored. Zacke noticed she kept looking around.

Lucas said uncertainly, "Well, can't you?"

"Maybe," Katie said, "I guess. What can you do?"

"I'm good at fighting," Lucas blurted.

Ariana looked confused, glancing at the skinny boy with glasses, covered in a grey hooded sweatshirt.

"Yeah, yeah," said Lucas. "I know I look scrawny, but I've been training for a while, and I can work myself into this crazy... well, I'm not sure exactly how to explain it."

"You can fight?" Katie said, realizing too late that it sounded like a sneer.

Lucas looked at Katie. "You don't even know me Miss Judgey Judgerton. I can also see people's thoughts sometimes."

"You too?" Ariana asked.

"So can I," said Zacke, "You said 'see' their thought. For me, it's like hearing them. How about you, Arian..."

"Ariana," Ariana corrected the pronunciation, "Yes. kind of, I always thought it was more of a feeling, than images, like I was inside the person. But yeah, and it's been happening a lot lately."

Katie was looking around again. Zacke said, "Katie, right? I'm Zacke and I can see thoughts sometimes. a Few times I've lifted some heavy stuff..." He paused, left off the craziest thing he could do. *No reason to tell them about that.* "How about you? What can you do?"

Katie said, "Why don't you go next?" pointing to Ariana.

Ariana scanned around, to make sure no one she knew was watching. She answered, "I can... I can stop things. Things from falling, or I can freeze them in mid-air. The 'feeling' thoughts thing, well, it's not a good thing when you have gross teenage brothers."

Katie smiled and the boys chuckled uncomfortably.

Lucas added, "You also make jerks throw up at will."

"Yeah, and that too," explained Ariana, "That never happened before."

Zacke looked to Katie again. "So what can you do?"

Katie had her hands folded on her chest, "Who says I can do anything? When you came to me in fourth period, you sounded a little crazy. So, what if you had a dream about me, about all of us?"

Zacke said, "A little late to play this off. I saw the look on your face when I talked to you. You looked like someone finally understood you. And you're here. So, what can you do?"

Instead of answering, she uncrossed her arms, put her palms out flat.

"Holy crap!" said Ariana, covering her mouth.

"What?" Lucas said.

"You don't see that?" Ariana shouted. To Katie she said, "Can I touch it?"

"Touch what?" asked Zacke.

Ariana moved closer, "The color surrounding her? You can't see it?"

"Wow," Katie said, "Even I can't *see* them. I imagine colors, but..."

Lucas asked, "What are we supposed to be seeing?"

"It's like a shield," said Katie.

Ariana added, "It's one solid color. Why is it green?"

Zacke reached out his hand near Ariana, "Oh wow, it is solid. That is so cool." Zacke, Lucas, and Ariana were all putting their hand along the shield. To an outside observer, it would have looked like their hands were floating a few inches from Katie's body.

"So, it's protective? Like a force field?" asked Lucas.

"Yes, but it's hard to control. Wow. I've never held one this long. So, green is like a base line, then different colors are more powerful.

They are kinda like layers. Different colors, different strengths. I can't believe one of you can see the colors."

"It's..." Zacke said, realizing it looked like he was following the contours of her body. He dropped his hand. "That's really cool. Anything else?"

"Whoa," Lucas and Ariana said at the same time, as their hands were pushed away.

"I can push with my shields too. But they were kind of weak until recently. I can't read minds, but sometimes I get glimpses of what's going to happen," said Katie.

"Wait. That's weird," said Zacke. "I just realized I can't hear any of your thoughts right now."

"Hey, me neither," Lucas added.

"You're right," Ariana said. She concentrated, looking back and forth to the other teens, "Nothing. I can't feel any of your thoughts. What does that mean?"

Zacke said, "I have no idea. I hoped comparing notes would give us some answers. I wonder why Ariana can see your shields when we can't. I wonder why this is happening to us. I wonder how none of us has officially met each other before today. There are too many strange coincidences."

"I can answer all of your questions," said Derek, startling them. "What you can do is pretty awesome, Katie."

Katie smiled, her face flushed.

"Who are you?" asked Lucas.

"I'm Katie's friend," said Derek, walking a few steps closer.

"Everyone," Zacke whispered, "that's one of the guys from the restaurant."

Lucas said, "I thought you said there were two."

"There are, my friends," said the man behind them, with a German accent.

* * *

Cody was waiting for the ref to make a call. The score was 27-7. They were crushing it tonight. He knew the Pirates coach was advising his linemen to go after him, hard. He couldn't hear him across the field, and didn't need his special talent; it was written all over the coach's red face. Cody had scored four touchdowns and three interceptions. He was on fire.

Cody decided he'd better cool it. His instincts were stronger than ever, and it felt a bit like cheating. It came so easy; he was afraid that someone would guess he knew what was going to happen a few seconds before it did. Cody thought about letting the Pirates score another touchdown.

Then he noticed the glow. He had just headed onto the field, about to huddle up when he saw the green glow from behind the other team's bleachers. The visiting Pirates were unhappy he even glanced their way. Boos rose from their stands as he entered the field, but he couldn't stop staring at the green glow.

It was coming from behind the bleachers. At first he thought it was a weird light effect from the crowd. But it felt familiar, somehow. He sensed something was about to happen. He got to the huddle, focused back on the game. He got through it, did the cheer with his troops. His friend, and linebacker Joey sensed something was wrong, but the huddle broke and they took their positions.

* * *

Behind the visiting team bleachers, Ehrhardt said, "There's no reason to be afraid."

"Although, with his sinister German accent, I'd understand why you might be alarmed. I'm Derek. That's my brother Ehrhardt. Hi Katie."

Katie said, "Hey."

"You know these guys?" asked Zacke.

"Yeah. I met them last night," said Katie, "They're okay. They know what's going on. They can help us."

Ehrhardt said, "And you must be Zacke, Lucas, and Ariana. Am I pronouncing that right?"

"Um. Yeah," Ariana said.

Lucas asked sharply, "How do you know our names?"

"Don't be mad," said Katie, "After you told me about your dream, I didn't want to scare you off. These guys told me a lot about what's going on."

"Like what?" Lucas asked. He had taken a fighting stance. Ehrhardt noticed.

Katie explained, "Like why this is happening. It's called a breakout. It's where a group of warriors is gathering in the same place."

"Warriors?" asked Ariana. "What does that mean?"

Derek took over, "You are all warriors. A few of you are warriors born with certain powers, in this life. You are new births. Some of you are ancient warriors reborn into your present bodies. That is called a re-birth. We can help you unlock these..."

"Step away from them!" John had arrived.

"This just got more interesting," said Derek, "Who might you be, big black bald man in a hoodie?"

John ignored him, for now, "Everyone, you need to get away from these men. They are not here to help you."

Derek looked around, "Wait, you're alone? They only sent one of you? To a breakout? The Amartus is losing badly."

John turned his attention to the brothers, "We'll never lose to you, Sazzo, or is it Caron? I haven't met you in these bodies."

"What is going on?" asked Ariana.

Katie spoke up, "Don't listen to him. Derek told me they would send people to confuse us."

John unsheathed the short sword strapped to his back, "Step away from them."

Ehrhardt shook his head, "No wonder your side is losing. You're still using swords." He pulled out a handgun with a silencer from the holster under his own suit coat, "This is the sword of today."

Ehrhardt shot three rounds at John. John moved with unbelievable speed. John leaped and twisted his body in midair, two shots missing him. He swung down the blade on the third bullet and deflected it into the ground.

Ehrhardt kept his gun aimed.

Derek whistled, "Well, that's a neat trick. Who are you, fancy black guy?"

"Figure it out yourself," replied John, stepping closer with his sword ready.

"Get behind us." said Derek, stepping in front of the teens. Ehrhardt moved too. As he did, he brushed against Lucas' arm.

An image flared in Lucas' mind: A bright hot memory of falling. The face that stared down at him was not Ehrhardt's, but he knew they were the same man. The man was firing a gun at the falling Lucas, three bullets ripping into him as he fell. Something shifted inside Lucas, and he felt stronger, sure of what to do. The flash disappeared.

Lucas stepped out of the group. "Caron. I see you in there. I've been waiting a long time for this." It was Lucas's voice, but different. Lucas was clearly surprised to hear his voice change as Ehrhardt looked around slowly.

A foot caught Ehrhardt's nose. Lucas had delivered a perfect round house kick. Blood gushed from Ehrhardt's nose and he went down. He finally managed to get back up on one knee. He gripped the gun awkwardly as he held his nose.

The three other teens stepped back, giving Lucas room. Derek went to help Ehrhardt, but froze. The younger brother stood like a statue.

Ehrhardt saw his brother freeze, "What is this?"

Ariana realized her hands were up, "Sorry."

Still frozen, Derek was helpless. Ehrhardt fired one more shot at John from the ground. Holding his bleeding nose, he fired wildly, hitting nothing.

"Get behind me, now." John ordered. Zacke and Ariana went behind John. Katie stood, frozen by indecision. Lucas didn't seem afraid of anything.

"Who's inside you, little man?" asked Ehrhardt, staring at Lucas.

"You know who I am," Lucas' voice was deeper than before.

Ehrhardt instantly did know, a cold shiver shot up his neck, "No. It can't be... I gave you a true death."

"Did you?" said the warrior, through Lucas.

Rage flared in Ehrhardt. He looked wildly from his statue brother, to the crisscrossing metal support structure of the bleachers. "Forgive me brother." Ehrhardt said.

He quickly shouldered his gun and dug his hands in the earth, speaking a mixture of languages. "Toke lurrikara tresti. Toke lurrikara tresti. Toke lurrikara tresti."

The ground began to shake. Lucas started to move at Ehrhardt, but they all fell to the ground with the violent shaking.

The screams from the crowds were immediate. The bleachers were made of interlocking metal pipes; a structured pattern of support bars built in the 1960s. They could hold up to 1200 people on either side of the field. But these stadium seats were free-standing, made of metal and wood nearly fifty years old. An earthquake of this size was too much for them. The metal began to groan and move.

They all writhed on the ground, unable to stand. Then the popping started. Pop. Pop. Pop. Bolts began to shear; metal supports began to clang against each other as they popped free.

A flash came to Katie. Megan. Face down. Blood. Katie screamed, "Megan. No!" she stumbled from the scene.

It was hard to stand, but Zacke and Ariana finally did, and moved away from the bleachers. Derek unfroze. He stepped awkwardly, now that the ground beneath him was shaking. For him, a few seconds had disappeared from his perception. Now he was unfrozen inside an earthquake. He looked around, confused.

John tried to get to Ehrhardt, but the shaking made it impossible to move in a straight line. The people were pouring out of the stands as they continued to shake. Both freestanding bleachers on either side of the field began to buckle.

The metal pipes that held up the bleachers gave way. Bolts popped and shot like bullets under the bleachers, ricocheting off each other.

The crowds' screams mixed with a deep rumble from the earth. The bleachers began to fall.

Ariana looked up and was frozen by fear. For a second she thought they would all be crushed behind the structure, but the chain reaction began and the bleachers started to crumble away from them, falling toward the field.

One person was moving against the crowds, running through the masses. Ehrhardt stood, and the shaking stopped. He raised his gun at John. The German was stopped when the blue and white uniform slammed into him, knocking him off his feet. The two bodies went flying together into the tall grass by the chain link fence.

It was too late for the bleachers. Both structures came down in a cascade of collapsing pipes and long wooden seats. It was hard to tell what was louder; the screams from the crowds, or the violent sound of wrenching metal.

They had all managed to get far enough away that they were not in danger from the collapse. John turned his attention back to Ehrhardt. He had flung the football player off, sending him tumbling into the deeper grass at the fence line. The German shot wildly, his arm shaking.

He got lucky on the last shot. John felt a burning in his back as the bullet ripped through him. He fell.

Ehrhardt stood a few dozen feet away, his gun now clicking empty. He shouldered it. Derek and Ehrhardt fled the field. Ariana and Lucas ran to John. Zacke ran to Cody in the tall grass.

Sirens were screaming in the night, fast approaching. Cody took off his helmet, and all four of the teens went to John.

"Help!" said Ariana, "We have to get him to the hospital."

John yelled, "No hospitals! I need to get to the station. Do any of you drive?"

They all shook their heads no.

"I have my learner's permit," Zacke offered.

John winced from the pain, "Good. You drive. The rest of you stay here and get your stories straight. You were behind the bleachers when you felt the earthquake. Say nothing of me, swords, or guns. And no man with a German accent. Do you understand?"

Zacke said, "We don't even know you."

"My name's John. Nice to meet you. I'm here to help."

"You're shot!" said Lucas.

John nodded, "Yes, Lucas. I need your help now. Lucas, Zacke. Please get me to safety. My friends will know what to do when we get there."

No one asked any more questions. In that moment, John inspired unquestioning trust. Lucas took John under his arm, helping him to stand. Zacke got on his other side to help.

John looked at Ariana and Cody, "You two, go back toward the field. Try to help those in need. I will be in contact soon."

Ariana was in tears. Cody was too stunned to do anything but obey.

Lucas and Zacke helped John to a small metal gate where he had entered.

They made it to Pete's truck. Zacke drove, John sat in the middle and Lucas kept pressure on John's wound as instructed. John was bleeding badly. They headed to the station. John called Pete on the way. Pete was not happy.

PART 2

"Many things simply are, whether you understand them or not."
~ Xemaricon Journal, Second Volume

CHAPTER FIFTEEN
WARRIOR INSIDE

Zacke drove through less traveled streets, taking a different route every time they heard another emergency vehicle.

The city was alive with traffic headed to the high school to pick up loved ones and see what had happened, but also clogged with people trying to flee the destruction at the stadium.

Two dozen blocks away, Lucas and Zacke finally got John to the old television repair shop. Zacke said, "I always wondered how this place was still in business."

Lucas said, "I never noticed this building at all."

John could barely stand, so he leaned against the wall and rang the bell. From the other side of the door, they heard a loud voice.

"Damn it, I was hoping that call was a sick prank." Pete opened the door. "Were you followed?"

"No, we took a curious route." John smiled as best he could, "Looks like I need to ask another favor, my friend."

Pete towered over the two boys, but spoke to John, "You brought two of them here? Oh, hell, get inside before you fall over. I've got you."

Pete picked John up like he was a small child. John groaned in pain. They made their way down to the basement and David was startled to see strangers entering the room.

Pete said, "It's alright. These are two of them."

David still looked worried.

Lucas looked around. "Wow. This is the first basement I've seen in real life."

'Hi, I'm Zacke." He said as he offered his hand to David, until he noticed John's blood on his hand, and dropped it awkwardly.

"Lucas," he said to David, still scanning the room.

"David." He didn't shake their hands, just looked them over with great interest. "I see the change in you, Lucas." Then he turned to Zacke, "Do you know who you are yet?"

Zacke replied, "Um, I don't even understand the question."

Across the room, Pete cleared a large work bench of small electronics. They crashed to the floor, and he laid John on the table, on his side, opposite the wound. John let out a yell and held his side. Pete ripped John's shirt off, threw it on the floor. Zacke saw the large tattoo on John's back.

He would try to ask John about it another time.

"I don't do transfusions," said Pete, "so we'll just hope you didn't lose too much blood. But I've got to get the bullet out. It's gonna hurt."

"Thank you, my friend," John managed.

"You keep calling me that." Pete reached under the bench for a large canvas bag. But if I get thrown out of the Sect because I helped you, any 'friendliness' will be over."

"I understand," John groaned.

"You, kid," said Pete, indicating Zacke. "Come here. I need you to use this gauze and apply pressure. Other kid, come unpack this bag and lay out the supplies for me. I gotta go wash up. It would be cruelly ironic, John, if you died of infection after your many lives."

John started to chuckle, but it hurt too much. "Ironic indeed."

The boys complied, and David came close to the table and watched them.

Zacke asked David, "What did you mean about knowing 'who I am'?"

John said, "He means your warrior self. Your core. We saw the change in Lucas tonight. Have you noticed your talents getting stronger?"

Zacke said, "Maybe a little."

David offered, "Zacke, you may be a new birth."

Lucas said, "A lot's been happening to me. I never felt quite like I did tonight. I felt like I was... more than just me." he finished laying out the contents of the bag.

David continued, "It's because you are becoming activated."

Lucas replied, "I know something is happening to me."

"Yes," said David, "You just don't know how to *believe* what is happening. It's real."

"Well, yeah, we just saw some Nazi guy pull down our stadium with an earthquake." Zacke asked, "what was he saying?"

David interjected, "Incantations, magic. The Rageto uses magic to augment their small talents."

"Ok, magic?" said Zacke as he kept the bloody gauze on John's wound, "Are we living some Harry Potter rip-off?"

John laughed, and regretted it, "No boys. Sorry, you're not wizards. You don't have magic. Your natural core talents come from the River. You are naturally drawn to the Amartus, my side. Only their side uses magic, the Rageto."

Pete said, "Stop talking, John," as he returned with thick latex gloves, and picked up the bottle of betadine. He took fresh gauze that Lucas had laid out, and poured the red liquid over the wound. It was hard to tell what was blood, and what was the strong antiseptic.

He handed John a different kind of bottle, "Sorry. This is all I have for the pain. And this is the only booze I have on hand. Drink up."

John did, and they waited a few minutes for the alcohol to hit his system.

"I will explain everything," John managed, "But I don't know if I'll pass out from the pain or not."

"You will," Pete confirmed.

"All of you are special, a part of the River. And you have a..." John screamed in pain as Pete put the metal device into his wound. They looked like needle-nosed pliers. Pete dug for the bullet. It was agonizing to watch, and Zacke turned his head away several times. John took more strong drinks, swallowing and then yelling in pain between gulps. Finally, the bullet came out. John passed out. Pete caught the bottle of liquor before it hit the floor.

Pete said, "You boys won't want to see me stitch him up. Go wait over there."

"Listen, man. Um, David. Can you stop staring at me?" asked Zacke.

David looked down, "I'm sorry. I just can't figure out if you're a new birth or an ancient."

Lucas pushed the glasses up his nose. "Alright. I'm tired of mysterious words being thrown around. Just tell us what's going on, please."

David nodded. "Both of you, come with me to the mirror. Lucas, look at your eyes."

Lucas stared into the mirror and said, "Holy crap!"

David said, "I assume this is not normal; that one eye is green and one is blue?"

"No," Lucas insisted. "Wait, I don't think I need these anymore." Lucas took off his glasses and looked at himself clearly in the mirror. "I've had glasses since I was five. When did this happen?"

"Probably tonight, because you're the closest to being activated," David said, "The strength of your warrior has improved your sight."

Zacke shook his head. "You just did it again. What is 'activated'? Why did John say magic?"

"Sorry, there's a lot to understand." David made the boys sit. Three chairs were arranged in a corner of the basement, "I'll try not to use shortcut words. You are members of a special group. You are part of what we call the River. It's a kind of flow of human knowledge and experience. That's why you get glimpses of other people's thoughts or emotions. Many of us are part of it; like a group consciousness that we all share. But some, like you and me, can see more than others. As you get stronger you'll know who you really are."

"I know who I am," Zacke said.

David nodded, "You know this body, this life. You were born 15 or 16 years ago and you have all the memories of your life so far. But you are much more."

"Thank God for that," said Lucas. Zacke gave him a quizzical look.

"God? Maybe. There are plenty of theologians on both sides that have all kinds of theories. But we don't usually talk in terms of gods and devils," David explained.

"Why'd you say 'thank God'?" asked Zacke.

Lucas replied, "Because now I know for sure I'm not crazy."

"Well this all sounds crazy," Zacke argued, "What we saw was crazy."

Lucas said, "Yeah, but up until, well, not that long ago, I thought I was actually crazy. Like voices in my head stuff. Now I know this is real."

"It is real," David reassured. "Has your warrior tried to speak with you, in your mind? In dreams, maybe? Do you know your true warrior name?"

Lucas thought for a second. "You know, now that you say that... I mean, not in any dreams I can remember, but this weird word has been rolling around in my head lately."

Zacke asked, "What word?"

Lucas shrugged. "Elgisard."

"Really?" asked Zacke.

"Yeah," said Lucas, "Whatever, whoever this is inside me, the name that comes to my mind randomly is Elgisard."

David corrected, "Not inside you. He is you. This ancient warrior was re-birthed into you, Lucas. You and he are one. Or will be, when you're fully activated."

Zacke said, "Sorry, sir, you'll have to explain better than that."

"I have some shards of his memories," Lucas said, "I can't tell when exactly he was born the first time, but I get flashes of like Viking ships and weapons."

"In time, you'll get more than that," David explained, "You will have the memories of every life he's ever lived, most of his accumulated knowledge. You never get everything back, and it's different for everyone. But you'll get all his strength."

"So, are you talking about re-incarnation?" asked Zacke.

"Not exactly, no. But that's probably the closest way to look at it."

"So why are my eyes two different colors?" asked Lucas, "Is this Viking guy, like, possessing my body? Is his soul joining with mine?"

David shook his head. "No. Whoever makes these cosmic rules, has decided that when you're around 16, your mind and body are ready to make the choice. Sometimes it manifests physically. Like your eyes. Until you decide, they will stay two colors."

"I have a choice?" asked Lucas.

"Yes. You can choose to deny this warrior's memories, to refuse to become fully one with your ancient."

Lucas seemed disappointed. "Then he'll just go away?"

"No. You and he are one," David tried to clarify, "When you die, you will either die with his memories and strength, or if you choose to live as you are now, as just Lucas, he will be with you, but dormant, sleeping, or locked away in a box. But all those ancient memories will fade. When you get old and die, your true warrior will go back into the River, to pass to another generation and they will make the same choice."

Lucas's cell phone lit up, "Oh, crap. It's my dad. I forgot to call him, it's on silent. Hey Dad. No... sorry. I'm okay. I meant to call you. I had to help a friend first. No, I'm not hurt. I just had... had to get out of there. No, don't come pick me up. I'm almost home now. Yeah, I love you too Dad."

"You should go," Zacke realized, "I better go too."

John had regained consciousness. His voice was slurred, "Boys, wait. Before you go," John strained through the pain. "Lucas, Zacke. I need to quietly check in with the others."

Zacke looked at his phone, "I don't have all their phone numbers yet, there wasn't enough time. I can message them through Facebook or something."

"Good," said John dreamily, "Not public, though, no one else can hear or see these messages. Tell them to stay close to family, and don't be outside their house alone. Lucas, you seemed to recognize the brothers."

Lucas was distracted. "In that moment, I knew them. I even think I saw one of them kill me. But that's all fading, like a dream... sorry guys, I really gotta go. I just lied to my dad about where I was."

"Go. Both of you. That stunt will have drained Caron," John explained, but he was fading again, "He won't be a threat for a day or so."

"And the other one?" asked Zacke.

John said, "They'll stick together. As you've noticed, there is strength in numbers. Everyone is more tuned in when we're close to each other. Even our enemies."

"Got it. Rest up," Zacke was at the door, "Oh, and thanks for saving our lives."

"Don't thank me." John was getting weak again, "I helped speed things up. You're all going to have to make hard choices soon."

John passed out again, and the boys left to see the current state of their town. Things like this just didn't happen in sleepy Sea Valley.

Zacke and Lucas knew that everything was about to get more dangerous.

CHAPTER SIXTEEN

MEGAN

Katie's stepdad Jason said, "Your mom's in there now. It's the ICU, so only one person can go in at a time. Kaitlyn, I know this wasn't your fault, okay?"

Great, she thought. *He's being understanding. Now I feel worse.*

"I'll go see her," said Katie, trying not to meet his gaze. She wanted him to know how sorry she was, but how could she explain? *Well, I was under the bleachers with some others freaks with powers, when this German dude made an earthquake.*

Any other time, the thought might have made her laugh. Not tonight. Right now, all she could think about was how Megan looked under those twisted bleachers, so small and covered in blood. Just like her flash.

"Hi Mom. How is she?" Katie said as she walked into the ICU room.

Her mother stood up and hugged Katie, tears streaming. "Thank God."

Katie sat down in the chair next to Megan, taking her hand.

Mom said, "The doctor said she should wake up any time. We just need to wait and pray. But only one of us can be in here. The nurse made that abundantly clear a few times. Stay as long as you want. I'll be with Jason."

"Okay Mom." The fact that her mother hadn't yelled at her made Katie feel terrible.

Her mom left the room and all Katie could hear was the hum of the machines. There were wires and tubes all over Megan. Her little step-sister's head had a bandage where a metal brace had cut her. Her cheek was bruised. She looked so tiny. A beautiful little doll pretending to be a patient. But this was real, of course. She didn't know what to say to her. Katie was quiet a long time until she finally managed, "I'm so sorry, Megs. Wake up soon, okay?"

Katie wiped away a single tear but she refused to cry more in front of Megan. *Keep it together.* Katie would cry plenty later. She left the room to face the parental storm. She had to figure out what she could tell them. As she approached, they were already in a whispered discussion.

It stopped when Katie walked up. Mom asked, "Where were you, Kaitlyn?"

"I was with her. I just had to go to the bathroom. She was sitting with a couple of friends," insisted Katie.

"Really? Explain this." Her mom showed her phone with some texts. "Megan texted me that she had no idea where you went. There are over 20 minutes' worth of texts. She's only 11, Katie. You're supposed to protect her."

The words felt like poison, but they came out of her mouth anyway. "I'm sorry I couldn't protect her from an earthquake!"

Jason kept his tone even, "You were supposed to stay with her, that was the deal when you went to the game."

Her mom kept questioning. Her tone was not gentle. "Also, how did you get here? Why wouldn't you wait for us at the stadium? We had no idea where you were."

"I told you on the phone," Katie tried to phrase it just right, "They wouldn't let me ride in the ambulance. She was already on the way to the hospital. By that time, all the cars were jamming up the parking lot and I knew it would be hard to find you. Some friends drove me.

They were parked at the other end of school, that's why I said I would meet you here."

Jason asked, "Who drove you, Kaitlyn?"

He's even using my full name. I wish he'd give me an excuse to be mad at him. "You don't know them," Katie dodged. *They're also the guys that started the earthquake.*

Mom's truth rays shot at Katie, "You're not telling us something."

Jason asked, "Was this about sneaking off with a boy? We just want to..."

"No it's not!" Katie let her anger flare, despite his maddeningly understanding tone. She knew she would regret it. "You know what, *Jas,* just believe whatever you want. Can I go home now?"

She could tell her mom was getting angry. "Watch your tone. Don't deflect the fact that you are in trouble by getting mad at us." Mom took a breath. "Yes you can go home. I need to get some things at home anyway, so I'll drive you. Jason and I will take shifts here at the hospital. I don't care what that nurse says, one of us is staying here tonight."

Jason nodded. He stood against the wall, arms crossed, his eyes wet. "I'm sorry Kaitlyn. This is just hard, you know? I'm glad you're not hurt."

Katie felt a sob rise. She hated when he ruined a good fight by being nice. "It's... it's ok, Jason. Thanks. I'm really sorry."

On their way out, Katie and her mom passed a group of football players. They were all still in their respective blue and white Waves, and black and orange Pirates uniforms. Apparently, an earthquake ended team rivalries.

Someone called over, "Hey, Katie, right?" Katie and her mom stopped as Cody came up to them, "Are you alright? Is your sister okay?"

Katie said, "Yeah. The doctor said she'll be alright. Where did you go?"

"We helped the emergency guys," answered Cody, "None of our guys on either team were seriously hurt. So, we stayed and helped."

"I'm Judith, Katie's mother. You are?"

"Oh, hi," he wiped his hand on his grungy uniform, "I'm Cody."

Katie explained, "We met on the field. He helped me find Megan."

"Hello," said her mother, warming just a little. "We have to go now, Katie. Nice to meet you, Cody."

"Okay. Later. Nice to meet you," said Cody, returning to the other players.

Mother and daughter walked out, and luckily for Katie, her mom didn't ask any questions about Cody. She couldn't explain that he'd also been the guy rushing past her, stopping the German making the earthquake. Or, how they had fabricated a story together. Luckily the scene had been too crazy, and no authorities questioned them.

Her mom started talking as soon as they got in the car, "I hate to ask, especially after all we've been through tonight, but will you be okay on your own for a few hours? Megan and Jason..."

"Of course, Mom. That's fine," Katie said as she stared out the window. She felt a familiar pang. The same one that hit her when Megan came first. But it wasn't as sharp as usual; Megan's healing was all that mattered now.

"We know you've been through a lot too," Mom put a hand on Katie's leg, like she did when she was younger. "Jason and I were just scared. We didn't know where you were. You said you'd get a ride, then all the cell lines were jammed."

"It just took a while to get there because of traffic." Katie asked, "The radio said no one died, right?"

"Miracle of miracles, no. But a lot of people were hurt. They moved some to Madeline Medical and Hope Hospital down the coast. It must have been terrifying."

"It was pretty scary."

"The weird thing was that no other buildings were damaged. Well, that's what they say tonight. I'm sure they'll find damage tomorrow," her mom insisted.

Katie secretly doubted it.

Her mom squeezed her leg, "I'm just glad you're okay. Jason is too. I'll pick up a few things and get back to the hospital. You sure you'll be okay on your own?"

"Yeah, Mom. I'll be fine." Katie nearly smiled. She felt like a kid again, her mom's total focus on her for the moment.

Once Katie was home by herself, she immediately got on her laptop, cruising the local news website. Over a hundred and fifty people were hurt. They estimated that nearly two thousand people were in the stands. The news was everywhere, even national news sites, Twitter, Instagram, everywhere. She jumped to Facebook, which has also ablaze with the news.

She went to the wall of each of the other four "special" kids she'd met tonight. She smiled at the thought of the other freaks, but then she thought of Megan. Not a time for smiling. They had all just met officially a few hours ago, so no one had any cell numbers. She made friend requests of them all, so they could exchange numbers by private message later. Then she got out her cell phone and texted the person she most wanted to talk to.

There were already three messages from Derek.

Are you OK Katie?

I know you need to be with family now. Text when you can.

I have so much more to tell you.

A blank, generic cartoon face was next to the name Derek. Apparently, he liked being anonymous online. When you knew people that could cause earthquakes, she reasoned that was a safer way to live.

Katie wondered why she'd even taken the ride from them. She felt a strange pull to Derek, but his brother had hurt her family. The German gave his excuses in the car, but he hadn't apologized. But, they were the ones that had explained things, and they felt true. Katie was a confused swirl of emotions.

Katie: Your brother hurt (she thought about typing step-sister, but changed her mind) my SISTER. Not ok.

Derek: I am very angry at him too. I'm so sorry. It was not supposed to happen that way. He is very sorry.

Katie: How's is the Nazi, anyway?

Derek: LOL. He does sound like a Nazi, doesn't he? He's resting. Takes a lot out of him.

Katie noticed he hadn't answered her question about how they could be brothers. There was a lot he hadn't explained. She changed the subject.

Katie: Who was the guy with the sword?

Derek: Ugh. The bad guy of our story. Bad guy who thinks he's a good guy. Too much to text. I'll explain more next time we meet. Remember: DELETE THESE TEXTS. You don't want your parents finding texts with words like Nazi or sword. The NSA has probably already flagged us both.

Katie: Seriously?

Derek: LOL. No. The government is run by idiots. Just delete them, all will be fine.

Katie: If I decide to forgive you and your "brother" for the earthquake, what's next?

Derek: I'll let you know soon. Stay safe, girly girl. Derek out.

She smiled at the girly girl line. The last few text chains, he'd been ending with that. It seemed old fashioned, but strangely adorable. So much had happened and Katie was exhausted. *What is it about him, anyway? You're probably being stupid. He just seems so... familiar.* She stretched out on her bed, and fell asleep thinking of Derek.

CHAPTER SEVENTEEN

REPORT

In the rented house, Derek smiled to himself, "Well, the girl still seems to be with us. You should have apologized in the car."

"MMMM," groaned Ehrhardt.

"How's the head?" asked Derek.

"MMMMM."

"I see," said Derek, "the healing spell seems to have fixed your nose. Any pain there?"

"HMMMMM."

"He'll be calling soon."

"HMMMMMM!"

Ehrhardt's phone rang. He lifted the wet towel from his eyes and handed the ringing cell to Derek.

Derek steeled himself and answered, "Earthquakes R Us. How may I help you? Yes, Elder Zamma. I know you don't think me funny. I just... no, no, he's resting. He had a busy night. Yes, we've been watching the news." Derek shook his head at Ehrhardt as he observed the conversation, "Do you really think that's... yes, of course our bathroom has a mirror. Give us a few minutes."

Ehrhardt's groan turned into a growl, "You're not serious! He wants a visual report?"

"This night just keeps getting better," said Derek.

Ehrhardt slowly rose from the bed, wincing in pain, and held the washcloth to his forehead.

Derek ignored his foul mood, "Are the candles in your suitcase?"

"HMMM," growled Ehrhardt.

"Ok to get them?" Derek asked, "I know how you feel about me touching your stuff."

"I'll get them," grumbled Ehrhardt.

They set up the three candles in front of the bathroom mirror. The brothers brought two chairs in and sat in front of the mirror. They held hands and began the incantation: "Pamje izgled gweld." They repeated the phrase three times. The elder on the other side was doing the real work, the brothers were just tuning into the more powerful spell of Elder Zamma. They both opened their eyes and stared at the mirror that now contained the image of their elder.

"What happened?" asked Elder Zamma.

They both bowed to their Elder.

"We've probably turned one, so far, a girl," said Ehrhardt, grimacing. Even the candlelight was hurting his eyes, "But we had to take drastic action when we were attacked."

Zamma was skeptical, "How many attacked you?"

Derek shifted in his chair, "Well, umm, one. Technically. But one of the boys is nearly activated. He's an ancient."

"Which ancient? Have we encountered him before?" asked Zamma.

Derek lied, "Don't know yet. The football boy tackled old Caron here. They had help. One of the Amartus showed up. I'm pretty sure it was Pentoss. He's still very handy with a sword. He's black this time, if you care. Caron shot him in the back."

Zamma thought of his last personal encounter with Pentoss. "Did you kill him?"

"Not sure. We went different directions," said Derek.

"And the earthquake? Why, Caron?" He did not wait for an answer and looked back to Derek, "Your talents are more discreet, Sazzo. You should have taken the lead. This is all over the news. Now, all the

American networks are covering that little town. We work better in the dark, you both know that."

Ehrhardt seethed, "An earthquake in California? Not much of a story. We'll get you some recruits. And if the rest won't come, a convenient aftershock will make a good way to end the problem."

"It was careless." Zamma stared at him. "You're supposed to be the responsible one. I'm very disappointed. How long until the Witness finds them again?"

Derek began, "About that..."

"Pentoss took the Witness," said Ehrhardt.

There was a long silence.

"I assume you're not joking," said the elder, "When?"

Ehrhardt replied, "It happened last night." He stared defiantly at his elder, saying nothing else.

"We thought it best to find him again before we mentioned it to you," Derek hastened to add.

The candles on the old man's side of the mirror flared, "And how will you find him? He's the one that finds people. How dare you not report this!"

"Enough!" Ehrhardt shouted. "How dare you send only we two, to root out five of them? We cannot produce miracles. You always expect too much, and give us nothing when we do your bidding. I'm sick of your empty orders. Come out of your little room and help us."

The elder stared. The candles in front of him shrunk back to their ordinary flicker. He stood, and leaned closer. The candles lit his face from below, and his face got larger, filling their mirror. Slowly, their mirror began to bow out toward them, just slightly at first, then more pronounced. Elder Zamma's eyes burned into Ehrhardt. "I will ignore your insolence for this night alone. Do not fail me again."

The mirror began to crack, the glass bending out much farther than was natural, and the elder's face was a mask of lines and cracks, a mosaic of rage. Ehrhardt and Derek shrank back in their chairs, their elder surprising them with yet a new trick to intimidate them.

Then the mirror exploded in a thousand shards. Derek and Ehrhardt shielded their eyes, but they both felt the shards cut their hands and faces. The candles blew out. Stale air rushed out of the void that used to be a mirror. Slowly, Derek got up. His shoes crunched on mirror shards until he found the light switch.

Derek was thankful that no glass went into his eyes, as he pulled a small shard from his cheek. He dropped it to the shards littering the floor.

"Well, that went well." Derek grabbed two white towels and threw one at his brother. Both had cuts on their faces, the white linen instantly streaked with blood as they carefully wiped.

"I'll get the healing spell," said Derek as he went to his bag.

Ehrhardt left the bathroom, and whispered to himself, "I will find a way to kill you, old man."

CHAPTER EIGHTEEN

FAMILY

Zacke shouldered his backpack, ready for class.

"Come on Zacke, got no time for your big brother?" shouted Zacke's shirtless brother Deke, walking off the sunny basketball court.

Zacke answered, "Sorry, Deke. Didn't see you. I got places to be. No time for hoops."

"Come on. Hold up," Deke said as he jogged to the fence.

He put his pack over the logo on his t-shirt as Deke made it to the fence. "What's up, bro?"

Deke asked, "Dude, were you at that game last night?"

"Yeah. Crazy, right?" Zacke said, hoping he wouldn't be asked too many questions. Then again, it wasn't like he was close with his brother anymore. "Where were you?"

"I was up in Santa Nina, hanging with some friends. Crazy night for me too, partying, etcetera," said Deke, offering no details. "Does Dad even know you were there?"

Zacke shrugged, "He's still in bed. He was passed out in his chair by the time I got home. Must have crawled into bed in the middle of the night."

"And I bet you put a nice little blanket on him and picked up all the beer cans and put them in the recycle," said Deke.

Zacke shrugged again.

"Dumb old drunk. He needs to move on from mom, already. She's the one that left." Deke changed subjects, "Anyway, come shoot hoops. I haven't seen you on a court for like a year."

There's a reason for that. "Nah. I gotta go. My ride's almost here."

"Alright. Hey, can you spot me a twenty until Tuesday?" asked Deke, "I want to contribute to the party tonight."

"Another party?" Zacke said, smiling, but without humor. He was about to point out the similarities between his partying and their dad's drinking, but didn't.

Deke got the hint anyway, "Don't judge, bro."

Zacke dropped it, pulled his backpack off his shoulder, fishing for the twenty.

Deke shook his head, "Seriously, Zacke? You still doing that?"

Zacke realized his brother had seen the "SV Explorers" logo on his shirt. He pulled the twenty from his zip pouch and passed it through the chain link fence. "Don't judge, bro."

That brought out a smile. "Yeah. Right. Just don't let my friends see that junior Po Po shirt."

"Whatever man. See ya." Zacke said, swinging the backpack over his shoulder again, covering the large logo on the back of his shirt. He made it around the corner to catch his ride.

The small white car was waiting.

"You'll call me for a ride, but you don't answer my texts?" Victoria said, leaning against her car.

"Yeah. Sorry about that. I figure I'd fill you in face to face."

Victoria rolled her eyes, "Get in, then, Mr. Zacke with an 'e'."

They pulled away from the curb, headed for the Police and Fire Academy. It was a huge complex set back from the highway at the entrance to their town. Atop a hill that looked out over Sea Valley, it was a state of the art training facility, one of only five in that half of the country.

On the way up the hill, Victoria asked, "So, why pick you up by a park? I know your address from your paperwork. Ashamed of where you live?"

"Yes," Zacke confirmed, "And who I live with."

"Wow, okay. Deep secrets. Alright, I'll drop that for now. But you never explained who those guys were, when I rescued you the other night. You also didn't answer my texts about whether you were dead under some bleachers." she poked him in the ribs. "*Were* you at the game last night?"

Zacke hesitated. "Yeah. I was there. Sorry. Things have just been crazy lately. I got home really late last night, but I wasn't hurt or anything."

"And those guys at work?" asked Victoria, "They looked dangerous."

"I really don't know who they are." Zacke didn't like lying. "Maybe they were trying to rob me or something."

"Hmmm. You are a bad liar, kid," Victoria said, glancing sideways at Zacke, "If you want my taxi service, you're going to have to do better than that."

Zacke rubbed his head. *Where would I start?* "You wouldn't believe all the stuff that's been going on. It's probably better if you don't know everything."

"Hmm. More mysteries," Victoria narrowed her eyes, "I saw your paperwork, so I know you're 16. Which makes me a cougar at 18. You can't have that many mysteries, kid."

"Lately, they're piling up."

They pulled up to the curb of the Police and Fire Academy. "You want to be a cop or fireman?"

"Cop. Probably," Zacke admitted, "I don't know. I'm just taking some Saturday Explorer classes right now. Took them all summer. I got the job to pay for it. My brother is really pissed I'm doing this."

Victoria smiled, "I see. It that one of the *reasons* you're doing it?"

Zacke shrugged and smiled.

"Alright. I'll be back at three. Don't forget you work tonight," Victoria added, "But the most important question is why haven't you asked me out yet?"

Zacke stuttered, "Um. Because you're my boss, and I..." he smiled, "I've never dated a cougar before."

"Okay, that was a good line. And I'm just a shift supervisor. No conflict there," Victoria added, "Better hurry, though. You don't ask me out soon, I will ask you. See you soon."

Victoria drove off leaving Zacke smiling.

* * *

"Is Ariana home?" Lucas said, feeling dwarfed by the large muscular boy standing in front of him. Lucas figured he must be about nineteen.

Ariana's brother eyed Lucas suspiciously, then gave him a baffled shake of his head. "Yeah. Hold on."

Lucas could hear the boy shouting Ariana's name through the house, and heard a muffled reply.

Her brother shouted louder, "Some white kid at the door for you. I don't know. He's waiting."

By that time, a few younger kids had peeked around the corner, and a woman floated by the open door suspiciously. Ariana came to the front door, her family literally at her back.

Ariana rolled her eyes at her family. "Stop staring. He's just a boy from school."

"Kinda cute," said her mother.

"Mami!"

Ariana closed the door behind her, leaving her family inside, and whispered to Lucas, "What are you doing here?"

"I didn't have your number," explained Lucas, "We need to talk about last night. You're the only one whose address I knew."

Eyes were peeking out from behind curtains. Ariana saw them. "Seriously?" she grabbed Lucas's arm and pulled him off the porch. "Sorry, my family is everywhere." She walked them away from the house.

Lucas asked, "Do you want to meet John, the guy with the sword?"

"I guess..." Ariana decided with a deep breath. "Yes. If he can tell me what's going on without an earthquake happening."

Lucas pointed back to the house, "Okay. Do you need to tell your family?"

Ariana yelled, "I'm going walking for a while!"

Her mom Josie popped out the door, "Okay mija, just keep your cell phone on." Josie smiled at Lucas, but he also detected a clear warning in her eyes.

Ariana and Lucas left to meet John. They walked to the old TV repair shop, furiously talking about what had happened the night before. Pete let them in, and led them to the convalescing John in the basement.

He was sitting in a chair, and rose slowly as they entered. Ariana walked up, wary of the men she didn't know. John's smile made her feel a little better. "Hello," he said, "I'm John. This is Pete, and this is David."

"Um. Hi." Ariana got to the point. "Can you tell me what's happening?"

John nodded with some difficulty, the pain still an issue, "Yes. But I'd prefer to talk to all five of you at once. My new friend David here is very good at finding people like us."

Ariana let her frustration show. "What does that mean? Why can we all do these things? Sorry, can I just get some answers now?"

John sat down again in his chair. "Of course, please sit."

"I'm sorry. I nearly forgot you were shot. Are you okay? I'm just frustrated." Ariana admitted. "And scared."

John smiled, "Of course. I wish last night hadn't gone so badly. I wanted to reach you all first. Anyway, some answers; you are all special. There is a struggle between my people, the Amartus, and the others, the Rageto. You might say it is a struggle between good and evil, but that would be too simple. The talents you feel growing, your special talents, are shared by only a select few people. It's my job to help you fully develop them."

Ariana's brow wrinkled. "What if I don't want to develop them?"

"That could be difficult," John said, "When people like us get together, our power gets stronger. But the other side, like those two men last night, they want to use your talents for very bad things. They give you a choice: join them, or die. You need to develop your talents to protect yourself."

"Will they come after my family?" asked Ariana.

John said, "No. Not directly. The core of who you are has been there since you were born. Without knowing it, the place where you live has been filling with protection all your life. It's kind of like your castle, deeply defended by your innate talents. You and your family are safe in your own home. They can't touch you there."

"Thank God," said Ariana, as if she'd been holding her breath. "If any of my family got hurt because of me..."

"They won't," John reassured, "Would you both come with us, to find the others?"

Both Lucas and Ariana looked at each other and silently agreed.

John looked at Pete. "Another favor?"

Pete held out the keys. "I figured you'd ask."

They left, and allowed David to guide them around town. They found Katie first. She lived just at the edge of town, on a road that wound through two hills. They stopped at a park near her home. Lucas went to Katie's door.

Katie was surprised, "Oh, hi. What are you doing here? How did you find me? I've been waiting for responses to connect online."

Lucas said, "The sword guy has a friend that can find people fast. Oh, the sword guy is named John, by the way. They want us together so they can explain what's going on."

Katie replied, "Oh. Um, okay I guess. Let me get some shoes on." she left Lucas at the door and slipped on her shoes as she texted.

First, to her mom: Out with friends.

She kept it short, knowing that they'd want her at the hospital. The next text was to Derek.

Katie: They're at my house. Want us all to meet somewhere. What should I do?

Derek: Go with them. Tell us where.

Katie: Ok

She finished her text and headed for the door, putting her phone away. Katie said, "Let's go."

Three of the five teens in the old white truck, they pulled up to a house at the bottom of a hill, surrounded by trees. They parked across the street, just in view of the front door. They watched as Lucas knocked and a woman with dark hair answered the door.

He had been distracted, but David glanced over to see the lady at the door. David went white, "No. No that can't be."

"What's wrong?" asked John.

David nearly yelled, "No! This is impossible."

They could see Cody at the door now, talking to Lucas.

David lost control, shaking, "No. No. No. No." he muttered to himself. Suddenly he bolted from the truck, running into the trees away from the road.

"What on earth?" said John. He got out and ran after David. Lucas and Cody both saw the commotion across the street, but couldn't clearly see what was happening.

John looked for David among the trees, calling his name. He didn't shout, since he had no idea why David would act this way. John thought maybe David had felt the brothers lurking around, "David?" he said as loud as he dared.

David stepped out from behind a tree, "Stop, John. I won't help you anymore. I'm leaving this city. You need to get all of them out of here, now. You can't let the brothers find them."

"What are you doing? What happened?"

"Get them out. Now. It may already be too late. Don't follow me, John." David ran through the trees, gone. John looked up the hill where the teens were, then back to where David had fled. Shaking his head, he reluctantly got back to the kids.

"What just happened?" asked Ariana.

"Our finder just left," said John. He went to their new addition, "Hello, Cody. I'm John. We have a lot to talk about. Will you come with us so I can explain everything?"

"Yeah, I guess," said Cody, "After last night I need answers. Why did your friend leave?"

"I don't know, but we need to find Zacke another way." John said, looking back where David had run off. "Does anyone know where Zacke can be found? We can't wait until Monday when school starts."

"They cancelled school for the whole week because of the earthquake," said Katie.

"He works at Ocean Burgers," offered Cody. John nodded and they were on their way.

In the back of the king cab truck, Katie was furiously texting.

"Boyfriend?" Ariana said in the back seat.

"Oh," said Katie, putting her phone away quickly. "Not really. Just a guy I know."

"Is this 'Derek' cute?" asked Ariana, smiling, trying to make conversation.

"Are you spying on me?" Katie said, angrier than she meant to be.

"Oh, sorry. I just saw the name." Ariana shrugged. "I didn't see what you typed or anything."

Lucas broke in, hoping to ease the tension, "Hey John. I'm not getting flashes anymore. Why?"

"Yeah, me either," said Ariana, "I thought you said when we're together, we'd be stronger."

John clarified, "You are. And the flashes will return. Some of you may even be able to read minds at will, eventually. But it always starts with the physical talents first. You are all tuning into the River. But it's like a journey. The talents grow stronger, but the flashes go dormant for a while. On this journey, the mental aspect is in a dark tunnel right now. The flashes will stop for a while, while your physical talents get sharper. The River knows your mind can only take so much. The mental talents will return once you're activated. I'm here to make sure you're ready for that."

"What if we're not ready?" asked Ariana.

"Sorry, but I'd like to wait until we're all together to answer all your questions."

They arrived at Ocean Burgers. They parked around back. John shifted in his seat, and winced at the pain, sorry he had moved so sharply. "Cody, would you do the honors and get Zacke? If he can't leave work, tell him to meet us there. This would be a good time for all of you to check in with your parents and let them know not to worry."

"Okay," Cody said, as he headed toward the front of the building. The rest of them got out to stretch their legs in the empty parking lot behind the restaurant. John got out of the old rusty truck slowly, to check his bandages.

He saw some of the teens call their parents, while others merely texted. *If their parents only knew what they were up to.* John knew this was the hardest part, the beginning. *They will have to decide to start keeping more and more from those they love.* John would have to be careful how much to share. The road forward would be strewn with nothing but trouble for all of them.

Cody walked in and scanned for Zacke. As usual, it was busy and he got in Zacke's line. Cody finally got to the head of the line, "Hey. Zacke, right?"

Zacke snapped his head up, "Oh. Uh. I didn't feel you. I mean *see* you..."

"Yeah, our new friend just explained why. Sorry I missed you at school on Friday, I got your note too late. Then the game happened. I wish we could have officially met some other way," said Cody, "But I need to tell you to meet us at the mission after work. What time do you get off?"

"Six. But I need to talk to you now." Zacke called over to a co-worker, "Hey Sarah, it's time for my break. Can you take over?" Victoria was busy at the other end of the open kitchen, but looked over, a little concerned.

At the far end of the counter, Zacke asked, "Dude, what is going on? Have you talked to the others since last night?"

"Yeah. They're all outside."

Zacke looked around, "You all shouldn't be here. Those guys know I work here. I've been watching for them my whole shift. Oh crap..."

Just then Cody and Zacke saw the two men walk in. They didn't get in line, just started scanning the restaurant.

Zacke pulled his visor down and grabbed Cody's arm, leading him around the counter to the back room.

Victoria noticed, and said, "Zacke! You know the rules about visitors."

The two men must have heard her and spotted the boys. The brothers weaved through the tables and chairs.

"Sorry, Victoria. It's an emergency," said Zacke, as he pulled Cody toward the break room. "Watch out for those guys."

Victoria turned to see the two men approaching. Derek and Ehrhardt began to casually walk behind the counter.

"Whoa guys." Victoria put her hands up. "You can't come back here." She put herself in front of the swinging doors.

Derek said, "Oh hello miss... Victoria," he saw her name tag, "This is Officer Lang and I'm Officer Sommers. We need to talk to those boys."

"Why?" she asked, noticing the quiet one rub his head.

Derek smiled, "It's about the stadium collapse at the high school."

"That was an earthquake," said Victoria.

"Yes," Derek replied smoothly, "but some of the team's equipment went missing during the confusion. We think these boys might have seen something."

Victoria crossed her arms. "I need to see ID, please." The quiet one showed silent anger, and she thought the man's face was scarred, maybe recently healed cuts? She didn't trust them. But the blond one, Officer Sommers, produced an SVPD badge. It had a strange green tint to it. But she doubted anyone would fake a small city's police badge.

Victoria said, "Alright, I guess. This way."

In the break room, Cody and Zacke furiously discussed their situation. That came to an end when they saw the brothers.

Cody said, "No!" and instinctively threw up his hands in front of him. The fluorescent bulbs overhead shattered, throwing the room into darkness. With no windows, it was very dark until a door was opened, the silhouette of Zacke and Cody running out the back.

The two men brushed off the glass and rushed to catch them. The back door swung shut automatically. Ehrhardt cussed in German as he fumbled for the handle.

The boys burst into the sunshine, and heard the German saying something as the back door closed. They kept running, just as they saw the old truck pull up. John yelled, "Hurry, get in!"

Cody jumped into the bed of the truck and Zacke tried, but caught his foot on the tailgate. He jumped again, and was sure he would tumble to the pavement. At the last second Cody grabbed his arm and pulled him in, closing the tailgate. The truck tires squealed and the smell of burning rubber filled their nostrils.

The back window of the truck exploded.

At the back door, Ehrhardt aimed the silencer-equipped gun again, but Derek stopped him. "No brother, we need recruits. Not dead teenagers."

"Hey, Officer dick!" a shout erupted from behind the brothers.

Derek wheeled around and was hit with a sloshy wet slap across the face. The wet mop enveloped Derek's head and he went down. He clutched at his eyes, yelling. Ehrhardt grabbed the girl's arm, forcing her to drop the mop. Ehrhardt screamed, "What did you do?"

"It's bleach water." then Victoria slipped from his grip and ran for the door. It closed as Victoria shouted "I'm calling the real cops!"

Ehrhardt pulled his gun again and might have fired into the back door of the restaurant, but his younger brother was still screaming. "Argghh! Brother, I can't see!"

Ehrhardt saw the hose and turned it on.

Derek took the water hose and ran it over his eyes, "Go around and get the car."

"We won't catch them now," Ehrhardt said, putting the gun back in his hidden holster.

"I know, damn it! I need to get back to the house for my eyes, another damn healing spell. Katie will lead us to where they're going. I better not be blind for the rest of this body's life! Hurry brother!"

CHAPTER NINETEEN

MISSION

John deftly handled the old truck, wondering how he would explain the window to Pete. Luckily the safety glass had shattered into tiny fragments. No one was hurt.

"He shot at us!" Katie said, carefully picking glass out of her hair.

"Yes, he did. Is everyone alright?" asked John.

"I'm okay," Ariana spoke first.

John called to the bed of the truck through the ragged opening, "Cody? Zacke?"

They were panting after the near miss, and the harrowing jump into the back of the truck. "We're good."

"I know this is all scary. After today, you will all be better armed against whatever comes." John asked Ariana, "Are you sure no one will be there?"

Ariana nodded. "Yes, the mission closes at four. I'm a docent every summer, the ranger will let us in. Should be deserted."

They had driven just outside of town, to the historic old Spanish mission.

"Alright," said John, "Is that the road?"

"Yeah." Ariana confirmed, "There's the back-way in. Take that service road all the way up the hill, then we can walk down into the mission."

John drove up the long winding road. Along the way were brown signs announcing that they were on the Camino Real. Ariana pointed the way and they ascended the small hill. They were met halfway up by a truck going the opposite direction.

The driver rolled down his window, "Sorry sir, park's closed."

"Hi Doug," said Ariana with a smile.

The ranger smiled back. "Oh, hey Ariana. How's your mom?"

"She's good." Ariana pointed to John, "This is a friend of the family. Can I give my friends a private tour?"

"Yeah, go ahead," the ranger said, "I'm meeting my wife in town for dinner. Will you watch the place for me?"

"Yeah Doug." she said, "of course."

Ranger Doug tipped his hat, "Have fun folks. You should have about an hour of light left." He drove on, and they parked at a make-shift gravel driveway on top of the hill.

"Why are we here, anyway?" asked Katie.

"To unlock your talents. And now that we're all together," John promised, "I will answer all of your questions."

"It's about time," said Cody, "No offense, but I really want to know what's happening to me."

"Me too," said Ariana.

They all got out of the truck and walked down the hill into the mission complex.

"Ariana, lead the way. Ask anything."

Katie started, "Who are you, really?"

"My name is John. My true warrior name is Pentoss. My true self was born a long time ago in a country that no longer exists. This body is thirty-seven years old."

"What do you mean true self?" Lucas asked.

"All of you are 15 or 16 years old, and have talents. A few of you are new births. Meaning that this is the first time, you are a blank slate. Whatever talents you have are totally new and not tied to any ancient warrior. The rest of you are ancients, re-births. Your talents were born a long time ago. I'm here to help you find out which one you are, and help you activate your talents."

Zacke asked, "So, some of us are re-incarnated, some of us aren't? Is that what the symbol on your back means?"

John looked puzzled at first, then remembered that Zacke was there the night he was shot, "My tattoo is the symbol of a re-birth. The great River is like a consciousness running through humanity. There are different philosophies about how and why it exists. But we know that knowledge flows through it, unique talents are born from it."

Ariana asked, "Is it like being born from heaven, or hell?"

John answered, "What we are, is not easy to label. Like Shakespeare's line 'there is more in heaven and earth than is dreamed of in our philosophy.' It's a fight between light and darkness, to be sure. But I wouldn't label it good and evil, or heaven and hell."

"The ancient warriors come from this river," asked Lucas, "but live inside us?"

"Yes." John elaborated, "Think of the river as a repository. Things go there to rest, and return when they are needed. A warrior born with special talents grows up, is fully activated, and chooses a side, The Amartus or the Rageto. When that body dies, the essence of the warrior goes back into the River, then is re-birthed into a new life. Usually around age 16, the warrior makes themselves known."

"Yeah, you could say that," said Lucas, "But what is a 'true death'? One of those guys said that."

John drew his short sword from the scabbard on his back. They all stopped, a few of them stepped back. "No reason to be afraid. This is Gwirionedd. It's a welsh word that roughly translates to truth. This is a relic. Only a relic can give a true death. When someone is cut with a relic, that warrior is prevented from returning to the river. This life will be their last. If you are killed with a relic, you and your warrior die a true death."

Zacke looked at the sword. "You always walk around with a sword on your back? Don't the cops stop you?"

John smiled. "I have been stopped, yes. But I must keep this in plain sight; Concealed weapons are illegal in California." He tapped the hilt. "Sword on my back, in the open, no problem."

Katie added, "Are relics always swords?"

"Good question." John put his sword away and they all continued walking down the scenic country path to the old buildings. "Relics can be anything, though they are usually weapons. They can only be made by a powerful elder; someone that gets stronger with each new life. The elders have deep natural talents. When they are re-birthed into new bodies, they activate earlier than most, and they get all their memories and talents back quickly. This is called a true birth. Since they've lived longer, they end up in charge. They gather disciples and try to find new recruits. They are usually born with the memories and talents from all their lives. Elders of the Amartus are like a council that guide us to knowledge and wisdom."

"What about the other guys, the rageta?" asked Zacke, "is that right?

"Close, the Rageto. Their elders are schemers, and are always at each other's throats. They are like warlords; they have their agents and sometimes war on each other. They want control. Always remember, those drawn to the Rageto have only small talents, and must supplement them with magic."

"Magic?" Cody sounded skeptical. "Really?"

Ariana smiled at him, "You can believe all the stuff we can do, but you can't believe in magic?"

"I call it magic as a familiar term, but it's like any of the sciences." John explained, "Magic has rules. Things that it can do, things that it can't. But the Rageto always use it for dark things."

"Yeah. Their 'sciencey' magic can do a lot. We all saw it," said Katie.

Zacke asked, "Why are we different? Who decided that? Where is God in all this?" His mind went to his mother, but he shook off the thought.

"The whys? Well, they're tricky. We've always existed. Some of us actively seek the others out. But eventually we gravitate toward each other. Who decides it? There are a lot of theories and philosophies about it in our world. But really, I have no idea."

Zacke stopped walking. "We're here for answers. How can you not know?"

John turned to face him, "I will give as many answers as I can. The Rageto want total domination, world control if they could manage it. They work in a structured system, with Elders who recruit and use teams of warriors. We are the Amartus. We are naturally stronger, but have been weakened over time by the battles we've lost, and the warriors that have defected to them." John took a breath. "I know that we are born and re-born from a universal consciousness we call the River. But how it all works, what the cosmic rules are? Sorry, for that, I'm the wrong guy."

Cody asked, "Don't you have a boss, or something?"

"Yes, the Amartus had the council of elders."

Katie said, "You're like our new leader, and you don't know everything?"

"I'm more of a soldier than a scholar. I know that's not fair, but if you've lived as many lives as I have, the cliché is true. Life is not fair. Sorry."

Cody wondered, "Will we have to fight their elder, too?"

"Probably not," John explained, "The brothers work for a man more dangerous than both combined. But the last time we met, I cut him with Gwirionedd. His current body must be in his 90's by now. He must protect it, since it will be his last. This elder will probably hide in his little hole. Good thing too, he has very strong talents and is a master of magic."

"Zamma," said Lucas, "Why did I just think of that word?"

"You're the most in touch with your ancient, so you've probably met Elder Zamma in another body," said John.

Lucas lost the grip on his thought. "I remember him being dangerous, but nothing else. Why? How come my ancient seems to... I don't know, like, ebb and flow. Just when I think I'm connecting, it fades away."

"Your full memories of all the lives you've lived may not come back for years. Whoever or whatever controls the River knows the mind can only handle so much at a time. I believe it's giving you time to process it all. Sometimes, there is a trauma connected to being activated, a mental block that's coming from your subconscious."

"Why do you call it the River, and not God?" asked Ariana.

"I think of it more as an instrument of fate, an older concept than the current idea of God." John tried to clarify, "The idea that no single being is controlling everything, but a sense that the universe will guide us, connect us together. But no one knows. Why are we special, with talents no other people have? I don't know, and despite our talents, we are still just humans. No one gets to know the secrets of why we are here. Lots of philosophical ideas, but there is no instruction manual. The River keeps its secrets."

Katie said, "So you're just as much in the dark as all of us? Great."

They finally arrived at the long main building of the mission. "Ironic that we're talking about God right now."

"Why?" asked Zacke.

John pointed to the apex of the building, the cross.

Ariana explained, "The church is the biggest building, and it's unlocked. I thought this would be a good place for answers."

John smiled and they all went into the building. "Ariana, do you know the history of this place? I don't want to bore you locals, but would you mind a quick overview for me?"

Ariana went into Mission Docent mode, "Sure, of course. This is the eleventh mission built by Spanish monks along the Camino Real Trail, originally founded in 1787. This is the largest and most restored of all the 21 missions. The original mission was built four miles from here, but an earthquake destroyed it."

They all paused at that, now that history and natural disasters were taking a new significance in their understanding.

Ariana continued, "It was sold a few times, left to rot, but fully restored in 1934 by several organizations including the Civilian Conservation Corps. It now hosts thousands of visitors a year."

John began the clapping, and the rest joined in. Ariana blushed. "I work here as a docent during Mission Days in the summer making fresh tortillas. Wow, I think I'm over-sharing now."

"Not at all," said John, "History is vitally important, especially to us. Many of you have been a witness to history throughout many lives, you just don't remember it yet. Thank you for the verbal tour."

"This is the largest building, the chapel, and now I'll shut up," offered Ariana, and let them look around.

It was a long rectangular space, with the altar and a priest's raised pulpit at one end. The other end had old furniture, cordoned off from the public by a velvet rope. There were heavy wood chairs and benches along the walls.

Since dusk was approaching, Ariana went to the altar and got candles from a hidden area. They all set up candles around the room, and the space warmed with the kind of light only candles can provide.

Zacke looked at the soft glow on the walls. The beamed ceiling and walls had delicate, intricate paintings. The alter was festooned with soft colors.

John said, "Let's all sit in a circle on the floor. I'd like to see how far we can activate you."

They all sat. Lucas asked, "What do we do?"

John said, "Just concentrate on your talents. They are getting stronger, but some of you may have had glimpses of these talents from a very young age; a random thought you heard when you were a child, making a door move without touching it. You all have small talents. You also have one big talent. This is the duality of existence."

"Like a main super power?" asked Lucas.

"Power can be unwieldy," explained John, "and power always corrupts. But talents can be shaped, honed. Your talents will get stronger as you use them, and your true self will be revealed. Only the Rageto think of what you have as 'powers.' "

Katie asked, "How do we start?"

"Just being close to each other should help. Your talents will draw out each other's inner strengths. Only you know what your talents are. Close your eyes and concentrate on that main talent. I want you to think of the first time you remember anything unusual happening."

Katie thought back to when she was six. Riding bikes with her friend. She had fallen over, and her friend's wheel was about to roll over her, but she imagined a green shield around her, and the bike rolled over her shield, never touching her. Her friend fell from her bike and their parents ran to help them. Her friend needed a Band-Aid. Not Katie.

Ariana was four the first time something froze when she thought of it. She was trying to help her mother clean. Ariana got the large glass jar of floor cleaner out from under the kitchen cabinet. It slipped from her hands and would have crushed her foot, but it stopped an inch above, frozen in space. The tiny Ariana picked it up with glee and put it on the floor beside her. She still remembered the baffled look on her mother's face.

Cody remembered the first Game Boy he got. The hand-held electronic was his favorite toy until he couldn't pass a level and the game sparked and shorted out in his hands. His mom returned it to the store, but the next one did the same thing within a week. Other things happened after that; a light going out, a school computer winking off, never to work again. Mom always said it was his "electric personality." Apparently, it was more than that.

Lucas' thoughts went to the first day of Kenpo Karate class when he'd nearly broken his sparring partner's foot... with his very first kick. That day he went home and thought of his childhood bully. He'd finally moved away, but his face still haunted Lucas. His anger had made him bite his lip and a few minutes later, his mom and dad came into a bedroom full of broken furniture and toys. He didn't remember how it happened.

Then his thoughts traveled back through a dark tunnel. He was standing on a shore, next to a Nordic dragon head that was carved into a ship. Then his mind sprang back to the mission. Lucas opened his eyes, frustrated as another truth slipped away from him.

Zacke didn't want to think about his so-called talent. His mind wandered to the first time he was playing hoops alone and felt the tingle. Then the memory of his mother walking into his room that night. The terrible screaming. Zacke slammed the memory into his metal sphere, locked it tight. He focused on the more familiar talent he knew best. His mind tried to focus on what the others were thinking, but he couldn't hear any of their thoughts. Then a flash, one of the brothers. Derek's mind felt close. Zacke could feel his own mind drifting toward his, glimpsing a thought. Then Derek's angry face pushed him out. Zacke's eyes shot open.

"Stay out of my mind, boy," said Derek, coming through the open doorway at the back end of the building.

The others opened their eyes, and John jumped to his feet, sword drawn.

"He's lying to you all," said Derek. He and Ehrhardt both stood inside the building.

John shouted, "All of you, get behind me."

Katie stood up on shaky legs, holding her head. She felt strange.

"Thanks Kaitlyn," said Derek, "Good work."

"Wait, what?" yelled Katie, seeing the accusing eyes of the others. "You shot at us! I'm not helping you now."

Derek smiled, "You really should understand technology better. I can track your cell phone easily. Always check your settings."

"I swear, I'm not helping them!" Katie could only hope they believed her.

John said, "It's not your fault, Katie. They tricked you. The Rageto are masters of deception and lies."

"Us?" said Derek, "We only wanted to talk, to tell you what's happening to you. To help you. This man lies, don't you Pentoss, or whatever your name is this life. Has he asked you to lie for him yet? Lie to your parents, maybe?"

John's eyes narrowed. "Nice try. I don't know what lies you told Katie. But you're too late. They are nearly activated."

"Good," added Ehrhardt, "Then they will remember what a liar you are. I wonder how many of their ancients you killed last time around, or the time before that. He is not your friend."

John said, "I only defend myself. The Rageto makes us turn on each other. Your elder recruited a few good friends. How is he by the way? Still nursing his wound, still hiding in his spider hole?"

Ehrhardt stepped toward John, anger flashing in his eyes, but Derek stopped him. "We're not wrong. He is. His kind are. You know how I can prove it? Their side is losing. Ask him how many Amartus have come back. Your elders, Pentoss, found true deaths. How many are left?"

"Enough to see the end of you," John answered, "We don't murder like you."

"John, what do we do?" asked Zacke.

"We fight." answered Lucas.

"I don't know how you came back, Viking." Ehrhardt spat at Lucas, "But I'll throw you back to the River as many times as it takes."

A deep memory came to Lucas.

He was standing on a beach in Galveston, Texas, the wind howling. He pulled his pitchfork out of what had been the younger brother Sazzo. He tracked them for weeks, the trains in 1900 proved to be surprisingly reliable. So had his information. He spotted the older brother, Caron. The storm was getting worse, and he could just make out the third warrior who was creating it. Caron hadn't seen his younger brother fall, his back turned and focused on the storm maker. He shouted Caron's name. The elder brother turned just as the pitchfork slammed through his chest. It wasn't a true death, but it would serve. Hopefully the River would refuse to spit out the brothers again. But, his victory was short. As he turned to take care of the storm maker, the winds lifted him high in the air and he was torn apart.

Lucas felt the warrior rise, as if the ancient Viking stood within Lucas's slim frame. He filled with strength and focus. "Hello, Caron. This time I'll finish the job."

Ehrhardt flinched as Lucas came forward. He sensed it wasn't just Lucas.

John shouted, "All of you, you'd better stand behind us. These two really don't like each other."

Lucas charged at Ehrhardt. He drew his gun, but Lucas was too fast and slammed into the German. He was knocked into the plaster wall, and the gun went flying across the floor.

Ariana, Cody and Zacke watched as the small Lucas lifted Ehrhardt and threw him across the room like he was a toy. The German's back smashed into a portrait. Both painting and Ehrhardt tumbled to the floor. Lucas calmly walked toward him.

Derek looked at Katie, "Kaitlyn, time to choose."

Katie looked defiant, then seemed confused, "You shot at us! You brought a football stadium down!"

"To stop maniacs like him," said Derek, pointing to Lucas, "I would never hurt you."

Katie blinked and was not at the mission.

There was fire all around. She fell from the five-story stone building and saw the younger brother, Sazzo's true face staring down as she dropped.

Then she was in a trench and she felt the bayonet in her gut, and saw Sazzo's smiling face.

Then she was in a jungle, in heavy rains as hot metal tore through her body. Sazzo came out of the dark, smiling at her, before she died

Katie snapped out of her memories. She smiled at Derek and walked to him.

John yelled, "Katie, no!"

Derek smiled back, "Girly girl. I knew you would..." he was cut short by Katie's hard kick between his legs. Derek doubled over in pain. From the floor, he managed, "Wait... don't tell me. Zhanna, right?"

Katie's hands went flat in front of her, and Derek slid across the stone floor. He smashed into the wall at the back of the building.

Ehrhardt ran for his gun, trying to avoid Lucas. John got there first and kicked it farther down the long room. Lucas fanned out to flank from the right. Katie stood her ground.

Derek got up, favoring his aching back. His hands were still over his privates. There was a fresh crack in the old plaster. "Of all the ancients... seemingly sweet, sweet Katie had to be you, Zhanna."

The girl-warrior said, "This time around, I'll let you have a true death with Pentoss' sword. I owe you that, my love."

Derek lost all his surfer boy charm. His true ancient revealed itself. His voice was full of rage, "None of you has seen what I can do yet." He closed his eyes briefly, concentrating. He smiled and opened his eyes. "Pajak Araneae Armata," he whispered, "Pajak Araneae Armata, Pajak Araneae Armata. You know, they say that every square mile holds about a million of these little guys."

Lucas wavered, then got ready to charge at the brothers.

Ariana covered her ears and yelled, "What is that? It's everywhere."

"What? I don't hear anything," said Katie anxiously.

"You can't hear that...? Wait, look!" Ariana pointed at the wall above Derek. Dark shadows appeared, changing and shifting. The candles revealed little, at first. Then, they could all see the shadows were moving. The shadow was alive, creeping closer.

Derek said in a calm, controlled voice, "I've chosen the most poisonous of them. Of course, most people hate them because they're just so darned creepy."

They all stared at the white plaster walls. Now, they could all see the blackness growing out of the corners. They stared at the black swarm quickly spreading over the walls and ceiling. It looked like one big blob at first, but soon they could see clearly defined legs.

Spiders of all types covered the far end of the room. Big hairy spiders, small deadly spiders, black arachnids fanned out toward them. They crawled with amazing speed. From overheard, spiders were already on their webs, headed straight down for them, unfurling their legs, as if hands reaching for its prey.

Ariana chanted, "Oh my god, oh my god, oh my god."

John yelled, "Run! Get out! We'll hold them off."

"I... I want to fight," shouted Katie, but she sounded less confident, like her ancient warrior had faded.

John said, "No Katie. Lead the others back to the truck, now!"

The room was half covered; floor, ceiling and walls. Katie, Zacke, Cody and Ariana dashed for the open door. They all ducked away from several spiders trying to web down to cut off their escape.

Katie pushed a shield in front of her and made an opening through the spider horde. They ran out the door, into the night. Derek directed half of the army out the door, toward the escaping teens.

John was busy sweeping his sword furiously, slicing spiders, cutting webs, making sure they didn't fall on his bare skin.

Lucas saw half the black mass leave the room, after his new friends. He ran for one of the heavy wood benches along the wall. He leapt on the arm and heard the crack. Two heavy wood clubs were now his to wield.

Ehrhardt casually walked to his gun. Everywhere the brothers moved, the spiders opened a path, like parting water. Lucas was swinging wildly with both clubs, cutting webs. Hundreds of spiders smashed against the wood, or flung like eight-legged baseballs against walls, as wet sounds accompanied each swing. Splat. Paff. Splat.

Ehrhardt aimed for Lucas and fired. The boy moved just in time. Lucas flipped over the speeding bullet. As he landed, he used the momentum and let one of his clubs fly. It flipped the length of the room and smashed Ehrhardt's gun hand.

The gun flew, sliding across the floor. A line of spiders skittered with it on the floor like eight-legged bowling pins, many crushed. Soon, the floor was all spiders again.

John yelled, "We should only have to fight for a few more minutes. Derek's talents are limited!"

"Don't give away all of my secrets," Derek said as he directed the last of the swarm at Lucas.

Ehrhardt got to his feet, and fled the room with Derek close behind him. John picked up the gun and he and Lucas fled the room. The spiders followed.

Outside, the mission was pitch black. Ariana led them, with Katie bringing up the rear. The ground was uneven, filled with gopher holes. Zacke tripped. Cody fell over him and Ariana turned back to help. Zacke tried to stand, "My ankle. I think it's sprained."

Katie stopped and turned her back to them. The feeling of being Katie and her ancient warrior self kept flashing back and forth. One second she was scared, the other she had the urge to fight. She stood her ground by Zacke and the others.

They all heard the two men approaching, "There's no place to go, Katie!" called Derek.

She was Katie just then; scared and out of breath. Ariana said, "Katie you have to make a shield." Cody yelled as he smashed a spider on the ground with his foot.

"I can't!" Katie yelled, but as the men drew closer, she felt her last reserve of strength swell. She blinked in the darkness and was sure the ground was moving toward them, on thousands of deadly little legs.

Her ancient warrior filled her again and she closed her eyes. Zacke was holding his ankle, looking around for spiders. Ariana saw the dome all around them. It radiated from her, a green glow in the night. Spiders tried to climb up the dome from the ground.

"What's happening?" Cody said.

"A really strong shield," answered Ariana. She looked around in a circle. The spiders were trying to climb up the green dome around them. The arachnids climbed over each other, their undersides and legs a strange green hue through the shield. Cody saw it too. To Zacke, it looked like they were crawling up a dome of invisible glass.

Then Ariana saw a new blue layer had radiated from Katie. It was a layering of colors, like a rainbow and went from green, to blue, then a sharp yellow layer added under that. The spiders began to fade.

Derek and Ehrhardt stopped at a tree, only a few feet away. Ehrhardt remarked, "Could she do that last time?"

Derek shook his head in wonder. "No."

"It would be advisable to fight another day," said Ehrhardt, "The girl is stronger than we thought."

By this time, Katie's eyes were open, and her ancient glared out at the brothers. Even in the dark, across the field, Derek felt a chill. "You are right, brother. But maybe this whole thing will end up being more fun than I thought."

Standing next to a tree, some bark splintered, the wood striking Derek's cheek. He spun around to see Lucas and John running toward them. John was firing Ehrhardt's gun. They ducked behind the tree, then Derek and Ehrhardt disappeared into the night.

The spiders had faded, like they hadn't been there at all. Katie's shield faltered, and she was just Katie again. She collapsed next to Zacke.

Katie muttered, "So tired."

Cody rubbed his arms furiously, looking all around for more spiders.

Lucas and John ran to them, "Is everyone alright?"

Katie looked around, sobs threatening. "So tired," she moaned.

"I know. Using so much of your talent can be exhausting," said John, "Let's get you home. The brothers have fled."

Ariana went to Katie and hugged her, helped her up. "It's okay. You saved us."

John said, "You met them before I had a chance to talk to you. They tried to twist the narrative. But you know who they are now, don't you Katie?"

Katie looked the direction the brothers had fled. "I don't like being lied to."

Cody kept rubbing his arms, sure he was covered in spiders. "Where'd they all go?"

John said, "Sazzo can conjure horrifying things. But it only lasts for a short time. With magic, the power of your will and concentration is key. It's hard to keep control of monsters for very long, even little ones. He tires, and the creatures fade. But, make no mistake. When they're here, they are real and very dangerous. He has a very dark imagination."

"Sure does. I hate spiders!" said Cody, shivering, rubbing his arms, still not convinced they were spider free.

"I'll take you home. You'd better call your parents. I won't tell you to lie to anyone. But you must be careful with the truth. Things are happening very quickly now."

"I might need some help." said Zacke. Cody and Lucas helped him to his feet. They all made their way back to the truck, using Ariana as their guide.

John said, "We must find another secluded spot, to continue activating you."

"What?" Cody said, "You've nearly gotten us killed twice. I want to understand what's going on. But this..."

Ariana said, "That's not fair. John is the good guy here."

"How do we know? Yeah, those other guys are crazy, but we only have John's word." Cody said, "Sorry, but I have a life. I want to get back to it, not have some crazy magic guy end me."

"I told you life's not fair." said John.

"You also said we have a choice," Cody shot back, "I choose no. I'll just deny my warrior, or whatever."

"The brothers aren't going to stop because you ask them nicely." John said, "There will be a choice to make later. Your fate will be your own. But right now, we must stick together."

Cody said, "No! I'm not going anywhere with you people. I'm done!"

They were nearly to the truck. Ariana said, "Look, Cody. We're all scared. But we have to stick together."

"Why?" Cody asked, "Because he said?"

"We have to trust someone. If you'd seen my warrior's memories..." said Lucas.

Cody shouted, "I don't want to see, or know, any of it! I just want to be normal."

"Well, you're not normal!" John shouted back. It was the first time John raised his voice, and they all stopped. "I'm sorry Cody. We are in real danger. This is your team now. You have two choices, fight them or die."

Cody stopped arguing. They all felt a chill from the stark assessment.

John's tone softened, "I'll take you home. We all need the rest."

Zacke and Cody got into the bed of the truck. Katie sat with Ariana and Lucas in the cab.

They were each dropped off near their homes. Doubts swam through their minds. They hoped that John was right about their homes being safe.

CHAPTER TWENTY

HOME

Ten minutes after Katie got home, she saw the headlights hit the front windows. She ran out the door. Her mom and stepdad got out of the car. Jason opened the back door and Megan got out.

"You're home!" Katie shouted and ran for Megan.

She hugged Megan as hard as she could, hoping her parents wouldn't see her tears. Her mom had planned to ask Katie why she hadn't been by the hospital that day, but she ended up just wrapping her arms around the two girls instead. Katie looked up at her stepdad Jason and motioned for him to come over. They ended in a real family hug on the driveway.

* * *

Zacke got home to a dark house. He limped on his ankle, checked his brother's room. It was a mess like always, but no one there. He looked in the fridge; hardly any food, of course. He made a peanut butter sandwich and looked through to the living room. His dad was there, lying back in his reclining chair. He could only see a few empty cans on the table.

He knew there would be more on the other side of the chair. He helped his father to bed, who at least made a sound of recognition before he was snoring in his own room.

Another night alone, he looked at the cell phone he'd ignored all day. Zacke laid in bed texting back and forth with Victoria while he messaged his ankle.

* * *

Lucas went through the garage door entrance into his converted room. There was a knock at the door. His mom and dad stood there, "Can we come in?"

"Sure. What's up?" Lucas asked. His parents hovered nervously.

"You know we don't want to bring up the past, honey. But you've been acting strangely. Never home, always tense when you are."

Lucas smiled. "Mom. Dad. I'm okay. I've met some new friends, actually. I think... I think I've finally found what I've been looking for."

* * *

Ariana's mother stood at the front door, and wouldn't let her come into the house, "Ah, mija. You don't call your mother? A text to your brother is not the same as calling me."

"Mami, I'm so sorry I worried you. There was a whole group of us. I was showing them the secret parts of the mission. Ranger Doug was around. We were safe." Ariana hated lying to her mom, even a little.

It took nearly a half an hour to calm her mother down. Ariana had missed dinner, but she joined her parents and brother on the couch with a slice of leftover pizza. She often felt surrounded by family, almost trapped. That night, it felt good to be close to family after the crazy day. She shook off the bad parts of the night and smiled as she took a bite. After all they'd been through in just a few days, she felt silly thinking about a boy.

* * *

Cody's mom wasn't home. He texted her, let her know that he'd made it home safe. John said they would be safe at home. But he made sure all the windows and doors were locked, made a full sweep of the house. It was his job.

He was the man of the house, and with mom working two jobs, and him always at practice, Cody always double checked. They couldn't afford a break in. He paused at the thought. There were much worse things to think about nowadays. He brushed his hand through his hair, imagining spider legs.

His mother's room had mirrored closet doors, so he checked the window lock quickly, and then shut the door, not daring to look at the mirrors.

Cody went to the small fridge in his closet, chugged the first beer, then got a second. He locked the bathroom door and took a shower. The bathroom mirror was built in, so he covered it with a spare towel. He looked very carefully for spiders. He checked the ceiling, behind the toilet. After he was satisfied, he soaped up thinking about the last few nights. *What a horrible power, able to conjure spiders.*

He shuddered and opened his eyed before he shampooed. Still safe from the eight legged creatures.

Compared to Katie, what use were his "talents?" Getting a random thought here and there. Sometimes starting old cars, more often frying whatever electronic device he tried to use. And the mirror thing. His mother had quietly removed most of the mirrors from the house. They never spoke of it. She just seemed to know. Cody had never seen anything bad in the mirror until now.

The few times it had happened before, he just saw a different place in the mirror: a meadow, a snowy mountain. Once he looked and saw the forest as a deer walked by. They had always seemed real, but pleasant; nothing like this old man.

He turned off the water, reaching for the perspiring beer can. Cody took two swallows. He belched, smiled at how loud it was. He'd make sure to wash out both cans and hide them in his small trash can. His mom had enough to worry about, and it was just a few beers. *If she knew how much some of my teammates drank...*

He had no idea what the old man meant, or who he was. But the feeling was getting stronger that he couldn't trust John. He tried to study the coach's playbook, but soon fell asleep. Happily, he did not dream of spiders.

* * *

John went to the station. Pete changed his dressing. "Yep, you opened up your stitches. Did you say spiders?"

"Wow, that hurts," John said, clenching his teeth, "Yes, spiders. It's a wonder no one was hurt. Now I must convince them to get together again. They're scared. I fear every day will be a battle now."

Pete put on the new bandages, "How are you going to do that? If I was them I'd take my chances in the jungle of high school nonsense. It's safer."

"Even if they decide to ignore their talents, bury them, they will still be hunted," said John.

"True. Speaking of that, you could just tell them the truth. They might rally to your cause faster."

John said, "That's too dangerous. Some of them may turn to the Rageto if they knew the truth."

Pete finished his work on John. "Again, I'm mister neutrality here, but take my advice; tell them before they find out, and think you a liar. Oh, and you can't stay here anymore."

John said, "Hmm. I guess I should have seen that coming. You've done too much already."

"Damn right."

John said, "I'll get a hotel room. With David out of the picture, there's no way for them to find me easily. It will feel good to get a night's sleep with no one trying to kill me."

"You sure your real talent isn't attracting trouble?" Pete smiled. "Take care. Our book problem will be solved tomorrow."

"The books leave for the next station?"

"Yes. Because the brothers are here, the sooner the books leave, the better. Imagine if you had a fully charged elder to deal with here, now, with this knowledge at their fingertips."

"Keep them safe, my friend. I'll see you again." John said, "If I fail, I'll see you the next time around."

"Don't be so fatalistic," Pete said, "You know what? Damn the Sect's neutrality. I want your side to win. Besides, I'm just an old man. I'm getting sick of having to learn who you guys are all over again."

John left for a good night's sleep. He walked to the nearest hotel. He couldn't tell these scared teenagers how small a chance they actually had.

* * *

At the station, Pete went to his small bedroom. He announced, "He's gone."

"Do you think he knew I was here?" asked David.

"No one knows you're here. And you're leaving tomorrow with the station crew, so no one ever will."

"Good." said David.

Pete stood silent, rubbing his chin and looked at the floor.

"You think I'm a coward?" asked David.

"What about your son?"

David closed his eyes. Tears appeared when he opened them again. "I want to run to him. I want to hold him tight. My son..."

"Then go to him. Explain everything."

"What do I tell him? What would I tell my wife? That my cowardice made me leave?" David shook off his tears, deciding he was unworthy of them. "I told myself they were safer without me. The truth is, I left because I was afraid she would reject me when she found out what I was."

"You got this all wrong, David," said Pete, "You told me you turned back, were going to choose your family when the brothers took you. Tell him that, make them understand. You were taken prisoner. He can't blame you for that."

"I blame me for that." David was quiet for a moment. Pete could see the bleakness struggling within him. "I left them. That's unforgivable. Even if they could forgive me, I can't."

Pete repeated, "They took you prisoner."

"Yes! And they broke me!" David shouted, immediately realizing he was shouting at the wrong person. "I'm sorry, Pete. Thank you. I know you're only trying to help. But I don't deserve to have them back. The brothers broke me. I'm no good to anyone now."

CHAPTER TWENTY ONE
THE BEACH

Lucas, Ariana, Zacke and Katie stood on the porch, waiting.

"Why didn't John come himself?" asked Cody, standing at his own front door.

"Ok, rude," Katie asked, "can we come in?"

Cody stood aside, "Yeah, but make it fast. My mom will be home soon."

"Afraid to have us freaks in your place?" asked Zacke.

"Well, some of you seem alright." Cody smiled.

"Okay, jerk. Thanks, I think," said Katie.

"No. Sorry," Cody searched for the right words. "I meant what you did last night was awesome. Scary, but awesome. I can't do anything like that. And you, Lucas, dude, you're like a skinny ninja. I can only, like, fry cell phones and break mirrors."

Zacke asked, "Break mirrors? Like with your mind?"

"No. Forget it. My point is, I don't fit. I'm not a superhero," said Cody.

"Like we are?" Ariana said, "None of us think we're heroes. We're all scared, Cody."

"You were the one that sacked the earthquake guy. How did you even know we were there?" asked Katie.

Cody's brow furrowed. "I'm not sure. I just knew. Someone gave me a weird note from Zacke that day at school, and then during the game I saw a green glow behind the bleachers. I just felt something, like a spidey-sense or something. So, I ran. That night... I wanted to kill that guy."

"I feel the pull too," said Zacke, "Especially when I'm around you guys."

"Yeah. Me too. But I feel like something's missing," said Katie.

Lucas said, "Right! Each time we almost get the truth, something interrupts us. I feel like we're in that show 'Lost.' "

"What do you mean?" asked Cody.

Lucas said, "Like, John says 'I'll tell you everything. Just come with me and I'll explain.' Then, bam, something crazy happens, and we don't learn anything."

Zacke laughed, "Man, I don't know what story we're in, but I want out."

"That's just it. It's kind of cool to be able to do this stuff," said Ariana, "But, mostly I'm just scared. I'm not afraid to admit it. Anyone else nervous about being 'activated'? Does that mean more of this, but worse? More guys coming after us? What do they want, anyway?"

Katie said, "I'm not sure. John says they want to recruit us. They tried with me. I was so stupid. Anyway, I can remember a few things from past lives, I guess, but only flashes. Like it or not, only John has the answers."

Cody said, "Yeah, but I feel like John isn't telling the whole truth."

"Why?" asked Zacke. Secretly, he was thinking the same thing.

"Just a feeling." Cody changed the subject. "Why are you all here? To convince me to come with you?"

"John did ask us to talk with you, but I'm here for me. I feel like we need to be together to get the answers," said Lucas.

Cody shrugged. "Okay. I guess. What's the plan?"

Lucas said, "John wants somewhere more secluded. Tranquilo Point should be pretty deserted on a Sunday."

"I haven't been there since I was a kid. That's where the ship wrecks are, right?" asked Katie.

"Yeah." said Lucas, "It's only a few miles outside of town, so if anything happens, we can get back to our houses fast. Plus, hopefully, those guys can't find us without their finder."

"They found us at the mission," said Ariana.

Katie said, "I'm so sorry about that. I know they're the bad guys now. I've changed all the settings on my phone. I won't even bring it tonight, just in case."

Lucas said, "I think we should all leave our cells in the car, turned off, just in case."

"What if they captured that 'finder' guy again? He can track us," said Lucas.

"Who are we talking about?" asked Cody.

Zacke explained, "Oh, that right. He left before we met up. The brothers were using a guy to find us. That's his talent. He escaped them and was on our team, but he bolted."

"Why?" asked Cody.

Ariana said, "No one knows. John was confused about it too."

Katie steered them back to the plan. "So, we're all going, right?"

"Ok, but I have to be back by ten." Ariana shrugged, "My mom's freaked out that I've been out so much. I'm running out of excuses."

They all laughed. Lucas said, "Yeah. It is weird to have these talents, but still have to come home on time."

* * *

John picked them up, and they headed a few miles west of town. He drove past the small train kiosk where he'd entered town, continuing down the road to another beach.

Tranquilo Point sits at the spot where the very long California coast takes a significant bend to the right, resembling a lazy elbow. Meaning "point of tranquility" in Spanish, the name is ironic; it's anything but.

Most people imagine warm, sunny beaches year-round in California. On the Central Coast, the temperatures are mild inland, but ruled by fog and wicked winds at the sea. The water is choppy, the surf uneasy. An infamous undertow sucks swimmers out to sea, to a likely death.

If a person walked out only a few dozen feet into the sea, the Pacific Shelf drops off, plunging hundreds of feet down; a steep canyon just under the water. Only a few feet from shore, there be monsters. Beautiful, majestic blue and grey whales migrate, but there are also many Great White Sharks. Tranquilo Point is beauty mixed with treachery.

There was nobody there on a Sunday in September, so they all found a quiet spot and started a fire. It was still daylight, but the fire had a purpose.

John addressed the group, "Fire can be a focal point; it will help your subconscious relax, bringing the warrior to the surface. The experience will be different for all of you, and this may take a few hours. Those that have ancients in them will hopefully awaken them. Those that are new births may get in touch with your inner talents. Let your minds open."

Zacke smiled. "Are you our Obi-Wan or Yoda?"

"That reference I get." John smiled back. "But none of you are Jedi... yet."

* * *

The two men from the Sect arrived, ready to transport the books to the next station. They drove a rusty freight truck that had been painted over many times to cover the rust.

It backed up to small ancient loading dock. The freight door shrieked in protest, reluctant to be rolled up. The men donned their lead lined gloves and entered the basement. Pete unlocked the thick plastic container that housed the ancient books.

David watched them carefully load the books, one by one. They were all wrapped in heavy blankets, each woven with what looked like metal threads. They carried each book up the stairs one by one.

"You sure I can't help?" asked David.

Pete answered, "No, sir. These must be handled in a very special way. The knowledge can slip out. Any little glimmer that gets back into the River could travel through the whole consciousness and end up with the wrong people. In fact, it would probably be wise if you leave until we're done. Why don't you go next door and get a soda pop or something? Just give us a little while."

David thought that was a good idea. He made his way up from the basement, averting his eyes from the ancient books of magic. His thoughts turned dark at the memory of the lost years with the brothers. *Dark magic, that damned charm.* He imagined using his other talent on the elder and the brothers so many times, but hope had faded over the years with that charmed weight around his neck. David wondered if they even knew what his other talent was. He hadn't used it in so long, he wasn't sure if it worked any more.

Better not think of them, not now. David tightened his thoughts, headed to the convenience store next door. David was so wrapped up in his thoughts that he failed to notice the televisions behind him, until he bumped into one. Dead for so many years, they were little more than props now. They still had screens, almost like mirrors.

An image flickered into existence on the dusty television screens. The three station attendants were too busy to notice that Elder Zamma had appeared in each of the screens. The building's bay door was open, and the faded wooded sign announced:

Bird's Eye TV Repair - 336 West Ocean

The elder didn't see who had focused him on this screen. *The football boy?* he wondered. Zamma had barely slept, casting constant spells to connect with anyone to open a window in Sea Valley.

The elder had been opening random windows in and around the small city, hoping to get lucky. Without their finder, Zamma used every spell he knew to locate his enemy. Now, he was viewing the repair shop. His luck was improving. He wished he could thank whoever had inadvertently helped him.

Zamma froze as he saw the men with curious gloves, carrying something that looked very important. He picked up his cell phone and made a call.

At the convenience store, David decided to splurge. He bought a Slurpee and a hot dog, thankful for the money John had given him. He felt another pang of guilt about leaving as he watched the TV repair shop from the convenience store.

David nearly choked on his hotdog when he saw the convertible pull up to the TV repair shop. He recognized the car, of course. He dropped the hot dog.

The brothers got out of the car.

* * *

On the deserted beach, they sat in a circle around the fire, and dusk was just threatening them with a pink glow through broken clouds. John got more wood from the back of his newly rented SUV and went back to the spot.

The tar on his feet and the cold September winds reminded him that he was on a California beach. Only chilly ice plant and tufts of scrub grass littered the otherwise sandy beach. They had all brought light coats or sweatshirts.

John had instructed them to bring something from their earliest childhood, but had not indicated why. They all had backpacks, and Cody pulled out a six pack of beer.

"Whoa! Hey. no booze dude." Zacke said, "I'm training to be a cop."

"It's beer, not booze. Beer's no big deal." Cody replied, "You gonna turn me in?"

John said, "No, Cody. You're only sixteen, and you need a clear head. Please put it in the car."

Cody shook his head, "Fine. Forgot I was with children. Be right back."

"Why is he being such a jerk?" asked Ariana.

"He's scared. We should all be scared. I saw what those guys really are in some crazy memories," said Katie.

John said, "They are very dangerous men, but you are stronger."

"I don't feel like it," answered Ariana.

"That's why I asked you to bring something from your childhood. It is a physical link back to your earliest days in *this* life. That will bring you closer to the last life you lived, and closer to your ancient," John explained.

Zacke asked, "But you said some of us are, like, new. Right?"

"Yes," said John, "But we can only know for sure when the ancients are awakened, or not. This will also help the new births to bring out any other talents you have. We'll need that when we meet the brothers again."

"Who are those guys, really?" asked Ariana.

"They are Caron and Sazzo. They are very dangerous ancients. I've battled with them over many lifetimes. Some of your ancients will have fought them as well. They work for an elder named Zamma. Luckily, the Elder is scared to leave his room, much like a hemophiliac that's afraid to bump into anything."

Ariana looked confused. Lucas explained, "Hemophiliacs can bleed to death really easily if they get hurt."

"Oh," said Ariana. "Really?"

"Yep." Lucas smiled. Ariana smiled back.

* * *

The elder Zamma was shirtless in his Italian home. He examined the old relic-inflicted wound in the mirror. The gash had stopped bleeding years before, but it had never fully healed. It felt tender to the touch and reminded him of the day he got it. He rubbed his finger across it and felt the special charge; like touching a tongue to a battery. He knew this would be his last body. Unless he could find the right spell, the one book that might help.

He had called the brothers in California nearly fifteen minutes before, to alert them to the shop he'd seen. *The boys should already be there, what is taking them so long?* he thought, just as his phone rang.

"Are you there yet? I can't see you." Zamma looked into his mirror, scanning the scene.

Ehrhardt answered, "Yes. You're sure this is a station? I don't mind the killing, but it's still daytime here. A busy convenience store is next door. It may be tricky."

"I don't care," answered Zamma, "Do what you must and get those books."

Derek said, "The Sect has been neutral for years. What are they doing in this small town during a breakout?"

Zamma let his impatience show. "I don't know. The Sect bastards have gone silent. Call me when it's done. I'll watch as much as I can from here." The elder clicked his phone to end the call.

He put on a fresh shirt. New pain came as the shirt brushed the wound. Zamma returned to watching the unfolding scene from his mirror, through the television screens. There were only so many angles he could see. He would have to trust the brothers, again.

* * *

Back at the station, Ehrhardt and Derek had cornered two of the men on the stairs. The silenced handgun made them fall before they realized they were shot. A package dropped out of each of their hands.

"Brother! We've finally found a station. The old man was right." Derek laughed at their good fortune.

They made it past the two bodies and down the stairs when a shotgun blast came from the corner. They both ducked and Ehrhardt came up, pistol aimed.

"Stop!" Pete said, a zippo lighter already lit. It was inches from a pile of books next to Pete. They saw the red plastic gas can at his feet. "You kill me, and these books all burn to dust."

Derek scanned the scene. "All we want is the Vitaeizicon. The rest of the knowledge can go back into the River. Burn the wrong book, and you die."

Pete laughed, "I know you'd kill me anyway. Drop your gun, or I burn them all."

"We don't need guns to end you." Derek smiled. "Zmija mhi-rizhonga cuska. Zmija mhirizhonga cuska. Zmija mhirizhonga cuska." A horde of serpents came into being with the incantation, slithering down the steps into the basement.

"Screw being impartial." Pete came into the open and let the lighter fall. He pumped the shotgun at the brothers.

Ehrhardt got a lucky shot off, and the lighter flew across the room, the flame snuffed out by the quick action. Derek ducked just in time, Pete's shot made splinters exploded from the door trim over him.

Pete said "shit," as the dozens of snakes lunged for him. He managed to get another round off before Ehrhardt shot Pete twice in the chest.

Pete fell, and the snakes covered him. There were cobras, rattlers, asps, and a dozen more varieties of slithering things. Ehrhardt's aim had been good; Pete was dead before he hit the floor. His face disappeared under a mound of serpents.

Derek went down the stairs and inspected the books. Unwrapping the bundle, he said, "It was a bluff. No gasoline on the books."

"There's gas in this can," said Ehrhardt. "Better make use of this. I'm sure I hear distant sirens already."

They bundled up the few books that were left. Ehrhardt recovered the lighter he'd shot, shocked it still worked. They poured the gas and lit the blaze as they escaped up the stairs. The snakes had faded, the fire now engulfed Pete's station. The room caught quickly, and the smoke was thick even before they made it out.

The sirens got louder. Derek spotted Elder Zamma's image in the old stack of televisions. They indicated the books, and Elder Zamma smiled. His image winked out and they left the station building.

Ehrhardt said, "Let's check the truck for more before the police and firemen come. Hurry."

Ehrhardt went to the truck as Derek unwrapped the bundle in his hands. The title said Vitaeizicon in ancient script. He turned it over and unlocked the clasp. The back binding was thicker than the front. Derek traced his fingers across the ancient metal clasps. He smiled, then wrapped it up again.

"There are three more here," said Ehrhardt, carrying his heavy stack to the car.

"Brother, a good day." Derek eased the car onto the street, driving slowly to avoid suspicion.

A few customers had come out of the convenience store, the smoke next door was very thick. Hidden from view, David's anger flared. *They have the books.* The Sect crew surely dead, his escape plan was gone.

He had to get to John. He looked at the sky, and thought briefly of unleashing his other talent, but the brothers had already driven away. He was powerless and alone. The smoke billowed out of the building. The sirens were nearly there.

David spotted Pete's beat up old truck and hoped the keys were in the cab. He got in and the keys fell from the visor. He peeled out, using his special talent to locate the others. *The beach.* He accelerated, heading west on Ocean Avenue.

* * *

The bonfire lit their faces. They sat, trying to concentrate. Katie opened her eyes and stared out. The sun had mostly disappeared behind the ocean, outlining the ghostly skeletons of the shipwrecks.

"I'm surprised they're still out there. When did they crash, like the '30s or something?" asked Katie.

Lucas was about to answer, when Ariana said, "'20s, between the World Wars. Seven ships; battleships, destroyers, all went aground in the heavy fog. After they rescued as many sailors as possible, they just left the ships there to rot."

Lucas seemed impressed. Ariana smiled, "I know stuff, too."

John sighed, "Again, focus on the first time you remember seeing your object; how you felt. Now imagine a door is opening behind you. This door leads to who you were before."

"We've been at this forever. I still don't see anything." said Zacke.

John bowed his head. "Listen. I know it's frustrating, but activating your talents is not easy. We may work at this for hours, then two days from now, one of you might activate overnight."

Cody slurped his can of soda, and kept his eyes closed. The warmth flushed through him. His head felt a little lighter, but he saw nothing in his mind. His memories turned to his dad, but he shut that out and took another gulp.

It had been well over an hour, and John sensed they were all holding back. "The hardest thing is to let go, to give over to something that's bigger than yourself. Wipe your mind of all your thoughts. Focus on the object, then the door to the past."

Cody snickered.

Ariana frowned. "Something funny?"

"Sorry," said Cody, giggling, "It just sounds like we're at some cheap hypnotist show or something. Sounds kinda Vegas."

Zacke opened his eyes. "What's the point? I don't see anything. My eyes actually hurt from being shut so long."

"I know it's hard," said John. He hoped the fatigue didn't show in his voice. "But I can't help anyone until your talents get stronger. We are outmatched right now. But together..."

Katie smelled something strange. "Cody! Give me that soda." Katie grabbed the can. "This is beer! Did you dump out a soda and put beer in this? What's wrong with you?"

Cody laughed, "You're so uptight."

Ariana said, "Guys, come on. Let's listen to John."

"We have to do this," said Lucas.

"Not sober," remarked Cody.

John's face registered anger, but quickly changed, like he'd heard a strange sound. He saw Cody had noticed, and quickly stripped his face of any emotion.

Cody looked back with suspicion. *John. You are hiding something, aren't you?* he thought.

Zacke asked, "John, you okay?"

"I'm fine. Let's take a break. I need to excuse myself for a moment." John walked off.

"Our moody Jedi Master," said Cody.

"I'm going for a walk," said Zacke.

"I'll go with you," said Ariana, jumping up.

Lucas watched them walk off. He felt an unexpected pang. He shook it off. *I'm sure it's just a walk.*

Katie said, "You're acting like a dumb jock right now, Cody. Let's not fall into stereotypes." She dug in her bag and brought out a compact.

Cody replied, "Like the girl that puts on make-up at the beach?"

"Shut up. It's a something I do when I'm frustrated. It calms me." Katie angled the compact mirror. It reflected light from the fire into Cody's face.

"Sorry," she said.

Cody lunged for it, but it was too late. The old man's face filled the mirror.

"Oh my god!" Katie exclaimed as she saw the face. She threw the mirror to the sand. The face got closer, like a camera zooming in, until it was just an eye.

Cody, Katie, and Lucas jumped to their feet. The mirror started to bow outward, to take the shape of the eye. The pale blue pupil looked around wildly. Lucas stomped onto the mirror and it cracked in the sand.

"What the hell was that?" asked Katie.

Lucas looked around. "Where's John? We have to tell him."

"He went over there, by the trees. Let's go," said Katie. "Come on!"

Cody stared at the broken compact mirror, blood pouring from it.

* * *

Back in his room, Elder Zamma screamed. Blood poured from his ruined eye as he reached for his cell phone. It dropped on the floor and he yelled again as he bent down to pick it up.

He held a white handkerchief to his eye as he dialed the number, "Yes it's me! I know where they are. The beach. Which beach? There are rusty shipwrecks just out to sea. I don't know. Idiot, Google it! Hurry!"

* * *

At a small group of trees, John let the news sink in, "Poor Pete. Did they get all the books?"

David said, "I don't know. They got some."

John reasoned, "If any books burned, it should take years for that knowledge to make its way back through The River and into our consciousness. Maybe a generation before the knowledge is put down on paper again."

"How far along are they?" asked David, "Anybody activated yet?"

"No. Cody and Zacke are stubborn." John sighed. "May take some time. Zacke is closed, like he doesn't want to be here. Ariana is special somehow, but I can't put my finger on why. Lucas and Katie are partially activated, but their talents and memories come and go."

Thick clouds were gathering overhead, making it darker. The only light came from the small light pole, next to the two portable toilets. David looked uneasily at the sky.

"You seem nervous, David. What are you not telling me?"

David looked around. "It's about..."

Katie and Lucas had made it up over the small dune, almost to John.

Cody followed behind the other two, slowed by the buzz in his head. "See? John's right there. I really have to pee," said Cody as he came around the other two.

"Everyone. Go back to the beach," said John.

Cody said, "Who's this?"

David turned his face away.

"Who is that, John?" asked Cody, his tone getting harder.

David came back into the solitary light on the pole, and faced Cody, "Hello Cody."

Cody looked closer. The last picture of his father was more than a decade old. The long hair confused him at first, then he saw it. "Dad?"

It sounded like a child's voice. Then his voice sharpened. He shouted, "Dad! What the hell are you doing here?"

Higher up the rise, Ehrhardt walked toward them, gun drawn. "What is this, now?"

Lucas froze, unsure what to do. "John?"

Cody faced his father, then turned to John. "You knew! You knew all this time! Is this some sort of trick to get me to help you? It won't work. I hate him!"

Derek, walking just behind Ehrhardt, grasped the situation. He held his amazement at the new revelation, and tried to turn it against them instead, "Ooh. Such Fire. I like that. You should be angry, Cody. I told you this man has been lying to you. He knew your father was alive, was close by, and he kept that from you."

"You're the liar," John drew his sword, "Cody, go get the others. Now!"

Cody yelled back, "I'm not doing anything you say, liar. When were you going to tell me?"

"I didn't know, Cody," John said, "He didn't tell me. David ran away when we picked you up that first day. I didn't know why until this moment."

"Of course he did," Cody spat, "That's what he does. He leaves people, like my mom and me, all alone in a Tarzana dump!"

David looked down, the pain etched onto his face. "I'm sorry Cody. It was wrong..."

"Shut up! I don't want to hear it," said Cody.

Derek said, "That's not the only thing he's lied to you about, Cody."

"Be quiet Sazzo," warned John, "Or I won't make your truth death quite so quick."

"I suspected it, but my elder wasn't sure. Why are you alone, Pentoss or John, or whatever your damn name is this time? Because you're the last one, aren't you?"

Katie asked, "What? What do you mean?"

Lucas shouted, "That's not true!"

"Don't listen to him," said John.

Derek continued stoking the growing dissent. "I told you, he lies. His side has lost, he's all alone. That's why he needs you."

A shot of lightning came from the clouds and incinerated the sand next to Derek. He flew into the air, back into the group of trees.

"Did one of us do that?" asked Katie.

Before anyone could answer, Ehrhardt lunged at David and smashed the butt of his gun onto David's forehead. He went down to the sand, unconscious.

Ehrhardt gripped the handle again and wheeled around for a shot at John. John was too quick for him, his blade jabbed under the trigger guard. John yanked the gun free, cutting Ehrhardt's finger nearly to the bone. A chunk of skin, along with the gun, went flipping behind Lucas to the sand. Ehrhardt yowled in pain.

"Holy crap, you are fast," Derek said, wobbling as he tried to find his feet. "Who did the lightning thing? I did not see that coming. Are you okay, brother?"

"No! Are you?" Ehrhardt said, wrapping his finger in a cloth from his pocket.

John had his sword raised. Lucas was in a fighting posture. He didn't feel his ancient, relying on his Kenpo training instead. John and Lucas made a rough circle around the brothers. Derek whispered his enchantment softly. "Kralj sato galak..."

Lucas took a step toward Derek, "He's saying a spell!"

Derek said, "Hey! Don't interrupt me. Spell? Let's be accurate. What I do is conjuring...."

John cut Derek off, "Run for the beach. We're stronger in numbers."

"Hey! I was talking..." Derek protested.

"I can take him here!" said Lucas, but he still didn't feel his ancient. His confidence wavered.

"John's right. Run for the beach." Katie sprinted downhill toward the sea.

Cody was still furious. He glanced at his father on the sand. He ran for the beach. Now, they were all running to join Ariana and Zacke.

"Wait!" called Derek. "It's no fun unless I set it up first!"

Ehrhardt walked to his brother, still holding his hand. "I have the charm for the Witness. I will chain him in the car. Can you handle this? Do you have a plan?"

"Yes!" said Derek dramatically, "I'm finally going to conjure... the T-Rex."

Ehrhardt shook his head. "This again, brother? I'm sorry, but that's just dumb." He gestured with his arms, mimicking the dinosaur's biggest flaw. "The T-rex has tiny little front arms."

"And huge scary teeth!" insisted Derek.

"You missed your chance, little brother. People aren't scared of dinosaurs anymore. Think of something else. Big enough to take care of them all at once, perhaps?" Ehrhardt put the charm around David's neck. He hefted the unconscious man over his shoulder. "Go take care of them. I'll meet you at the car."

Derek sighed as Ehrhardt walked off with David. Derek walked down to the beach, muttering to himself, "I think dinosaurs are scary." He looked to the ocean, over the multiple rusting hulks that used to be ships. They gave him an idea. "Hmmm. Through adversity, comes innovation. Something cooler than a dinosaur. Let me think, this one could be interesting."

As Derek walked, he stared out into the water and thought of the proper conjuring spell. The most powerful words. Derek spoke fourteen languages. Words of power were different in each language. He had to get this just right. He whispered it slowly to himself, over and over; "Urod calamar teuthida, Urod calamar teuthida, Urod calamar teuthida."

The beach was dark, but he knew the rest of them were there. Derek announced, "Hello all! You know that thing that bad guys do in movies? Where they talk, and talk about their plans, or grandstand and you're not quite sure where it's going? I always thought that would be a great trick to use. Well, at least, to stall for time."

They all looked around, but nothing happened. They glanced at the ocean, the moon peeked from behind the clouds, now lighting a small swath of the beach.

Nothing. Silence.

Derek continued, "I'd been saving a very special conjuring for just such a night. Just curious, when you think scary, do you think of Dinosau... oh, never mind. This will be better."

Zacke and Ariana were close to the water, the others halfway between Derek and the lapping waves. The dying fire backlit Derek. As they scanned behind Derek, something caught Zacke by the leg and pulled. Zacke fell flat, and was yanked into the water. Ariana grabbed for him, but he was underwater in seconds. She screamed, "Zacke!"

The clouds parted briefly, so she used the glimpse of moonlight and scanned wildly for him. Then a giant tentacle lifted from the water. They all spotted Zacke struggling to get free. The tentacle suckers moved and writhed around his tall frame.

John and Lucas rushed toward the water.

"Is that a giant octopus?" Katie yelled.

"Giant squid," said John. "Katie? Can you put a shield around Zacke?"

Katie just stared. "I don't think so. He's... he's too far away. It's moving too fast."

John looked at his sword, furiously trying to form a plan. Before he could think of whose talent could best help Zacke, the other tentacle wrapped around John's chest, and squeezed. John felt white hot pain as his recent wound flared up. He dropped his sword and was lifted off the sand. Pulled to sea, they all watched the giant shape take John. The squid's elongated head rose over the outline of the rusty wrecks.

Lucas had no idea how to help. His eyes darted back to Zacke, still airborne in another tentacle. Lucas felt ocean spray hit his face as one of the eight arms reached out of the water. He ducked just in time, landing next to John's sword. Lucas fumbled for it as the creature changed its mind, and went for Katie.

Everyone on the small beach watched as the giant squid rose higher. It kept rising until its elongated head rose a dozen feet above the water, its eyes the size of dinner plates, illuminated in the small sliver of moonlight.

The beast was massive. The old wrecks looked like toy boats compared to the monster. Lucas remembered a nature program, the massive beak made for chopping its prey, the tongue-like radula lined with teeth, even more razor-sharp teeth that lined its cheeks. If Zacke of John came close to its mouth, they were dinner.

The two tentacles whipped around, smashing the rusting hulls just off shore. The creature used the multiple legs to push closer to the beach. The ancient wrecks gave way before it, with a shrieking of rusty metal.

Katie tripped as a leg reached for her, and was sprayed with a hot blue liquid as Lucas cut into the appendage. Katie screamed, as the wounded arm receded into the ocean. Zacke landed hard just feet from them. Ariana rushed to help Katie up.

"What happened?" Lucas got Zacke to his feet.

"I don't know. It let me go. Where's John?" asked Zacke.

Ariana pointed out to the water. The tentacle that held John was getting closer to the huge head. The main body was rising higher out of the water. Lucas wondered how enormous the squid's teeth must be, since that's where John was now headed. They had to act quick.

Zacke looked around frantically. The girls were near each other on one side of him, on the other, Cody stood like a statue. He looked back and forth from Derek to the squid, like a man in a trance.

"Cody! Help us!" shouted Zacke, and Cody seemed to just notice them, like he was coming out of a dream.

Cody's head was buzzing from the beer he'd been sneaking, vaguely hoping this *was* all a dream. His father. The monster in the ocean. "What... what can I do?" he said in a whisper. He looked back for his father, but he and the German were gone.

Zacke saw the look in Cody's eyes, and how he was standing, "You're drunk!" Zacke looked away in disgust. He focused on John.

Lucas said, "Katie, can you push a shield at it?"

"It's too far," she yelled, as they saw John struggling with the tentacle, almost to the creature's mouth.

Zacke said, "Ariana, freeze it."

Ariana shook her head. "It's too big."

Zacke looked into her eyes. "You can do it."

She wasn't convinced, but Ariana faced the beast and concentrated, holding out her hands.

Lucas still held John's sword, absently. "What now?"

"I have an idea. Be ready," said Zacke.

The beast was getting closer, the legs spraying ocean mist at them. It startled Ariana, but she tried harder. Then, it froze. Like pausing a movie, the creature froze. John, silhouetted by moonlight, was also frozen in the air. Even the water droplets around the massive beast were suspended.

Zacke closed his eyes, sighed, then opened them again. *I have to do this*, he thought. He grabbed Lucas.

Lucas felt himself lifting off his feet. "What the..."

Zacke lifted Lucas like he was an infant. He said, "Brace yourself, and hold on to that sword!"

Zacke flung Lucas as hard as he could. Lucas was airborne, John's sword straight in front of him. It felt like flying, but Lucas couldn't enjoy the moment. He concentrated on helping John. Lucas aimed the sword straight and held tight.

Cody stared. Up the beach, Derek's mouth dropped open.

As Lucas flew straight for the creature's huge elongated head, Katie stared at Zacke.

Zacke wouldn't make eye contact, "What? I said I could lift heavy stuff, sometimes."

Lucas held the sword as straight as he could in front of him. John was still suspended in mid-air, and the creature was just coming out of Ariana's freeze when Lucas cut deep into the squid. Unfrozen now, it began to flail and John fell to the water, the tentacle vanishing.

The rest of the beast winked out of existence. A dozen feet in the air, Lucas plunged into the water. He barely held onto the sword, and gasped for breath as he searched for John. He remembered the undertow that could sweep them out to the deep waters.

His adrenaline was still going, as he spotted John a few feet away. John was headed straight for him. They swam for each other, narrowly avoiding rusted bits of old battleship just under the water. He kept a tight grip on the sword as he swam for John.

"I'm here," said John as they found each other. They held onto each other tight. John took the sword, and sheathed it. They headed for the shore.

On the beach, Derek felt his legs give way, and nearly fell over. "I think that's enough for one night." he said to himself.

Cody shook off the beer buzz. The crazy night was filled with monsters and all he could think about was his dad. A flush of anger accompanied the thought, but another feeling surfaced.

He looked back to Zacke, Ariana, Katie and the moonlit sea beyond, noticing how apart from them he felt. They were looking out to sea, trying to gauge how close Lucas and John were to the shore. He glanced back to the receding Derek, then ran after him.

Derek looked weak. He did not seem surprised that Cody was next to him.

Cody asked, "Can you teach me how to do that?" Indicating the beach, and the place the monster had been.

Derek raised his eyebrows. "I can try."

"What will you do to him?"

"Your father?"

"Yes."

Derek shook his head. "You don't want to know."

"You don't understand." said Cody, "I want to help."

Derek stopped. He looked back to the ocean. No one on the beach seemed to notice Cody was gone. Derek silently offered his hand.

Cody took it, and helped Derek to the waiting car. He got in the back seat with his father, still passed out. David was chained, and had a strange necklace around his neck. The Rageto apparently had their newest recruit.

Back at the water line, as the waves broke on the dark shore, Lucas and John helped each other onto the sand. The others went to help them. The two heaved and strained, finally laid out on the cold sand. The others collapsed on the sand around them, their adrenaline fading.

"Are you guys alright?" asked Katie.

"Yeah, I'm okay," said Lucas.

"I'll be fine," managed John.

John stood, one hand holding his wound. He'd lost the bandage and there was fresh blood.

They all stood, and realized the brothers were gone. So was Cody. Even in the moonlight, they could see John's exhaustion. "You worked together. Thank you all for saving me."

Lucas said to Zacke, "Nice throw. Anything else you're holding back?"

Zacke avoided the question. "Thanks," he smiled sheepishly, "It only works sometimes, when I'm stressed, mostly. You can guess why I don't play sports anymore."

Ariana looked out to sea, "Is it going to get scarier than that? I don't think I can take much more."

"She's right," said Katie, "John, we're not ready for this."

John wiped excess sea water from his smooth head. "You have to be ready. Derek is a liar, but he is correct about one thing. I haven't told you everything. It has to be us, because we're the only ones left to stop them."

CHAPTER TWENTY TWO
TRUE COST

As they left the beach in the rented SUV, John insisted he was alright. Everyone could see the blood and knew he'd torn his stitches. They were all silent for a long time.

John finally spoke, "I'm sorry I didn't tell you everything."

Lucas said, "You couldn't tell us we may be the last six? Oh yeah, maybe just five; since Cody went to the dark side. We're the only ones in the world that can stop those guys?"

"Yes," said John. "I've been searching. There may be a few more Amartus out there. But, I haven't found them yet. It's just us."

Ariana felt the weight of their situation. "We have to hope our talents, powers or whatever, fully activate soon; before they come for us again."

John answered, "Yes. And they will come for us. They have David again. His best talent is finding us. I don't know why Cody went with them."

Katie asked, "Did I hear that right, that David is Cody's dad?"

"It was news to me too," said John. "I had no idea."

Zacke sounded exhausted. "Now they've got Cody and his dad. How will we fight them?"

Lucas added, "Why is this all up to just us? What about those Sect guys? Pete was on our side."

John said, "Pete was unusual. The Sect are fiercely neutral. They see their roles as chroniclers, sometimes as referees. Never will they fight on either side. The attack at the station might draw them in somewhat, but we can't count on that."

"So we are totally alone," confirmed Ariana, looking out the dark window.

John said, "You are the best hope because what is happening here is new. Our numbers have been dwindling for decades. They are winning. But two new births are never born in the same place; it just doesn't happen. And five warriors total, a mix of ancients and new? I think it's a first in human history. The River is giving us a sign."

"I'd take an instruction booklet over a sign any day, thanks," said Zacke. "You said we get stronger when we're together. But what if you're wrong?"

"That super-strength was awesome, Zacke," said Lucas.

John asked Zacke, "Are you sure there weren't other strange things? No other talents in your past?"

Zacke snapped, "We have more important things to talk about!"

"All your talents should have shown themselves in some way. David said he was a late bloomer. David and Cody being related is also rare. The brothers are famous ancients, since close relatives being warriors is uncommon. These all must be signs. But what do I do with them?" John looked in the rear-view mirror at Zacke. "Don't worry. I'm sure about you, Zacke. You're very important to what's happening. I feel it. Your other talent will show itself."

Zacke returned the stare. "John. I can't. I'm sorry guys, I'm done."

"Me too," said Ariana. "I can't do this anymore."

John was quiet for a few minutes. When he spoke, there was a flatness to his voice "I'm not Rageto. I won't force you into a destiny you don't want. You must choose to embrace your warrior. But they will come for all of you again. Whether you embrace it, or not."

"Then what choice do we have?" asked Katie.

John said, "They won't come to your homes."

"What? We just stay in our houses forever?" asked Ariana.

"They came to my work," said Zacke. "What if they come for our families? It's a small town, you know. What if they attack our parents at the grocery store? They don't seem to have any boundaries, John."

"I don't know," said John, holding his side.

Katie yelled, "What do you mean you don't know? We're in high school, John. You throw this crap at us, people try to kill us and you don't know what to do?"

John stopped the car, and pulled to the side of the road. "You're right. This isn't fair. You were born into a struggle that goes back eons. The River controls much of our lives. It has chosen you. This is not a movie. This is real. Strange and unbelievable, with dangerous things happening. But real. You are the last chance to defeat people who have tried to kill you. We can win. That I know. Your strength grows when you're together."

"But we're not together," said Katie, "Cody chose to go with them, being stupid like I was. What does that mean? What do we do about that?"

John got back on the road, "We rescue them. David and Cody both. Then we set the terms for a final battle."

"Cody doesn't want to be rescued. And we have no idea where they are. He said he, like, blows up cell phones, so we can't call him."

"After a few hours Cody will want to be rescued. The brothers have a hard time hiding their true nature. Cody will sense it quickly. And then, we take them."

They all looked at each other, wondering if John was going crazy, or if this was just a new kind of normal.

* * *

Pulling into the city, Cody was still asking questions. Ehrhardt was driving, and Derek was sitting in the passenger seat, nodding off. The conjuring had taken its toll. David had woken up with a headache and once again found himself in chains, the charm around his neck.

David cried out when he'd first seen his son in the car. Cody wouldn't speak to him. David openly sobbed.

"Stop your sniveling, Witness," said Ehrhardt. He nudged his brother, "Wake up Sazzo. We're almost there."

"He's really out of it. Has Derek ever done that before?" asked Cody, trying to ignore his father's sobs.

"Never a squid. I watched from the car." Ehrhardt explained. "The larger and more fantastical, the harder it is on him. I've seen him conjure a pack of wolves, Elephants, an alligator, a swarm of locusts."

"The locusts were fun," said Derek sleepily.

Cody asked, "Those were all real, right?"

"Oh, yes. Quite real," confirmed Ehrhardt.

David pleaded, "It's not too late to change your mind, Cody. Be angry with me, hate me, but don't join them. You don't know..."

Derek slammed David's head into the back of Erhardt's seat.

Cody was startled by the sudden violence, but didn't say anything.

Ehrhardt said, "You speak again, Witness, and we gag you. Don't talk to the boy."

"He's my son."

Derek slammed his head again. "You are not in the position to bargain or demand, Witness."

"Why... why do you call him 'Witness'?" Cody tried not to look at his father.

Ehrhardt replied, "Oh, just a pet name. He has Witnessed many things. Maybe we should make you our biographer, Witness."

Derek added, "Name's more exciting than David, anyway."

They arrived at the house and Ehrhardt asked, "Can you make it to the door, brother?"

"Yes. But once inside I'm going to sleep for a while."

"A good while, brother. Giant squid? Very impressive," Ehrhardt said, actually smiling a little. The smile sent a chill through Cody.

"Ah, shucks. Thanks bro." replied Derek.

They marshaled David into the house, turning on the lights as Derek said, "Sorry kid. We'll talk more when I wake up. You'll have to chat with Ehrhardt here. Pardon the sparse living conditions. It's a furnished rental house until we finish our business here. Hotels ask too many questions when you have a prisoner."

"Go rest, brother," said Ehrhardt.

"After I secure the Witness in his room," Derek said, as he lead David down a hallway.

David looked back to his son, but Cody looked away.

When Derek and David were out of earshot, Cody asked Ehrhardt, "What will you do to him?"

"Use him to find the others again," Ehrhardt answered. "He's very useful that way. We have an elder we must consult. He will let us know what to do with the Witness after. Elder Zamma doesn't like disobedience."

They heard one door close, and then a second; Derek must have gone to bed. Cody noticed a few old books laid out on a side table. He made a mental note to ask about them later.

"How long will he sleep?" asked Cody.

"Hard to say," Ehrhardt replied. "Would you like a beer?"

Cody wasn't sure if this was a test, "Umm. Sure?"

"I know your age." Ehrhardt went to the kitchen. "The best thing about being one of us, is that we don't play by the same rules. Also, America is backwards. You can join the army at 18, but not drink until 21? Ridiculous. In Germany, we drink at 16. You will like German beer."

He pulled a Weihenstephan from the fridge and grabbed one for himself from the counter. Cody smiled. It was the first time he didn't have to sneak a beer.

"You Americans drink beer too cold," said Ehrhardt. "This is not my favorite, but the best I could find for sale locally."

"I guess I kind of get how this works," said Cody, "but it's still weird. So, you're German and Derek is so, like, California dude. But your ancient warriors are brothers."

"It's true. That's always the strangest part. The finding each other again across the world. Of course, when we grew up, this time, me in Saxony and he in San Francisco, we were just living out regular teenage lives. I was planning to be a lawyer. Derek was... well, Derek didn't have much of a purpose. Just liked to chase girls and play video games."

Cody asked, "How did you find each other?"

"We Rageto are more organized, that's why we are winning the great struggle," explained Ehrhardt. "We have elders that help find us. We are unlike the Amartus, the foolish children stumbling in the dark. We use magic to strengthen our powers. They rely on their feelings and their vague notions of each other. Eventually they run into each other. But by then, we are there to convince them to play for our team."

"But to have a brother from another country. It's just strange."

"True." said Ehrhardt, taking a long gulp. "We never know where the River will deposit us. Or, in what bodies."

Cody examined the walls. They weren't covered in pictures, but magazine and newspaper articles. Some were framed, others were tacked up with push pins. Cody got up with his beer and looked at them.

"That's Derek's idea. He's very sentimental. Takes them on all our trips."

Cody saw the pattern "These are all stories of disasters, death."

"Yes. The best skill we have, is that none of the inferiors know we exist. We are the masters of our own fate. We won't let anyone control us. We are the ones that control. We live privately exciting, but publicly quiet lives. We also get to witness history as it unfolds. We even unfold some ourselves."

Cody looked around at all the cuttings. Indian Ocean tsunami 2004, Haiti earthquake 2010. Airline disasters. Several framed items with individual police stories. "So, your brother likes disasters? Whoa, is that the..."

"Hindenburg? Yes." Ehrhardt shook his head. "No one likes disasters, or loss of life. It's not good for us, but sometimes action must be taken."

"What do... Wait. You mean, you guys did all this?"

"Yes, Cody," said Ehrhardt, joining him by the wall of memories. "Sometimes, we had no choice. You see, when there is a new ancient detected, re-birthed from the River, we are there. But as you've seen, it's hard to control their new powers. That makes these re-births very dangerous. Sometimes we must destroy them. Sometimes inferiors must die as well."

Cody looked at the front page from 2004. The headline cried, "Over 200,000 Dead." He looked back to Ehrhardt, who finished his beer, got another and sat on the couch.

Ehrhardt stared at the same headline, "Yes. Terrible mistakes are sometimes made. Inferior life lost. But we pay for that, I assure you."

"You said that before. What do you mean?"

"I don't believe in God. Any creature that would make a world like this, is a deity I will not worship. But be it fate, or cosmic forces, the River; whatever you call it, it has a terrible sense of justice. We are punished for taking inferior life the next time we are re-birthed."

"How exactly?"

"Sometimes it's a terrible deformity. Imagine having amazing powers, but born blind. Or missing both legs. Then sometimes... sometimes you are born into cruelty. We both have a lot to be angry about, concerning fathers."

Cody asked, "Yours left, too?"

"Oh no. My father was a builder. Houses and office buildings. A good German businessman. Everybody liked him. No one knew that he beat us. No one found my mother's body when she went missing. But I knew. I knew because he killed her in front of me." Ehrhardt gulped his beer. "Turns out there are worse things a father can do to his only son."

There was a long silence.

"I'm... I'm sorry," Cody offered.

Ehrhardt was still lost in memory, "The last life, the one where I earned that monster of a father, I had only killed a few thousand inferiors. But this life I've killed a quarter million more. What horrors await me next time?" He was no longer speaking to Cody, lost in his own dark thoughts.

Cody had only taken a few sips of beer, which now felt sour in his stomach. "Well, I'd better be getting home. I'm surprised my mom hasn't called already. Can I use the bathroom first?"

"Sure." Ehrhardt's phone went off. Before he answered it, he pointed Cody to the bathroom. "through there."

Cody took a deep breath when he locked the door and spotted the mirror. It was a cheap looking model from a department store. It was leaned against the wall where a built-in mirror had been. Cody quickly put the small mirror face down on the counter.

All that was left of the larger mirror were a few shards in the corners. He wondered what could have broken such a large built in, but was relieved he wouldn't see the old man again. He finished going to the bathroom, washed his hands and opened the door.

Ehrhardt was standing there. He slipped his phone into his shirt pocket, "Elder Zamma wants to meet you."

Cody asked, "Now? I really have to get home."

"It's alright, Cody. He's already here." Ehrhardt made Cody go back into the bathroom. He tipped the small mirror back up.

Cody's heart raced. It was the same old man he'd seen in other mirrors. This time he had a bandage over one eye. The old man was smiling. Another cold chill shot through Cody. *These guys shouldn't smile*, he thought. The elder's voice was old, but clear. Like he was in the same room.

"Hello, Cody. It's nice to finally meet you."

CHAPTER TWENTY THREE

PARENTS

As usual, Zacke didn't know what to expect when he got home. He hadn't bothered to call, knowing his dad would be out of it by now. When he opened the door, he saw the glow of the kitchen light and soft 1950's jazz music playing. He went into the kitchen to find his father finishing the dishes. "Hey Zacke."

Zacke looked around for beer cans, "Hey Dad. You... you feeling okay?"

He chuckled softly. "You mean because I'm not drunk?"

"Sorry," Zacke said, "I'm not trying to start anything."

"I know son. It's okay. I know how I've been. And I know it's not enough, but I'm sorry. I've been selfish."

Zacke shifted his weight from one foot to another. "It's okay, Dad." But it wasn't okay. Month after month of the same old dad behavior, and now 'just like that' he was going to change overnight? Zacke felt anger flare, but battled a quick internal battle; he did want his dad to change. If this was the start... "So, what's different today? Why now?"

"Because it's time. I've been wallowing in your mom leaving for too long. I'll try to do better. This thing just hit me harder than I thought. After all this time, you'd think...." his dad trailed off. "...Well, no excuses."

"I'm really..." Zacke avoided his father's eyes, "I'm really sorry, Dad,"

"No! Not this again," his dad said louder than he intended. He quickly softened his tone. "Don't blame yourself, Zacke. It's not your fault. Your mother... well, she's sick. It's not okay what she did, what she called you. Don't blame yourself for that."

Zacke didn't know what to tell his father. Not telling his dad everything felt like a lie, which made him feel even worse. Zacke answered, "Dad, don't blame yourself either."

"I'm trying to stop feeling sorry for myself. Booze just masks the problem. I know that." His dad took a deep breath. "So, no beer tonight. I can't promise I won't screw up again. But, hey..." he stepped aside. "...I did the dishes."

Zacke smiled. His dad changed subjects. "You see your brother? It just goes to voicemail when I call his cell."

Zacke shrugged, "He's stays up north a lot. With friends, I guess."

"He thinks I'm weak, I know," said his father.

"He'll get over it." said Zacke, "I don't know, we don't talk much since I gave up basketball."

"You should get back to that. You were good. It's all you used to talk about. Especially when you started beating your older brother on the court."

Zacke smiled, thinking of flinging Lucas at Derek's conjured monster, "Yeah. I guess I'm just over it. Trying to concentrate on school and the Explorers."

"School's important," said his dad.

"You still okay with the cop thing?"

"Sure. You know I don't feel cops are bad. I know what your brother thinks, but he's young. I've known very good officers, of all races. I'm a white man who married a black woman. Your mother and me, we believe it's what's inside that counts."

What exactly is inside me? thought Zacke.

"I'll always be standing right behind you."

"Thanks Dad."

"With a beer in my hand."

"Ouch. Too soon, Dad."

"Yeah," said his dad, "first night not drinking in a while, I guess I need more appropriate jokes."

"Now it's awkward." Zacke smiled. "I'm gonna take a shower. I'm glad you're back, Pops."

"Me too. Come on, give me a hug like we're a normal family."

"Just don't say like the Cosby's."

"Can't go there anymore. We'll be a different sit-com," said his dad.

Zacke didn't tell his dad it felt like he was in a horror movie. Or at least some dark fantasy story, compete with weird agendas, crazy bad guys and secrets. Lots of secrets.

They hugged.

"Why are you damp?" asked his dad. "Go swimming in the ocean with your clothes on?"

Zacke thought of the slimy tentacle. "Yeah, didn't mean too, though."

"Don't do stupid stuff for girls," his dad warned.

If you only knew, thought Zacke. "Okay Pops, shower time."

"Yeah, and I should probably go to bed. First of many nights getting some sober sleep. Kinda looking forward to that. Zacke, seriously. You okay?"

Zacke smiled. "I'm okay, Pops. Just tired."

"Not getting into trouble, right? Your brother has got that one down already."

"Nothing serious. There were girls at the beach, but it's not like that. A lot of weirdness around it."

"There always is," said his dad. "Woman are beautifully, dangerous creatures. Man is not meant to know their nature."

"Night Pops."

"Night son."

Zacke enjoyed his shower, but it didn't wash away the craziness of the night. He went to bed and woke up an hour later in a cold sweat. He dreamed it again, not giant calamari or spiders. He dreamed of the night his mother first found him. The night everything changed. He thought about what his father said, 'what's inside that counts.' Zacke wasn't sure what that even meant anymore.

* * *

Ariana came home knowing she was in trouble. Her father stopped talking when she came into the kitchen, which meant that the talking was about her.

Her mother Josie asked, "Where have you been?"

"Sorry Mami, Papa. My phone died."

"Everyone has a cell phone. You couldn't borrow the skinny *wedo's* phone?" said her father, arms crossed. "Is that who you were with?"

"I was just out with friends," Ariana said.

"You know the rules, mija. It's past 11," her mother scolded, but Josie rolled her eyes toward her husband. Ariana got the signal that she wasn't in real trouble.

Her father asked, "Are you serious with this boy?"

"What?" Ariana said, "No. No, we just met."

"Exactly," said her father. "Boys we don't know, doing lord knows what."

Ariana said, "I'm not having sex, Papi. Is that what you're worried about?"

Her father said, "I worry about everything. Now I worry about skinny white boys."

"You want me to kill him, Papi?" said her older brother, popping his head in the kitchen.

"If he touches her, I'll do it," confirmed her father.

"Shut up, stupid hermano," said Ariana, then turned back to her parents. "Papi, Mami, we're just friends."

" 'Friends' means different things to boys and girls," her father insisted.

Ariana knew she shouldn't be, but she was getting angry. "You're just worried that I'm going to do what you did!"

"Be careful," said her mother. "Little girl, be careful. I was sixteen when I got pregnant, but we were married."

Ariana tried to regain calm. She couldn't tell them she was scared. But she knew if her mom was getting mad, she'd gone too far. "I'm sorry. Really. He's just a friend."

Her brother lost interest and left to watch TV. Her parents relented. Ariana ate in the kitchen, then helped her mom with the dishes. Her father went to bed. Josie usually didn't stay up this late, but Ariana was glad, because what she most wanted to do was talk. She wondered if her mother could sense it.

"What is wrong, mija?"

Ariana dried the plate. "Nothing. Everything. I've just been thinking about how fast things change."

"At your age they change fast, at my age they change in a blur. Like that." she snapped her fingers.

"Do you think that we always stay the same?" asked Ariana. "I mean, what if I feel like someone else is in my head, trying to tell me what I should do."

Her mother smiled. "We all do that, mija. Sometimes the voices will be me, or your father. Even your grandmother. Sometimes it will be the deeper part of you, guiding you."

Ariana considered that. "A deeper part. Yes. That's what I mean. But what if this deeper part felt like a different person?"

"Oh, mija," her mother laughed. "Of course it does. It could be that your soul is guiding you, telling you what is right. I believe God is guiding all of us. Or it may be the past lives you've lived."

Ariana wasn't sure she'd heard correctly. "Wait. You believe in past lives?"

"We're Catholic, we believe in the Resurrection." Josie leaned in, "But don't tell the Pope that I also believe in reincarnation. This can't be the only life we've lived. We are born knowing so much. God's little joke is that we are trapped in a baby's body, and must learn all over again. We forget who we were before. But the core of who we are never changes."

Ariana smiled, knowing how right her mother was. "I didn't know you felt like that."

"You never asked." her mother shrugged, rinsing the last of the dishes. "Plus, you will be a woman much sooner than I would like. It is time to talk of these things. How do you feel about it, mija?"

"I'm confused." Ariana wanted to tell as much truth as she could, "I feel an... an energy filling me that I've never felt before. I feel pulled to things that I never even imagined."

"Good things, I hope," her mother handed Ariana the last plate.

"I think so. But lately, I feel like there is someone else in my head, fighting to make decisions."

"But it's all you, mija," said her mother. "Don't forget that. Even if it sounds like two voices in your head, and that happens to me all the time, remember it's your core. And your core is all goodness."

Ariana smiled, "Thanks Mami. I like your core too."

* * *

Katie knocked on the door. "Mom? Jason? Can I talk to you for a minute?"

They were already in bed, Jason reading on his Kindle and Mom watching TV.

"Of course," said Jason. "Come on in." Mom turned off the TV.

"How's Megan?"

"She's fine, she's in her room," said her mother. "Megan's supposed to be asleep by now, but I doubt she is. She'd love it if you'd talk to her."

"My next stop," said Katie. "I just wanted to say sorry."

They both looked at her in stunned silence.

"Hey, it's not like I *never* say sorry."

Mom still couldn't speak. Jason said, "No. No, of course not. It just hasn't been your favorite word for a while."

Katie said, "I've been going through some weird stuff lately. But it's not fair that I take it out on you. I can just be a bit... well, I'm not very nice sometimes."

Jason asked, "This weird stuff, is it girl stuff? You want to me leave the room?"

"No, nothing like that. Can't explain it all. But, I wanted to apologize to both of you. Especially you, Jason. I don't hate you. You're, you know, all right."

Jason nodded. "I'll take that."

"You're actually kind of cool sometimes," Katie elaborated. "I just feel like... like two different people sometimes. It's hard to explain."

They both smiled. Her mother said, "It was back in the time when giant monsters roamed the earth, but we were teenagers too. We get it."

Katie thought of the beach and shuddered at the word monster. "I just wanted to say that, whoever I happen to be, I intend to be nicer."

"Thanks, Kaitlyn," said Jason.

Mom added, "That means a lot. That earthquake must have really scared you."

"A lot of things have been scaring me lately," admitted Katie. "It will get better, right? I'll stop making dumb decisions?"

"Lots of good stuff is coming. Fifteen and sixteen, they can be fun, and tough. There are some more bumps coming." her mom promised.

"Greeeeeat. Well, I better go see Megan. Oh, and you can call me Katie again."

More stunned silence.

"Some new friends have been calling me Katie lately. I don't mind so much."

Jason and her mom looked at each other and nodded awkwardly. They all said goodnight.

Down the hall, she knocked on Megan's door. It was dark under the sweep of the door but Katie knew that Megan read every night, much later than she was supposed to. She knocked on the door, but there was no answer. "Megan, it's just me."

"Come in," Megan's voice whispered back.

Katie entered and saw the towel by the door. "The old towel to block the light trick. Classic."

"Hey," said Megan, looking like herself again, except for the small butterfly bandage on her forehead.

"Hey yourself," said Katie, coming close to the bed. "I just wanted to check on you, kid."

"I'm alright." she was re-reading her favorite book, *A Wrinkle in Time*. If she was reading a comfort book, she probably wasn't 100% alright.

Katie sat on the edge of the bed. "It's not like me to say sorry. That was just pointed out to me. But I am. I'm sorry I left you that night to go talk with friends. Seeing you in that hospital. Well, you scared me, kid."

"I'm not a kid," Megan warned. "But, you shouldn't have left me."

"I know. I'm sorry."

"You seem different," said Megan. "What's wrong with you?"

Katie laughed, "It's been a weird couple of days. I don't feel myself. I'm not even sure what 'myself' means anymore."

Megan smiled. "I feel like that sometimes."

"You do?"

"Yes!" Megan became animated. "I'll be in middle school next year. I'm like actually popular right now. What happens to all that?"

Katie completely understood; the fun of fifth grade, and the terror of sixth grade memories rushed back to her. "Kid. Sorry to say, it all starts over. Total popularity reset. Middle school is hard, and other kids are total jerks."

"You're in high school," Megan smiled. "and you're still a jerk sometimes."

"Good one!" laughed Katie. "Sometimes? How about a lot lately?"

Megan rolled her eyes. "I was trying to be nice."

Katie pointed to Megan's head, "Does it still hurt?"

"Not really," Megan touched her small bandage. "But Mom and Dad say I can stay out the rest of next week. I don't want to miss too much school, but it's kind of nice."

"I was surprised they kept the high school closed all week. But I'm kinda glad too."

Megan put her book on the night stand, but she already knew the answer would be no, like always. She asked anyway, "Want to watch a movie?"

Katie was exhausted, but she said, "Yes. I would love that. Your pick."

Megan tried to hide her excitement, but Katie felt it as her little sister rushed to the bookshelf across the room.

They watched *Hocus Pocus* until they both fell asleep on Megan's bed. After midnight, their mother came in and turned off the TV, pulling up the blankets to make sure they would be warm for the night.

* * *

Lucas came in through his side door. It was a few minutes before there was a knock at the door connecting the house and converted garage.

"Hey Lucas," said his mom, his dad standing behind her. "Can we come in?"

"Yeah, sure." Lucas said, "What's up?"

"Nothing's wrong, honey," his mom said. "Unless there is."

His dad said, "We've noticed you keeping late nights."

"Mom. Dad. I'm fine, really."

"We made the agreement when you moved out here that we would give you space. You had a tough year. But you being so close to the earthquake and the stadium, we worry. You're the only kid, you know. We have to smother you whenever possible." His mom noticed his clothes, "Why are you wet?"

Lucas thought quickly, hating how much he had to lie to his parents, "I went to the beach." *How should I put this?* "I went swimming with friends. Forgot my swim suit."

The parents exchanged a glance. His dad asked, "Did they throw you in?"

"I didn't get beat up on the beach or anything. My new friends are cool. Intense, maybe, but cool."

"You've grown so much this year," said his mom, brushing a stray hair on his forehead, like she did when he was young.

"And look at those muscles. Just like his dad." Dad flexed his muscles, looking more like a washed up old wrestler, nearly eighty pounds overweight.

They all laughed, but both parents seemed uneasy and looked around at the equipment. The bed was only a small part of the converted garage, which resembled a private gym more than it did a teenager's bedroom.

"I know what you're thinking." *Sometimes, I actually do.* "you're worried that after last year, the next step is weird friends and drugs."

Dad said, "The thought had occurred to us."

"I've met some new friends," said Lucas, "and they are definitely weird. But it's nothing like that. No drugs. I'd never do that."

"Honestly, we're more worried about all this," said his mom.

Dad added, "We helped set this up, let you sign up for martial arts to help your self-esteem. But..."

"You think I'm going overboard?" Lucas asked.

"Maybe a smidge." Dad arched his eyebrows comically, always the one to lighten the mood.

His mom said, "Your sessions with the doctor are nearly done. We just worry; it's kind of our job. We also don't want you to get into any trouble you can't get out of with that bully. We know he moved back."

Lucas always wondered why they never used his name. "Billy doesn't worry me." *Unless I lose control and kill him.* "Last year I was really messed up. I thought it was about Billy. But I think I just needed to find the real me. I'm close. It's hard to describe. Anyway, I have no plans to fight Billy."

"Good," said his dad, "You come from a long line of lovers, not fighters."

"I'll say," said his mother provocatively.

"Mom, gross."

"We just don't want this to be about revenge. And we don't want you to try and hurt yourself again." Mom had finally gotten to the point.

Lucas considered what his mom said, because in the beginning, it was about revenge. All he could think when he punched the bag, was Billy's face, turning his stupid verbal attacks into pain. Humiliation. But that was when he thought he was hearing voices, convinced he was crazy. Now, he knew there was a real warrior inside him.

Lucas shook his head. "It's not about revenge. And I'll never do that thing again. I know how it hurt you guys. I was just confused. I'm clear now."

His mother smiled, and Lucas thought he saw the beginning of a tear, but Dad changed the mood.

Dad said, "Here I come..."

Lucas rolled his eyes.

"I'm gonna do it, can't stop me." said his dad as he bear hugged Lucas. He whispered in his son's ear, "Do these new friends include girls?"

Lucas freed himself of the hug. "Yeah. A few. Well, we'll see. It's early days with that." He thought of Ariana walking on the beach with Zacke. He shook off the disappointment. "Girls are one thing I can't train for."

"That's for sure," said his dad.

His mother eyed his father, "Watch it, honey. Or you get none tonight."

"Mom! Uber gross. Okay, both of you get out of my room. I don't need porn talk from the parents."

"It's natural, Lucas," his mom began the familiar talk. "When a man and woman love each other very much..."

"Mom! I wish I had siblings so you could gross them out."

Dad said, "Nope, all for you. Give us a little time. Another year and nothing will shock you."

Lucas couldn't stop smiling. "Love you guys."

"Love you too," said his mom as she hugged him.

His father shook his head, "Ehh. You're ok. Let's say a strong *like* and leave it at that. Better get out of those damp clothes, buddy."

He thought of the huge, slimy monster in the ocean, "Yeah, I think you're right."

Lucas shook his head at his silly parents. His silly, funny, awesome parents. He wondered how long until he remembered his parents from other lives. That was a strange thought, and his mind opened up with a new line of questions. How many parents had his true self had? Dozens? Hundreds?

He went to his parents and hugged them again. They hugged back in surprise.

"Haven't gotten an unsolicited hug like that for a while," said his mom.

Lucas replied, "Well, you deserve it. You're the best parents I've ever had."

They all smiled as his parents left his room.

He decided to train for one hour before bed. This time he thought of Cody's face when he hit the bag.

Traitor.

* * *

Cody let himself in the back door of their small house, head swimming with all that had happened. The lights were off except for the single lamp in the front room; which meant Mom wasn't home from work. No need to explain where he'd been. How could he explain? *Oh, nowhere really; just saw a giant squid attack my new ex-friends and oh yeah, saw Dad who we thought was probably dead.*

He unloaded his pockets. His wallet was not there. *Did I leave it at the brother's place?* Cody didn't remember taking it out of his pocket all night. He thought of everything the old man had said, the promises he'd made if he joined them. *Can I do this?* He was still figuring out the next step when he heard his mom's car in the driveway.

Cody scrambled to make sure there were no signs of the weird night he'd had. He popped a stick of gum in his mouth to hide the scent of beer.

A few minutes later, he heard, "Hi baby. You still up?"

It was after midnight. He replied, "Yeah, no school all week. Remember?"

She hugged Cody, "Thank God you were okay. When I heard about the stadium, then couldn't get you on the cell, I freaked out. I've only got one of you, you know. Haven't seen you much. Sorry, both jobs are crazy right now."

"Yeah, we're both busy," Cody said, thinking of recent events.

She detected his strange mood, and knew one thing would fix it. "You hungry?"

"Actually, yeah. Starving. I think I forgot to eat," said Cody.

"You?" Mom was shocked. "I got the second job just to support your athlete's stomach."

"Been a weird night." Cody looked in the fridge. "What can I make you? You worked all day."

His mom said, "Don't be silly. I'm the mom. I've got a tri-tip in the crock pot."

"Oh my god," he'd been so distracted, he hadn't noticed the smell. Cody hugged his mom tight, "Tri-tip? I love you so much."

His mom took the hug, a rare thing these days, and laughed, "I'll just get into my PJs."

Cody went to the kitchen and warmed up some Pinquito beans and put some bread in the oven. He got the tri tip out of the crock and put it on the cutting board, covering it with aluminum foil until it was ready to slice.

His mom came back into the kitchen, "Oh, that does smell good."

"What do you want to drink?"

"Jack Daniels," Mom said, "but I'll settle for a diet coke."

Cody asked, "You sure? I think you have some wine left."

"Naaa. Soda sounds good. It'll keep me awake for my homework."

"You're amazing," said Cody, "two jobs, and online college. I feel lazy."

"School is your job. Just focus on that. I've got the rest."

The meat had rested, the juices collected back into the middle of the roast. Cody cut it, got the bread out of the oven, "You shouldn't have to do this alone. It's not fair."

"Life isn't fair, baby," confirmed his mom.

"Do you ever think about... him?"

"Your father? Of course I do. We were married for five years."

"You're still married," said Cody, realizing the gravity of what that might mean in the coming days.

"Technically. But after all these years, I know he's not coming back."

"Plus, you wouldn't let him, right?"

His mom gave Cody a strange glance. "Why the new interest in your dad? You haven't wanted to talk about him in years. What's up?"

Cody shrugged, "I've just been thinking about him. What happened, I mean exactly?"

"I've shown you the note, about leaving 'being for our own good,' all of that stuff. But really, he just left. I don't like to speak bad about your dad, but what he did was cowardly."

"What would you do if you saw him again?"

His mom considered that. "Hmmm. If he was in the street, I might accidentally speed up. 'Oh, I didn't see him, officer. My long-lost husband, you say? What a strange coincidence.'"

Cody laughed.

"Sorry. I know he's your dad. It's up to you if you want to discover who he is. But, we'll probably never see him again. He's been gone twelve years. You were four when he left. No birthday cards, no phone calls, no nothing. For me, he's not worth finding."

"Sorry to bring it up."

"It's okay. You're old enough to ask questions. I just don't have a lot of answers," his mom said. "This tri tip is awesome by the way. I'm probably going to dream of cows."

"That would be awkward," laughed Cody.

"I've had worse nightmares. You sure you're okay, baby?"

"I just... I never want to hurt you like Dad did."

"You could never do that. Come here and give your mom a hug," She covered his forehead and cheeks in kisses while he squirmed. She finally let up. "I love you."

"You too, Mom."

"It's okay to think about your dad. It's up to you how to think about him. You'll have some choices to make about what kind of relationship you have, if you ever find him."

Cody thought of his father less than a mile away, chained in a small bedroom. "Yeah, I guess I will."

CHAPTER TWENTY FOUR

THE PLAN

The next day came, and as soon as everyone woke up, texts began flying back and forth.

Katie: is it okay to text?

Zacke: I think so. Does anyone have John's #? Does he have a phone?

Lucas: He does. I have it. Sending...

Ariana: Hey. Has everyone recovered from last night?

K: Umm, no. Still freaked out.

Z: I think we all are.

L: I feel the same.

John: Is everyone alright?

K: John? You text?

J: It's the 21st century. Of course I text.

A: Is it ok? Will anyone see these but us?

L: I doubt it. Governments are not as efficient as many believe. The Rageto use older ways to find their prey than monitoring texts.

A: I guess magic is easier than hacking cell phones.

J: We shouldn't use cell phones anyway. We should meet.

Z: I told you, I'm done.

A: Me too.

J: Please give me one more chance. I'd like us all to meet in a safe place.

Z: Maybe. But where? They crashed my job. They seem to show up wherever we go. And they have David, who can find us.

J: We finally have an advantage. Last night's stunt will put Sazzo out for at least a full day. One brother won't hunt without the other. We have today to make our plans.

K: Do we have a plan?

J: I do – but I'll need your help. Where can we meet that is safe?

L: I thought you were the leader – aren't you the Splinter to our Ninja Turtles?

J: Not sure I understand that reference.

L: I know a place. I'll call John with the location, and he can pick you all up.

A: No sea monsters?

J: No. They'll stay in today. The German wouldn't face Lucas's warrior without his brother.

A: Do you think Cody will come?

J: I don't know. Cody has no cell phone. I plan to try to persuade him privately today. I'll bring him along if I can.

L: No. I don't want the traitor there.

J: Everyone can be redeemed.

L: No. Cody is not invited.

Z: Sorry John. I agree. If I'm gonna come, I want to know everything – and NO Cody.

They all agreed. John relented about bringing Cody. Lucas suggested his converted room, since John said their houses were safe. Within the hour John, Lucas, Zacke, Ariana and Katie were all present.

"Are you sure we're safe here? Wait, is this a gym?" asked Ariana.

"No, it's my bedroom. Yeah, we're safe. My parents are shopping out of town. Should be gone for hours," said Lucas.

"We'll be safe from the brothers here." said John, "You've lived here all your life, so you've been quietly releasing your strength throughout your home. They can't attack us here."

"I hope so," said Lucas, "They're powerful. I didn't expect that squid stunt last night."

"Some stunt," said Katie. "If he can do that, how are we going to win?"

Ariana added, "What does winning even look like?"

Zacke joined in, "She's right. Even if we destroy them, which means actually killing other people, they will still come back in some other body. Right?"

Ariana said, "I told you I'm done. I only came because you said you'd tell us everything, John."

John said, "You're right, I did. It's time to be completely honest. We are in a bad situation; much worse than I first told you. I am the last of my kind, the sole keeper of the Amartus. At least, until I found you. Their side has been very effective at either killing us when we are re-birthed, or giving us a true death. Now I have you."

"Then it's hopeless," said Katie.

"No. I think something new is happening. I think the River is trying to restore balance. I think all of you are a sign that we will win."

"But, you only have one relic, and I don't want to kill anyone," said Zacke.

John said, "Even if we destroy them without the relic, that gives us at least fifteen years before they come back, re-birthed into another body."

"How does that work? It's still confusing," asked Ariana.

John said, "When someone with a warrior within them dies, their ancient is cast back into the River. It may take a few days, or even months before they are re-birthed into a new person. Sometimes years. When that new body is 15 or 16, they will come into their talents. That gives us time to rebuild the Amartus."

"It's kind of creepy," said Katie, "It's like we have other people inside us."

"I know it seems that way. But it's just the essence and memories of your ancient. You are who you are now, the person your parents raised you to be. You are you, and the ancient is raised *with* you. You become one only at the point where you accept the essence of your warrior. A choice you will all have to make soon. Lucas, I think, has already made it."

"I have," said Lucas. "But I don't feel any different. I still don't have the memories, and the talents come and go. It feels like... like a short in the wiring."

"It will come," John assured, "Once you've opened yourself up to accepting all that you are, the memories and talents will flood in, and never leave. It may be any numbers of things in your mind, or some past trauma blocking a full activation."

"If I'm a new birth, how will it work for me?" asked Zacke.

"From what I've seen, I think you and Cody are the new births. Your main talent hasn't manifested itself. I've seen incredible strength before, but I think you are something new. The new births have no core ancient to rely on, so it comes slower. But sometimes, it also manifests deeper; like building a new foundation. This is your first life as a warrior, I expect your talents to be unique and impressive."

Zacke was skeptical. "Really? Feels more like a curse. It freaks me out. I don't know how else to say it."

John smiled. "It feels that way for all of us, especially the first life. I've seen new births that are stronger than re-births. You'd think that with more lives and experiences, the talents would grow. But when new births show themselves, they begin very powerfully. That's why we must know which is which. The Rageto will target the new births, once they are sure. That's why they chose Cody. Plus, he was also emotionally compromised."

"What do we do about him?" asked Ariana, "If he's turned, can we ever get him back?"

Katie said, "I think so. I mean, I came back when I realized I was being stupid."

"I believe so," John sighed. "But we have two bigger problems. They know that your home bases can't be attacked. David can find us. They may try to pick us off one by one. Not usually the brother's style. More likely, they will try to draw us to one place."

"Well that just sounds awesome." Katie didn't hide her sarcasm. "How?"

"Caron, or Ehrhardt as he calls himself, is usually bolder." John furrowed his brow. "But this time, it's Sazzo, or Derek, that seems reckless. It may be something in his up-bringing this time around. They attacked you at a very public place, and were willing to hurt thousands to get to you. I don't think they'll hesitate to do the same thing again."

"What about the game this Friday? Will Cody show?" wondered Zacke.

"They cancelled the game because of the stadium." said Lucas.

John said, "Good. We don't have to worry about all those people being in danger."

"Wait," Ariana stood up. "Oh my god, what about the homecoming dance? It wasn't cancelled. They're combining both school's dances this year. There will be over five hundred kids in the auditorium."

John was distracted by something out of the corner of his eye. He looked at the three full length mirrors. He noticed there were also three on the opposite walls. "Why all the mirrors, Lucas?"

"Sensei says it's good for precision." Lucas jumped to his feet. "Why? What's wrong?"

John stared at the mirrors, scanning back and forth carefully.

They all looked, but all that stared back were their reflections. Then, a subtle darkness shaded the glass. To Ariana it looked like a faint shadow passed behind their images in the mirror. She turned around to look behind her, but only saw the opposite mirrors facing her.

Lucas said. "I saw it too. What does it mean?"

"Oh my God, is this like the mirror on the beach?" Katie's stomach turned when she remembered the old man, the eye, the blood.

"Does anyone have something of Cody's?" asked John, scanning the mirrors.

Katie said, "Uh, yeah. He dropped his wallet. I thought you could take it to him."

"What's going on?" asked Zacke, looking from mirror to mirror.

"Mirror viewing. It's a rare talent. Only two people I know can do it. Objects can be triggers for certain talents. Give me the wallet."

Katie handed it over, and John flung the wallet at the mirror closest to him. The mirror flashed green when it hit, and a ghostly image of a man showed for a second, until the wallet tumbled to the floor.

"Zamma. I know it's you!" John pulled his sword. "I can smell you from here."

A deep, unpleasant laugh sounded around the room. The mirrors vibrated, "How foolish, Pentoss. You should know by now that nowhere is safe from me."

John responded, "Leave us, spider. You'll get a true death soon enough. My blade longs to meet you again."

Zamma chuckled again, and Ariana's hair stood up on the back of her neck.

"Children," sounded the mirrors. "I ask you all to come to me. This foolish man is doomed. Come join us. It's your only chance."

The mirrors continued vibrating, a dull hum sounding through the room.

Lucas said, "Sorry, whoever you are, but we're on team John. Get out of my room."

John swung his sword at one of the mirrors, breaking it.

Zamma's voice rang out, "That's not nice. Simple choice, children. Join or die."

"Neither, creepy voice guy." Zacke spoke to the mirror, "You know what, I don't like bullies. You just helped me make up my mind. Team John all the way. Now get out."

"Pity." the voice said.

The vibration gave way to shaking. The mirrors undulated on the wall.

John yelled, "Everyone duck!" The mirrors began to shake violently.

Lucas and John put their backs to the mirrors, forming a shield on either side of the others. All five remaining mirrors exploded toward the center of the room. They all closed their eyes. John and Lucas braced for the impact of shards imbedding into their backs. Their faces were all covered, expecting the worst.

When the shattering noises ceased, they slowly opened their eyes. Lucas and John felt nothing. They all looked around at the destruction to see the glass shards stopped in a perfect circle around them. A dome shield had been temporarily erected around the group. Katie put her hands down.

"That was awesome! Katie, how many colors was that?" asked Ariana, reaching out to touch the vanishing shield.

Katie breathed hard. "I just threw the whole rainbow of shields up."

"You're getting stronger, Katie," said John. "More memories and talents should come to you soon. Is everyone okay?"

"Who... what the hell was that?" Zacke asked, standing and checking for cuts.

"Hell? You're not far off. That is an evil elder; the functional father of the brothers. Zamma is his name, and he has been talking to Cody."

"Cody talked to that?" asked Katie.

Ariana looked suspicious. "How do you know that?"

John answered, "Because I met with Cody before I picked you up."

Ariana said, "Wait! Because of my stupid mouth, he knows the perfect place to hurt a lot of innocent people."

"Homecoming." Katie confirmed.

John looked around at the destruction, and knew there would be much more to come if Zamma got directly involved. "I learned some surprising things when I met with Cody. I need to ask you all to do something. You're not going to like it."

PART 3

"The past is shadow. It stands behind you."
~ Elder Giddeon, after the battle of Uruk

CHAPTER TWENTY FIVE

LOYALTY

Cody kept reliving his conversation with the elder.

He'd thought getting glimpses of the old man was bad, but he'd never been so scared to talk to anyone in his life. He now knew what people meant when they said a 'cold chill'. His spine went numb when he'd heard the elders voice through the mirror.

Mom at work, he'd been going through old scrapbooks. He barely remembered his father. Now, looking at photos of their family trio playing on the beach, in the park, smiling, it brought into focus how serious everything was. Seeing his father's happy face in old photos, Cody realized how much he had aged. The long hair totally changed how he looked.

Cody had fantasized about reunions before; some were tearful events, most ended with Cody punching his father in the face. He never imagined he would see his dad like he had, in the back seat of the car. He was completely broken.

There was no turning back now. The next hour would be hard. The elder explained they needed proof of loyalty. Cody guessed at what they would ask him to do. He hoped he was wrong.

Cody thought of his mother briefly, but clamped down his mind and decided even a thought of her shouldn't be exposed to the craziness of what came next. He rode his bike to the brother's rented house. Cody knocked on the door, and Ehrhardt let him in. "Hello, Cody."

"Hey," he tried to keep his voice calm, but his heart was thumping wildly, threatening to betray him.

"Sazzo wants to see you." said Ehrhardt.

"I guess I should get used to Derek's warrior name. He's awake?"

"Yes. But he has a terrible headache, and is in a bad mood. Best do what he says. Don't make him angry."

Cody tried to lighten the tension. "I wouldn't want a sea monster to eat me."

Apparently, humor was lost on Ehrhardt, who led him toward the bedroom without another word. They passed through the living room, where Cody noticed the books again. "Will you teach me how to use those?"

Ehrhardt glanced at the books and made an odd expression. *Should I not have mentioned the books?* Cody thought.

"Once you prove yourself, your training will begin. You will be taught magic and how to strengthen your powers."

Cody liked that they called them powers, it felt more honest than John.

Ehrhardt continued, "All books belong to the elder. He will decide what you learn."

Cody clarified, "After we kill the others?"

"Yes. Does that bother you?"

"No." Cody lied, but he had to show strength. He feigned calm as Ehrhardt opened the door. Derek was sitting in a chair, and the dark curtains were drawn. Derek clicked on a table lamb.

"Don't stare. I know how terrible I look. The bad thing after a big conjuring is that no amount of aspirin will help. Only time cures these things. I remember conjuring a whale once, a long time ago. You know... I've just recently noticed how much I tend to make speeches. I sound like a two-bit villain. Funny. Do you know why they call it two-bit? Two bits is a quarter, and..."

"You're doing it right now, brother," said Ehrhardt.

"Damn. You're right. So, Cody, do you know what elder Zamma demands of you?"

Cody remembered the discussion in the mirror, "A test of my loyalty."

"Yes. Can you guess what it is?" asked Derek.

"I... I think so."

"You must not hesitate," Derek got up from the chair, and uncovered a large hanging mirror on the wall. Zamma was there, watching quietly.

"What do I do?" asked Cody.

"Ehrhardt," said Derek, "Your gun please. It has one bullet. Oh, and in case you change your mind and try to turn the gun on us, we will kill you on the spot."

"Don't trust me, huh?" asked Cody, but couldn't bring himself to make a joke.

"Not yet," answered Derek. "You see how I used just two words there? I'm getting better at keeping my sentences short. It's going to take some work, but..."

"Stop talking," Zamma commanded.

Derek frowned. Ehrhardt handed the gun to Cody, still equipped with the silencer. The German said, "The safety is off. Don't put your finger on the trigger until you're ready to fire. Then press it into your target. It's .45 caliber. One shot will do."

Cody took the gun and looked around the room, confused.

Ehrhardt went to the closet. Two thin wooden doors opened accordion style to reveal David, arms duct-taped to a chair.

A cold chill went down Cody's spine, "You do want me to kill my own father."

Ehrhardt nodded. The closet had been covered in thick plastic from top to bottom. Derek said, "The head's too messy. Put the gun to his heart."

Ehrhardt pushed the center of David's chest to illustrate.

David stared at his son. He was gagged, but his eyes spoke clearly. David knew his life was over, one way or the other. He stared into his son's eyes and tried to communicate understanding and forgiveness.

Derek added, "There is a thick piece of wood behind him when the bullet goes through. The one shot will..."

"You're over explaining again," said Zamma from the mirror. "Cody, kill the scum that walked out on your family all those years ago. Kill him to honor all the sacrifices your mother had to make while raising you, alone."

White-hot anger shot through Cody as he heard the old man lie. *I believed it all those years.* But hearing the lie spoken, to get him to kill his father enraged Cody. He put the gun to his father's chest.

Cody visualized every electronic wave he felt around him. In his mind, they flashed a bright green. The lightbulb in the lamp exploded. Ehrhardt and Derek were flung back as they felt a wave of electric charge fill the room. The mirror cracked and Zamma was gone.

Swinging his arm toward the heavy curtains, Cody fired the one shot. He threw the gun across the room. Derek and Ehrhardt were still on the floor, recovering from the electric pulse. They heard a window imploding into the house, and the front door burst open.

Ehrhardt moaned, "What have you done, boy?"

David was unconscious from the electrical pulse. Cody had his pocket knife out and cut the duct tape, freeing his father.

Ehrhardt tried to stand, reaching instinctively for his gun, but the holster was empty. "You stupid boy, I'm going to rip..."

"Caron!" A voice rang through the small house. It was Lucas' voice, but it wasn't. "I'm coming for you!"

David was loose except for his gag, and regained consciousness. He got up from his chair and went for Derek.

David lifted Derek to a standing position and punched him in the stomach. Derek doubled over, and David threw him into Ehrhardt. They were a pile of brothers on the floor, as father and son left the small room.

Ehrhardt reached for his second gun in the holster under his right arm. This gun had no silencer.

John, Lucas, and Katie were in the front room, "Car's outside, go!"

"I want to help!" said Cody.

John replied, "The plan worked. You've done enough. Go!"

Ehrhardt came out of the bedroom firing. John deflected one bullet with his sword. Lucas ducked and was headed for Ehrhardt, when two more shots rang out, aimed for the fleeing David and Cody. To Ehrhardt's surprise, the bullets stopped dead and fell to the floor. A small green flash appeared where they hit Katie's shield.

Derek stumbled out of the bedroom, nearly pushing Ehrhardt over in the small, narrow hallway. Ariana focused on Derek. He started to speak a conjuring, when his stomach rumbled. Projectile vomit spewed at the wall. Derek doubled over, and a second wave of vomit landed on his shoes.

Lucas tried to kick the gun away. The German pulled back to avoid the move and his elbow connected with the wall. His gun flew from his hand, toward the kitchen.

Zacke stood at the front door, guiding father and son safely out the front door.

Ehrhardt landed an unexpected left jab and Lucas went down.

The brothers stumbled to the kitchen. Ehrhardt looked for the gun.

Derek had recovered from the stomach pain, and stood the best he could, dizziness threatening to overtake him. He felt his rage rising; he made a low growl and grabbed a kitchen knife.

Ehrhardt didn't see the gun immediately, but he did see Lucas charging toward him. He grabbed a knife from the block on the counter and Lucas and John joined them in the small galley kitchen.

John used his sword as a defensive weapon to block Derek's attacks, the length of his weapon little use for attacks in the tight space.

Ehrhardt used every skill to battle Lucas. Lucas's body was just a skinny fifteen years old, but the warrior inside him made up for it. Lucas grabbed two blades from the block, meeting every blow from the German.

Lucas used the cabinet doors as weapons. When Ehrhardt lunged, Lucas used his foot to swing open a lower cabinet door. It hit Ehrhardt in the knee. Lucas kicked the door for greater impact. It worked. The German stumbled back.

Derek was pushed into Lucas. Derek lunged for another knife, and was sparring with both Lucas and John. The younger brother backed up, near Ehrhardt.

Derek jabbed his left hand at John, but overextended his reach. John used the chance to duck to one knee, and sliced across Derek's stomach. It wasn't deep, but Derek dropped one knife and held his wound.

Lucas slashed a deep cut across Ehrhardt's arm. The German yelled in surprise. He and Derek backed out of the kitchen together, John and Lucas aggressively pressing the attack.

Ehrhardt looked worried as John advanced. There was no time for magic. The fighting was too fast.

Ariana and Katie stood outside the kitchen, unable to help. They feared they would just get in the way. Zacke started the vehicle in the driveway, making sure David and Cody were secure. David had removed his gag, Cody next to him.

"Do you have a license?" Cody asked Zacke.

Zacke shrugged, "Learner's permit."

Back inside, the fight was now in the small dining room, which was empty except for a table, a few chairs, and a large mirror on the wall. John tried to glance to see if Zamma was there.

Ehrhardt was done messing around, and growled with rage as his jabs and slashes got more aggressive. The brothers were still backing toward the wall of the dining room. Lucas had landed a few thin cuts on Derek, and Ehrhardt had slender lines of blood showing through his shirt sleeves.

Then Lucas bit the inside of his lip and tasted blood.

Ehrhardt saw the change in the boy's face, recognized the ancient berserker Viking warrior, shining through Lucas. He could see a shadow of all the past faces he had known of his enemy, flashing, super-imposed over the boy he was now fighting. A chord of fear went through Ehrhardt.

They all knew what was coming next. The berserker rage, about to spin out of control mentally, become unhinged. Ehrhardt knew he might not survive; remembering the times he had not.

Derek shouted, "Zamma help us!"

Lucas made a final lunge at Ehrhardt, but both men were pulled backward off their feet. They floated off the hard wood floor and were sucked into the mirror. They disappeared as though it was an open window.

Lucas leaped at the mirror, to follow them, but it was just a mirror again, and shattered. They were gone.

The ancient in Lucas became unglued, insane. John backed away and grabbed the books lying there, fleeing the house. The girls ran out with him, frightened of what Lucas had become. John ran out the front door, and closed it behind him.

They all went to the SUV and stood there while they heard destruction unleashed inside the house. John looked around uneasily for neighbors. Luckily, no one was on the otherwise sleepy street.

Ten minutes later, there was quiet and Lucas stumbled out of the house. He righted himself and tried to pretend nothing had happened. Lucas made it to the car.

David said, "Son, take this necklace off." Cody took the charm necklace from his father's neck. It felt strange and heavy.

John snatched it out of his hand. "This needs to be destroyed. I'll see to it."

David leapt out of the vehicle. Before anyone knew what was happening, streams of lightning bolts fell upon the house, like a waterfall made of electricity. The house caught fire in several different places. David climbed back into the car to stunned silence.

David fell back against the seat. His breathing labored, he managed, "I wasn't sure I could still do that."

CHAPTER TWENTY SIX

LAST CHANCE

Ehrhardt laid on the floor. "Thank you, Elder Zamma."

Derek and Ehrhardt were in Zamma's chamber. The cold dusty stone floor was a welcome change from the heat of the fighting. But the rest only lasted a moment as they were lifted like rag dolls and flung up to the ceiling, pinned by Zamma's power.

"You were attacked, tricked by a boy, lost my books, lost the Witness again, and all you have to say is thank you?" said Zamma in a cold, hard voice.

Derek squirmed against the ceiling, "Thank you... very much?"

"Enough!' shouted Ehrhardt, "They are nearly activated, strong, united. We are only two, What do you expect?"

He pushed against Erhardt's throat with an invisible hand. "I expect success."

Derek said, "Elder Zamma, let him go. Stop acting like Darth Vader. I have a plan to finish them."

They abruptly dropped the full ten feet, from ceiling to floor. They landed on an ancient rug, but it still hurt when they fell. Ehrhardt's and Derek's gashes oozed fresh blood.

"Stop bleeding on my rug," said Zamma.

"Then heal us, oh loving elder." Derek held up his bleeding arms. "Holy shit! What happened to your eye?"

"On the beach, I was viewing the scene through a small mirror. When it cracked, it did this to my eye."

"Why don't you heal it?"

"I tried. Something is strange about the boy's mirror ability. I can't explain it. Hopefully the Vitaeizicon will have the answer."

"Well, could you heal *us*, at least?"

"After I hear this plan," said Zamma.

They both slowly rose to their feet, brushing off the dust. The brothers winced in pain.

"Have you forgotten your manners?" asked Zamma.

Ehrhardt fumed, "You expect us to bow when we are injured?"

Derek put a hand on his brother's arm, suppressing his own anger. They bowed together, refusing to let the elder see how much it hurt.

"Astound me with your brilliant plan, Sazzo. And don't tell me you were planning on attacking their school dance."

"Umm..." Derek said, changing tactics from plan A, "Okay, I have another plan then. Firstly, I didn't lose your books."

"No? where are they?" asked the elder.

"In the trunk of the rental car," Ehrhardt said angrily. "We left decoys out in case the boy was lying. He was, so it's a good thing we did."

"Fine. And your plan?"

"We can't turn any of them," said Derek, "that's obvious now."

Zamma agreed, "Exactly. I want you to wipe them out."

"Now wait," said Derek, "There's another solution. We bring them here for a consuming."

"That's too dangerous," said Zamma.

"A consuming requires a relic, and a rare spell," Ehrhardt reasoned, "Plus the subject must be awake. So, we can't knock them out."

"No." Derek said, "But they can be bound. They are not fully activated yet. Their real strength, is numbers. They will be alone, powerless and subdued."

Zamma considered it, "There is such a spell in the Vitaeizicon. I would need that book."

"Brother, your plan is overly complicated. The Amartus are nearly wiped out," said Ehrhardt, "let me kill them all. We can't let this attack, this betrayal, go unpunished."

Derek replied, "Come on brother, we can do this. There are only four Rageto elders left. A consuming would give elder Zamma an advantage over the others, a way for him to finally rule them all. These kids are powerful. You would get all their powers added to yours. Not to mention, I could bring you Pentoss. You could give him a true death."

The elder stroked his chin. "Which means my fate would be reversed, and I would not suffer a true death after all. This damned wound would finally heal."

Ehrhardt shook his head. "This is a mistake, brother."

Zamma challenged Derek, "You can't beat them in the field, and they're not even fully activated. How do you propose to get them here?"

"One at a time, of course," said Derek. "They are still on the run. They've attacked us, so they know we'll come after them."

Ehrhardt said, "Yes, they suspect you'll attack at this coming home dance."

Derek smiled, "So we will. But not how they expect. They think there is safety in numbers. We will turn that against them."

Zamma stared. Ehrhardt seethed. Derek smiled his most charming smile.

"I will allow you to try. This dance is on Saturday, yes?" Zamma went to a large hour glass and began casting a spell. At an Elder level, the brothers knew he didn't have to speak aloud. They had no idea what spell he was casting.

"I will heal you and you can rest here. Plenty of time to get you back to California. The portal was destroyed from the other side, so you'll take the other jet. But, if this doesn't work, if anything goes wrong, then Caron; you will reduce the entire city to dust. I'm lifting my ban from 2004. Nothing survives."

"Understood," said Ehrhardt, still bleeding on his own shoes.

Zamma finished the spell. "No more failures. This glass will run out at one minute before Saturday turns into Sunday. You have until then."

"And then what?" asked Derek.

Zamma said simply, "Both of your brains implode."

CHAPTER TWENTY SEVEN
MEETING

John and the others made it back to Lucas's converted garage. His parents still weren't home, but he warned them that the last text he'd got said they only had an hour of privacy left. John looked through the books they'd taken before the brothers' rental house burned down.

"What about those books?" asked Ariana.

John replied, "No. As I feared, these books are useless."

Cody said, "But they displayed them like they were important."

"They suspected you were disloyal, so they used decoys," John said. "These are old leather bound books on horticulture."

"What?" asked Katie.

Ariana answered, "Flowers and stuff."

Lucas was impressed with her knowledge and gave her a smile. She smiled back.

"Now we need a final plan," said David. "They will come for us."

"Can we use other spell books?" asked Zacke.

"The Amartus don't use magic. I was only hoping to keep the books out of Zamma's hands. Magic is of the Rageto, that's how they become corrupted."

"So when you say battle, you mean we may have to actually kill people? I'm not okay with that." Ariana crossed her arms.

"It's self-defense if they come for us," said Zacke, "no one wants violence."

John said, "It will come down to us or them. We must all be prepared for that."

"I am," said Lucas.

"No! I'm not killing anyone," said Ariana. "Maybe we just made it worse, made them angrier."

"They would come for you no matter what. If we hadn't saved David, they would still hunt us. They know that none of you can be turned now."

"I'm just glad the plan worked," said Cody.

John turned to face Cody. "You played a dangerous game when you left the beach."

"I had to save my dad," Cody said. "I can work out how pissed off I am later. You needed info on where they were."

"You're a good actor. I was fooled," said Lucas.

David said, "It was still too dangerous, Cody. After all those years with the brothers, I've seen what they can do."

"I saw those articles, those trophies," added Cody. "I looked up some of those 'accidents' online."

John nodded, "They've killed hundreds of thousands of innocents trying to get to people like us."

"Why didn't you tell us that?" Katie asked.

John answered, "I suspected, but it's hard to prove it. Natural disasters happen. Some of them aren't natural. Now you know how far they'll go to destroy breakouts. They are cowards at heart, hiding behind their magic."

Zacke asked "How are we supposed to know what to expect, since Cody and me are first timers, new births?"

John said, "You are the mysteries in our equation. We know Cody has talents, one has something to do with electrical energy. We still don't know what your main talent is, Zacke. Because you're a new birth, we won't know until it appears."

Zacke didn't respond. He felt guilty not telling them what he could do.

"You can't speed up this process? Activate us sooner?" asked Ariana.

John shook his head. "No. I've done all I can. Being around each other this much, using your talents, it should have sped up the process. But it's like some of you are holding back. There's something I can't see."

Katie snapped, "Holding back? We've done everything you told us and we've almost been killed four times. My sister got hurt. Remember? Because of me."

David spoke up, "It's not John's fault. He's been trying to help you. I've seen these men do evil up close. None of the blame rests with us. If one of them pointed a gun at your best friend and said 'don't move or I'll kill them,' and then you flinched, would it be your fault that he shot your friend? No. The man holding the gun is responsible. *They* are our enemy, and they will come for all of us."

They all went quiet, imagining the next fight.

David looked to John. "We're running out of time. The brothers told stories of warriors linking. Could we attempt that?"

"No." said John, "It's always ended in disaster."

"What is linking?" asked Zacke.

John rubbed his bald head. "In theory, if the circumstances are just right, some warriors can link. They feel each other's talents. Legends say they can even share them for a short time. But I've never heard of it actually working."

"There are seven of us, only two of them." David reasoned, "If we could link, we'd be unstoppable."

"You don't understand!" John shouted, filled with a bitter old memory. "I'm sorry. I didn't mean to yell. I saw three warriors try to link once. In China, in the 1540's."

They were all startled. The old date and place made their situation real.

John continued, "They were the best; clear headed, fully activated, experienced. They linked. At first, they were fierce beasts, defeating ten foes each. Then, one by one, they bled from the eyes. They died screaming before their foes cut them down."

The stark story brought home what they were up against. No one knew what to say.

"Those warriors were the best, and they failed. We must rely on our numbers; seven against their two." John shook off the old memory. "They'll make one last attempt. They'll give the choice again: join, or die. When we say no, they will try to wipe out this whole town."

"Everybody we care about," Katie whispered.

"Yes," said John. "You didn't ask for this to happen to you. I know. I don't want this responsibility either. I've seen too many warriors fall. But if they wipe us out this time, that's it. The balance will be forever tipped their way."

Ariana thought of her family. She stood up. "Then let's end this."

CHAPTER TWENTY EIGHT

THE DAY BEFORE

They'd heard nothing from the brothers for days. John suggested their elder had pulled them half way across the world through the mirror. They needed time to heal and get back for the final fight. That was true for everyone.

They all agreed to stay in their homes where it was safe. David reasoned it would recharge them and hopefully a small rest might be what they needed to finally activate. John hated waiting around, but David took over nursing duties and told John he needed to rest and heal from his injury.

David had hoped Cody would come to their hotel room so he could finally explain why he'd been absent from his son's life. But three days in, no Cody.

Before they knew it, it was Friday afternoon, only one day before the dance. They'd made a tentative plan, but it felt flimsy to Zacke. He would have to trust John and his lifetimes of knowledge. He still felt guilty, especially after what John had said about one of them holding back. He knew it was him.

There was a knock at Zacke's door. Two men stood on the porch. He recognized one of them from the academy. "Hey Officer Jack."

"Hey Zacke. This is Detective Jenkins."

Detective Jenkins said, "Hi, Zacke. I'd like to ask you a few questions. Since Jack here is your sponsor at the academy, he asked to come along."

"Sure," said Zacke. "Come on in."

They did, and his father was concerned until they explained that they were investigating the two men at the restaurant.

His dad asked, "Why didn't you tell me about this Zacke?"

"Well, you were..." Zacke looked at the officers, "...busy. It's been kind of crazy lately. Besides, when those two guys came in, I ran out the back."

"You didn't see anything else? How about the car? Did you see what they were driving?" asked Jenkins.

"No, they parked in front, I went out the back. Sorry." *Sorry I'm lying to you. I hate this, but what else can I do?* he thought.

Jenkins took notes. "What did they want? What did they say to you?"

"I have no idea what they wanted," said Zacke. "They didn't really say anything. They came in and went behind the register. I thought they were robbing the place."

"Witnesses said they seemed to be looking for you and the friend you were talking to." Jenkins consulted his notes, "Cody Nichols."

"He was there. But I don't know him very well, just from school. He ran out the back with me when the guys came," said Zacke.

Officer Jack added, "Zacke, are you sure there's nothing else going on?"

Zacke felt a thin layer of perspiration appear. "Not really. I'm sorry I can't be more helpful."

"Alright." Jenkins handed Zacke a card. "Here's my card and that's the case number I wrote on the back. I've already spoken to Cody and Victoria Masala, your shift manager. Call me if you remember anything else."

"Okay," said Zacke.

As they left, Officer Jack said, "See you tomorrow at the academy. The fire guys are showing off their new camera system."

Zacke had nearly forgotten. He was planning to spend all day getting ready for the big fight. But he still had a life, and he was determined to keep things as normal as he could. *If that's even possible.*

His dad looked at him when they were gone, "You weren't telling them everything. What are you holding back Zacke?"

"Nothing. Just drop it Dad, please."

"You want to be a cop, and you're lying to them? You're better than that, Zacke."

"You don't know me! You haven't talked to me in months without slurring your words!" Zacke yelled, surprised at his own outburst. His dad stood and took it.

"Dad... I'm sorry..."

"No, Zacke. I'm sorry. Mom leaving has been hard. I didn't handle it well. I'm the dad. Well, I haven't had a drink for a few days. I'm working on it."

"It's alright. I'm sorry, Dad. Things have just been hard lately."

"Everything's tough when you're a teenager. What can I do to help?" asked his father.

"Nothing Pops. Just typical teenage stuff. Mostly."

"Hmmm. Well, if you change your mind." He put a hand on Zacke's shoulder. "Zacke, you can tell me if this is about your mom, the anger I mean. It's no one's fault she went off the deep end with that church. I know she tried to make it about you, and I think someday she'll ask us to forgive her."

Zacke dodged. "Yeah. Ok. Well, I got homework and stuff."

"I thought school was out this week?"

"It is. I just have to keep up on my reading for next week."

Dad nodded and Zacke went to his room. Locking his door, he closed his eyes. *"Mom wanted to make this about me?"* He thought. *It is about me. I'm the reason mom left.*

* * *

Lucas had been eating like a pig all week. He wondered how many calories his ancient required. Before his parents got home, he'd walked to the neighborhood convenience store for some junk food, a splurge, since mom was trying to buy fewer sugary treats. He'd gone the long way around to avoid walking by Billy's new house.

It was frustrating that he couldn't become the warrior at will. There were still flashes, and a few shards of ancient memories. He thought about what John said; someone holding back. He knew it was him. He was thinking about the past year as he rounded the tall shrubs.

He was ambushed by Billy and two of his buddies. Before Lucas could react, his arms were behind him. His bag of junk food spilled on the lawn. They took him to a grassy strip between two houses.

Billy had his typical cocky tone, "Hey Lucasfilm, we never finished that conversation."

"That's because you were covered in puke." Lucas was laid on his belly by Billy's two friends. The friend laughed as Billy sat on Lucas' back. Billy used one of his hands to hold Lucas's wrists.

He used the other to punch Lucas in the kidney. "Talking back these days? That's cute."

Lucas kept quiet. *I could take all of you, right here,* he thought. But old feelings rushed back. He felt helpless, ten years old again, when Billy first started bullying him.

"I saw you with some new friends. The black one looks pretty hot. You finally got your first boyfriend? I know you wanted it to be me, but sorry, I'm straight."

Control, Control.

Billy's maddening arrogance continued. "I've always been curious; do you shower in between doing each other? Do you watch gay porn to get in the mood?"

Lucas tried to sound casual, "Yeah. I watch tons. I saw you in a couple. You're even smaller than I thought you'd be." He got another punch in the kidney for that.

"Okay, that was kinda funny," Billy admitted. "Frankie, I'll bet you have to take a leak, right? Piss on Lucas' head. Just don't get any on me."

Screw control. He tightened his muscles, ready to slide out from under Billy. He was just about to bite the inside of his mouth, when the shouting in his mind began.

CAN YOU HEAR ME? YOU KNOW WHO THIS IS, AND NOW YOU KNOW SOMETHING ELSE I CAN DO

It was Derek's voice. Every word in his head was like a wire hacking at a raw nerve. Lucas yelled, still pinned under Billy.

MY BROTHER AND I ARE THROUGH PLAYING. YOU WILL SUR-RENDER TO US TOMORROW AT 8 O'CLOCK OR WE WILL KILL EVERYONE AT YOUR LITTLE DANCE

Lucas screamed louder. Billy's excitement grew, assuming the yelling was because of him. At first, it made all the boys laugh, but they could tell something was wrong. Lucas writhed on the ground.

"What did you do to him?" asked Jonesy.

Billy shouted, "Nothing. He's faking."

His other friend Frankie looked around, "Better let him up Billy." Billy finally got off Lucas, but Lucas stayed on the ground.

Lucas put his hands to either side of his head as the excruciating mental message continued.

ALL FIVE OF YOU WILL BE THERE, OR EVERYONE DIES. BRING PENTOSS, AND EVERYONE DIES. BE LATE, AND EVERYONE DIES.

Billy towered over Lucas. "Freak. Grab his shoes, Frankie."

Frankie pulled Lucas's shoes off and began tying the laces together.

"Hey, what are you doing over there?" said one of Lucas' neighbors.

"Oh, sorry ma'am, just helping a friend," said Billy, "I think he's sick."

They left quickly, as the woman got to Lucas. He was still moaning on the ground. When the talking stopped inside his head, the pain began to recede. He cleared his eyes, and looked around for the boys. They were gone.

"Are you okay, Lucas?" asked his neighbor.

"I... Yes," Lucas managed, getting to his feet and realizing that his shoes were gone. "Thank you Mrs. Patel. I'm fine."

She looked at the boys far down the block now, "You want my pellet gun to take care of those pests?"

Lucas tried to smile, but the adrenaline that had been building up was starting to wear off. "No. But thanks for the offer."

He saw his shoes dangling over the telephone line, and walked away in his socks.

Lucas didn't go home. He walked in the opposite direction of Billy, straight to his psychologist's office. He felt his phone vibrate and saw the group texts.

Zacke: Did you hear that?

Katie: Yeah, I think we all did

Ariana: Hurt my head. What do we do?

Lucas didn't engage in the conversation. He looked up and saw that Dr. Mason was just locking his office for the day.

Mason said, "Hey, Lucas. We don't meet today."

"Doctor," Lucas looked straight into his eyes. "Sam. I need an appointment right now. A special one."

"Are you going to actually talk to me this time?" the doctor smiled. "I have enough model ships."

"Yes. I'll talk. I'm ready for hypnotherapy."

The doctor stopped smiling. "Okay. Why don't we just talk first?"

"You can ask me anything you want, and I'll have to answer. I'm tired of holding back. Sam, I need this."

The doctor unlocked the office. "I can't pass that up. You sure about this?"

"Yes. But you have to do something for me. Regress me as far back as I can go. It's important."

"Early childhood memories? What are we looking for?"

"You'll know when you hear it," said Lucas as he thought, *I hope this works.*

* * *

Cody and David sat on the bench in center of the hotel courtyard. They were surrounded on four sides by the three-story hotel, while they listened to the fountain just behind them.

Cody spoke first, "Thanks for meeting me."

"I'm glad you wanted to meet. I know how angry you must be with me, and I need to explain what happened."

"John came to my house and told me that the brothers grabbed you. But I'd already decided to save you," said Cody, arms folded, staring at the glass elevator as it moved up and down. "But it doesn't explain why you left in the first place."

David took a deep breath. "I thought I was doing the right thing, to keep you and your mom safe. But I was an idiot."

"Yeah, you were." Cody shifted on the bench. "We would have been safer together."

"You're right. I realized that, and was headed back. That's when I was taken by the brothers in a train station. They kept me prisoner and used my talents to find people like us."

"But I saw that lightning storm you made. Why couldn't you get away? Even just to make a phone call? Anything to let us know what happened."

"When we were hunting around the world, I was tightly controlled, chained most of the time. They beat me down for years, until I had no hope. The thought of you and your mom being safe, and away from all this craziness was all I could hold on to. But I had to bury that deep, so they couldn't use you against me. I was afraid to use my talent, for fear they would make me use it on others. Elder Zamma is very powerful, and very cruel. They made me wear that damned necklace. There was a powerful spell so I couldn't take it off myself."

"You had no idea that I would have these talents, powers, whatever?" asked Cody.

"No!" said David, "It's very rare for the River to choose two people from the same family. The Sect may have records of it happening before, but I've never heard of it except for the brothers. Whatever the reason, I think it means something."

"What? Even our powers..." Cody trailed off as a humming began in his head. He saw his father's face change as well, when the shouting began in their minds.

CAN YOU HEAR ME? YOU KNOW WHO THIS IS, AND NOW YOU KNOW SOMETHING ELSE I CAN DO

Every word was like a hot metal pin poking into their brains. Father and son both held their heads.

MY BROTHER AND I ARE THROUGH PLAYING. YOU WILL SUR-RENDER TO US TOMORROW AT 8 O'CLOCK OR WE WILL KILL EVERYONE AT YOUR LITTLE DANCE

ALL FIVE OF YOU WILL BE THERE, OR EVERYONE DIES. BRING PENTOSS, AND EVERYONE DIES. BE LATE, AND EVERYONE DIES.

They sat on the bench, a few other hotel guests passing with concern. The mental hum, and pain, finally receded. David said, "Are you all right?"

Cody rubbed his forehead. "Ow! Now we know he can do that."

"Let's get to John. I don't think we were the only ones that heard that."

John had already texted everyone by the time Cody and David got to the room. Soon, everyone gathered at David and John's hotel room. Lucas didn't show, and wasn't answering any texts.

Zacke asked, "Are they serious?"

"Always." John said, "But it's a trap, and they know that we have no choice but to end this."

David said, "No choice? I'm not letting Cody near those monsters."

"Not your call, dad," said Cody.

Ariana said, "But if we don't show, then they're going to kill everyone."

"If you do, there are still no guarantees," said David, "These are evil men."

Katie insisted, "Then we have to destroy them."

"Even if we could, it would be too dangerous around all those people," said Ariana.

"Not if you put a shield around them," said Zacke.

Katie replied, "You mean the auditorium? I can't do anything that big!"

"Maybe not," said John, "but you could put a shield around four people. You could all meet them as planned, then Katie could throw a shield while Lucas and I finally destroy them."

"Use them as bait, you mean?" said David.

"They'll be safe inside Katie's shield." said John, "We have to at least act like we're giving them what they want."

"Where is Lucas?" asked Ariana.

Katie looked at her phone. "He's still not answering his... wait, he just texted me. He says 'Off the grid for a while. I got their message too. I'll be there, and ready to finish it.' "

"I'm in too," said Cody.

David sighed "John, do you have another weapon I could use?"

Cody asked, "Dad? You want to fight? But what if they take you again?"

"I won't let them. You're not going without me. Besides, I have a lot to pay them back for," said David.

"No, Dad, you should stay here..."

"Not your call," said David firmly, but Cody saw the worry in his eyes. He couldn't imagine what his dad had been through. Cody's long held anger was turning into something like pity for his dad.

John said, "Sorry David, just one relic. You'll all have to rely on your talents. In moments of crisis, activation sometimes comes all at once."

David offered, "I wish you'd consider my idea again. They could link..."

"No!" John snapped. "Sorry, David, no. It's far too dangerous, even for ancients at full strength, linking warriors is a bad idea. Plus, we don't have a hub; one warrior to focus everyone's talents and funnel them through all of us. It could kill us all."

"Dad," Cody interrupted. "Can I talk to you outside?"

David furrowed his brow. "Sure." They walked out of the hotel room and let the door close automatically.

"I want you to stay here. I just got you back. We can't trust the brothers. They'll probably kill you on sight."

David put his hands on Cody shoulders, "Son, you're only fifteen with talents you can't fully control. I'm not planning to leave your side again."

"I was so mad at you." Emotion threatened to choke off Cody's words. "Now I find out you were basically a slave, all this time. Those monsters. I can't lose you again."

David pulled his son into an embrace. Tears came for both. David cradled the back of Cody's head like he was still a little boy. "It will be okay, son."

Cody pulled away with more force than he meant to. "Will it? How can you know that? I'm begging you to stay behind."

"I'm sorry, son. I can't do that."

Cody's tears went dry and he felt the old anger rise in him. He wasn't sure why. He said, "Fine. Whatever. What time do we meet outside the dance tomorrow?"

David said, "Seven."

"Okay. Kinda need to cool off right now."

Cody walked off.

David stared after his son, wondering how anger could affect a person over time. *What have I done to my son?* The old shame of leaving his family crept back into his thoughts, as David used his key card to go back into the room.

As Cody neared his house, he couldn't shake the angry feeling. Then he realized why he was mad. *The brothers. It's their fault.* The familiar knot of anger burned, but it was for them now. He was relieved he didn't have to hate his father anymore.

He went into his house, and walked directly to the garage, finding the hammer from the tool box. He then went into his mom's bedroom. The closet doors were mirrors, and one side was open. Cody assumed she was in a hurry dressing, but one sliding mirror door would do just fine. He concentrated on the old man's face. His own reflection faded and was replaced by the old man's room. *That's getting too easy. Not sure I like that.*

The old man was facing away from Cody, looking out his own window. His head cocked to one side and he swung slowly around to stare at Cody. Cody winced when he saw the old man's ruined eye. *Did Lucas do that on the beach?*

"Is this bravery, or stupidity?" asked the old man, walking down the few steps to get closer to his own side of the mirror.

"I want to make a deal," said Cody. He hoped it sounded brave, but he felt icy fingers play with the nape of his neck.

"That time is over. You can't be trusted."

"Neither can you," Cody replied.

"True."

"Tell the brothers I will join you. But you leave my father alone. Forever." Cody knew what weight the idea of forever held in this new reality.

"Father. Yes, that was a surprise. Two from the same family given powerful gifts from the river. It's very rare, you know. That's why I value the brothers so highly."

"I'll surrender tonight," said Cody, keeping his tone even.

"That's not possible. They will not return to your little town until tomorrow." said Elder Zamma.

Cody didn't want the old man to take control of the conversation. He smiled. "Not powerful enough to get them back here through another mirror?" Cody realized John was right, they were pulled a great distance.

Anger flared in Zamma's good eye. "My private jet is bringing them back. They arrived a mess. But they are fully healed now. And very angry. They will be there soon enough, boy."

He stared at the old man's eye. "Okay... tomorrow, then. 6:30 at the auditorium. But only Derek. I don't trust the German. There's a room in the same building, a dance room. Tell him... do you want to write this down?"

The old man stood very close to his mirror. His good eye bore into Cody. "I'll remember."

"Okay. Do you agree to this... arrangement, then?" Cody hoped he didn't sound like he was reading dialogue from a bad movie script. *I hope this lie works.*

Elder Zamma had wondered how Derek was planning to get any of them alone for the consuming. Now, the boy was creating the perfect trap for himself. "Of course. I'll contact Derek right away. 6:30. It's a date."

The hammer swung and shattered the mirror. Shards big and small rained onto the carpet. A few large pieces stayed in the frame on the sliding door.

On the Elder's side, his mirror had a new crack. "There are easier ways to end the conversation, boy," Zamma said aloud. He imagined how painful the consuming ceremony would be for the teenager. He smiled as he went to his cell phone and called Derek.

Back on Cody's side, he cleaned up the shards. He didn't know how he would explain it to his mom. He would have to invent a good story.

Lying to his mom again made him sad. Not telling her about dad was even harder. He went to his room, got a beer. He hesitated before he popped the top. When he thought of the fight ahead, he gave in and opened the can.

A few swallows later, Cody had drawn the longest knife from the wood block in the kitchen. He hid it in his room. He said aloud, "No one will ever hurt my dad again. By seven o'clock tomorrow, the others will only have the German to worry about."

If Cody's plan worked, Derek would be dead at 6:31.

* * *

Dr. Mason lowered the lights, closed the blinds to his office. The hypnotherapy session began.

"Just listen to the sound of my voice. Nothing else, only my voice. Do you understand?"

"Yes," Lucas answered.

"Okay, I want you to go back a few years. You are going to see everything just the way it happened, but nothing can hurt you. Do you understand?"

"Yes."

"Do you remember the first time being bullied? Go ahead and nod your head if you remember. Yes? Alright. Let's go back to the first time you were bullied. Can you see yourself?"

"Yes."

"How old are you, Lucas?"

"I'm ten."

"Good. Now who is trying to hurt you?"

Lucas spat out the name, "Billy."

"What is Billy doing?"

"He pushed me on the ground. He's sitting on my chest. He's calling me a fag." said Lucas, his voice cracking.

"It's okay. Nothing can hurt you now. Does he do this every day?"

"Yes, but sometimes just with words, insults, like that."

"Let's move ahead to about a year ago. Do you remember being in the hospital?"

Lucas paused before answering, "I don't want to talk about that."

"I know. But you are safe. What happened, Lucas?"

Long pause. "I took pills."

"What kind of pills, Lucas?"

"Aspirin. I swallowed a whole bottle of them."

"Why aspirin?"

"It's the only pill we had a lot of."

"What happened next?" asked the doctor.

"I woke up in the middle of the night. My ears were ringing. I went to my parents' bedroom and told them what I did."

The doctor continued drawing Lucas out, probing for answers. His voice remained calm, controlled. "What happened next?"

"We went to the hospital. The doctor at the hospital gave me something to make me throw up. It tasted really bad. It worked, and I kept puking. Spaghetti tastes disgusting coming back up. And the aspirin burned."

"What next?"

"They pumped my stomach. They put a long tube down my nose all the way into my belly. It hurt."

"How long were you in the hospital, Lucas?"

"A week. They put a tube in my wiener. I stayed in bed to pee. It hurt when they took it out."

"How are you feeling while you're in the hospital?"

"Bad. Sad. My stomach hurts. I have a lot of Jell-O. They keep feeding me lots of Jell-O."

The doctor asked the question he'd been building up to. "Why did you do it, Lucas?"

There was a long pause.

"Do you understand the question, Lucas?"

"There is no hope." Lucas said.

The doctor pondered his response. He didn't want to push the boy in the wrong direction. "Why?"

"There is no way to... untie the knot." His face was troubled. Deep inside, Lucas knew it was important to say the right words. The truth.

"My parents are nice. They can't understand the ugliness. They can't know what it's like. Billy is like a god. The whole school worships him. He..." Lucas trailed off.

"Go on, Lucas."

"He's good at sports, he's good looking. Even the teachers treat him differently. Grownups can't see it; they can't see what he is inside. Day after day this shiny God is calling me names, pinning me to the concrete, pulling my pants down, throwing me in trash cans. Everybody hates me. No one will talk to me. Billy and his gang turn everyone against me. The school God decided I am a fool. I am tainted.

They look away. They all smell death on me. They stay away. They think I will rub the stain on them. They don't want to be punished by a god."

"Is that why you refused to go back to school at first?"

"Yes," Lucas' voice was shaky. "My teachers don't understand. Grownups forget. My parents believe me, but they can't help me. They don't understand casual, everyday violence."

There it was. He stared at the small fifteen-year-old Lucas, and felt there was an old soul in the boy.

"Let's come back to the present now."

"Okay."

"Would you ever hurt yourself again?"

"No."

The doctor closed his eyes. So much time with Lucas, and the boy finally opened up. He could have helped Lucas sooner, if the boy had let him use hypnotherapy as his first tool. This was a special boy, who'd been through some tough things. Sam was just glad he could be a small part of the process.

The tone in Lucas' voice changed, "You've gotten your answers. You have to keep your end of the bargain, Doc."

The doctor's brow furrowed. "Lucas, are you still under, still in your safe place?"

"Yes... and no."

The doctor had never seen a patient float in and out quite like Lucas. He wasn't sure how he was managing it. "I remember the bargain. Why do you want to go back so far into your past?"

"I can't tell you that," said Lucas.

Strange, thought the doctor. "You must be open and honest, Lucas."

"I know. I can feel the change beginning," said Lucas, "It's better to show you. I need to go back. I think I can now."

Lucas was right; any trauma, even the earliest types were best brought to the surface. But the doctor still wasn't sure what Lucas wanted to show him exactly: Lucas' mother and father were lovely, concerned parents. He was sure there hadn't been any abuse, or anything like it.

He wasn't sure what Lucas was after, but he started the process to go back farther. "Okay Lucas. I want you to go way back now. Remember, nothing can hurt you. Do you understand?

"I understand."

"I want you to relax and think very hard to your very first memory. Can you see it in your mind?"

Lucas was quiet for a long time, and his voice thickened as he answered, "Yes. But it's dark."

"Where are you?" asked the doctor.

The deep voice answered, "I don't know, across the water. Father says I need first blood."

First blood? That's strange. Hunting, maybe? the doctor thought. Lucas' dad didn't strike him as a woodsman.

"Look around you. Do you see anything you recognize, Lucas?"

"Who is 'Lucas'? I can't see over the side of the ship."

"You're on a ship. Okay, do you see anything else?"

"I see a dragon," said the deep voice.

"A drawing of a dragon?"

"The front of the ship is a dragon."

Lucas spoke to himself in the new, deeper voice, "Lucas, are you sure you want this?"

Lucas responded in his regular voice, "Yes. I'm ready."

"When we become one, you will change," said the deeper voice again.

Lucas asked in his own voice, "Will I still be me?"

The deeper voice answered, "You will be both. All my memories, all my skills, you will know. Are you certain?"

Through clenched teeth, Lucas' fifteen-year-old voice said, "Yes."

The doctor was beginning to sweat. *Incredible. Schizophrenia? The boy showed no signs of this before.*

Dr. Mason said, "Okay... okay, Lucas, I want you to come back to the present now. When I tell you to wake up, your eyes will open. You will feel calm and refreshed. Do you understand?"

"I do understand," Lucas said, with some semblance of his own voice, but strengthened as though joined by someone else, as if two voices were trying to speak at once.

The doctor wiped his brow. "Okay Lucas, wake up."

Lucas opened his eyes, all tension from his brow gone. He looked around, but it seemed like he was still somewhere in his own mind. Lucas' eyes darted back and forth, like he was seeing amazing things flash before him.

Lucas blinked, and looked at the doctor as if just noticing him.

Dr. Mason stared into the boy's bright blue eyes. He consulted his file and found the general information sheet. *I'm right. His eyes should be green. He looks older, too. What is going on?*

Mason asked, "Lucas, do you remember what we just talked about?"

Lucas stared at Dr. Mason. The surprisingly blue eyes sparkled. Lucas laughed a full-bodied laugh, a deep sound that was out of place for his thin frame.

"Doctor, I remember everything."

CHAPTER TWENTY NINE

THE MORNING OF

Victoria rolled up in front of Zacke's house on Saturday morning, "Okay," she called through the open passenger side window, "now I'm pissed. You got someone to cover your shift tonight, and you continue to blow off my texts."

Zacke stood at the car door, "Not true, I texted you back last night."

Victoria got out her phone and read, " 'Things are crazy, explain later, gotta go.' is not a proper response to twelve texts. I feel like I'm your stalker. Seriously, I almost resorted to calling you." She took a breath. "Get in, kid. I'll take you to your cop school."

"Really? I was sure you'd be too mad to drop me off." Zacke opened the door and got in.

"Close, but your dreamy green eyes are kinda worth it. Yeah, I just used dreamy in a sentence. Deal with it." She took off as soon as Zacke buckled up. "God, I sound like such a girl. Okay, kid, so you get exactly one chance to tell me why you're avoiding me. Be honest, is it because I'm white?"

"No!" yelled Zacke, "Who cares about that crap? My dad's white."

Victoria said, "Okay. Good. What is it, then? I'm not trying to be pushy, but I like you and I hate that whole coy flirting thing. If you don't like me, just be straight."

Zacke sighed. "I do like you. A lot. I will say your bluntness kind of freaks me out sometimes..."

"Ha!" Victoria blurted, "Awesome."

"... this has nothing to do with you. No, wait," said Zacke, "Actually, it does. Because I like you so much, you should stay away from me."

"That makes zero sense," said Victoria, making the last turn headed out of town, up the hill toward the Police & Fire Academy.

Zacke fidgeted with his uniform's tie. "I know it doesn't make sense. If I told you what was happening, you wouldn't believe me. It's not safe to know me right now. Okay, I know that sounds like some movie line that's supposed to make you more into me, but I mean it. I'm just messed up right now; my father drinks because I made my mom leave, which he doesn't even know about. I have no control over what's happening to me, and I'm scared a lot of the time."

Victoria looked over. "Not to be a jerk, but you just described everyone I know. At least, if they could be honest with themselves. Except the thing about your mom. What could you do that would make a mother leave her kid?"

"She saw me do something. It scared her. She freaked out."

"Like psycho stuff?" said Victoria. "Did you kill someone?" Victoria's seemed intrigued, not worried.

"No, nothing like that. It wasn't even bad, just weird..." Zacke paused, "Look, I like you. I don't want to scare anyone else away. If you knew what was really going on..."

"Okay. I'm in." said Victoria.

"No. No..." Zacke shook his head. "...What does that even mean? You don't know what's going on."

They had arrived. She pulled up to the curb. Victoria leaned over and kissed Zacke, then pulled back. "I know people Zacke. You're a good one, you just need a little training from a girl-of-the-world like me. I have feelings about good people. Call it my super power. Whatever's going on, I'm in. Crazy shit, I can definitely handle."

Zacke smiled, despite the looming danger. He did not tell her that was his first real kiss. "You're going to regret this. But I'll tell you what, if I get through this night, I am so going to date the crap out of you."

Victoria smiled back, "I'm holding you to that, kid."

Zacke got out of the car. As she drove off, she said, "And that was a pretty good kiss for your first time."

Zacke smiled. *She knew it was my first kiss.*

Victoria drove away and Zacke went into the presentation. Half an hour had passed when he realized he'd not heard a word, still thinking about Victoria. "Sorry, what does that switch do?" Zacke asked the boy next to him.

Fire Instructor Steve repeated, "Folks, we are only doing this presentation today, so listen up. These switches control the automatic jets for each room of the fire tower. As I've already explained, the seven-story fire tower has individual rooms that mirror real fire situations. Some look like hotel balconies to practice fighting hotel blazes, some look like family living rooms. Others have balconies where we can rappel up and down. These switches can flood each room with fire jets, from pipes mounted to the concrete walls. The fires can either die down on their own, or we can bring up the hoses and use them for practice scenarios. The new camera system can monitor all of it."

Another cadet spoke up, "But we're gonna be cops, why are we even learning the fire side?" It was Billy, who had just moved back and joined up. He stood with another kid Zacke didn't know.

Steve answered, "As I've already stated... seriously folks, you need to listen up, we are cross training in many areas over the next few months. Emergency services work hand in hand. No, you will not be training for fire, but this is a multi-million-dollar tower built for many uses. For instance, police academy members will be training logistics, and crowd control in this tower, not to mention advanced students will be doing hostage scenarios. There are lots of opportunities for both Police and Fire to work together."

Zacke raised his hand, "Sir? Will the interns who have guard duty at night be responsible for guarding this control room, as well as the police side of the campus?"

M.J. Sewall

"Yes, Explorer..." the instructor looked at his name tag. "...Good question, Zacke. The newly assigned teams will be doing guard duty for the entire campus. It will only be for a few hours until regular staff arrive to guard overnight. Your battalion instructor will have all the assignments. There will be sheets for both fire and police sides."

The demonstration went on for the next hour and Zacke tried to concentrate. But with Victoria filling his head, not to mention the looming battle to come, it was no use. He just hoped no one else noticed him zoning out.

After the presentation, they were allowed to split off and look around the campus, or go check their guard assignments for the coming weeks. Zacke looked over the fire tower controls more carefully, as did Billy and his friend.

Billy said, "You're Zacke, right?"

"Yeah." Zacke extended his hand. He assumed Billy would shake, since they'd never formally met. But he just stood there, looking Zacke up and down. Zacke put his hand down.

This close to Billy, Zacke confirmed his original impression; Billy was a total jerk. Zacke got the first flash of someone else's thoughts in a while.

...wonder if they really are gay for each other?

Zacke spoke before Billy could, "Sorry dude, I'm straight. You can stop checking me out."

Billy's face reddened. His friend started laughing, "Hey!" Billy shouted, then realized there were others still hanging around, "Screw you. I know you're gay for that Lucas kid. I saw you guys together."

"Lucas? Yeah, he's a friend," said Zacke. "Billy. There's this thing called projection, when you accuse someone else of something that you yourself gravitate toward. It's cool to come out of the closet, man." This made the friend laugh again, and Billy turn redder.

Billy got in full tough guy mode. He pushed his finger into Zacke's chest, "Watch it kid, or you're gonna get it just like Lucas."

Is Lucas hurt? Zacke would not let this jerk off the hook, especially if he'd hurt his friend. Zacke held up his hands. "Whoa, dude. 'gonna get

231

it?' That sounded kinda gay. It's cool. I'm all for equal rights, nothing to be ashamed of. We welcome openly gay cadets here." Zacke's face was serious, fully of compassion.

Zacke imagined Billy had cartoon steam coming out of his ears. His friend couldn't stop laughing. A few other people noticed, and Billy noticed them noticing.

Billy took a step closer, "That's it. I'll give you two black eyes, right here. I don't care who..."

Zacke shook his head. "Dude, it's okay if you're gay, but *black* eye? We do not tolerate racism in the academy."

Billy's red face changed to one of panic. "Wha... what? No, I didn't mean. I mean, I didn't...."

Zacke said softly, "I'm just gonna walk away now. I won't report you... this time." Billy's friend had walked away in hysterics.

I better text Lucas to see if he's okay. Zacke began to walk away, but the memory of Lucas came back of him, planting the sword into the giant squid.

He turned back to Billy, "Oh, and trust me. You do *not* want to mess with Lucas."

CHAPTER THIRTY

DANGEROUS NIGHT

It was still bright outside, but the day was making the transition toward the dangerous night. Derek and Ehrhardt arrived at the side street before six o'clock.

Ehrhardt insisted, "They won't show. And if they do show, they won't turn, no matter what we threaten."

"Then you will get to destroy them all one by one, then we wait for the next breakout." Derek went to the trunk and got the book.

"Why do you need that?"

"Brother, I have been holding back," announced Derek, "I've been planning a surprise for you. I'll reveal it tonight for your birthday."

"It's not my birthday," said Ehrhardt.

"Not this body's birthday," Derek said, "your first birthday."

"We used the Julian calendar back then. You have to adjust for..."

"My god brother, you ruin everything." Derek closed the trunk and kept the book wrapped in the heavy cloth. "But I am not going to let you spoil my mood. It is going to be a very good night."

"If you say so, brother. I'm still jetlagged from the long flight back."

"I feel refreshed." said Derek. "They will pay for destroying both our portal back, and the rental house. We will not be getting that deposit back. But, we've got the books, we have a plan to punish these cockroaches. Plus, I have that surprise for you."

Ehrhardt frowned. "We've parked two blocks away so they won't see the car. Do you think Cody will really give himself to you?"

"Probably not. But if it's a trick, we'll have been here, waiting, in place and 'ready to pounce', as they say."

"I've never heard that expression," said Ehrhardt.

"You speak as many languages as I do. It means *Bereit zu streiken.*"

"Ready to strike," said Ehrhardt, "Why didn't you just say that?"

"Because I was born American this time. *Gotten heimel*! You're exhausting."

Ehrhardt said, "I will wait at a distance, to make sure they are all there."

"I will go see if Cody is a liar," confirmed Derek. "If he's not, I will bring him to the others."

"What about the consuming? I thought..."

"Part of the surprise! Either way, he will die, then we kill the others together with your scary earthquake power. Then we finally get to have our lives back. This trip has been exhausting."

"Yes, but they will come back eventually, in the future within other bodies," Ehrhardt said. "We have no relic to give them true deaths."

"We can't have everything," said Derek. "This is nearly the end for the Amartus. We will win."

"Then I get my surprise?" asked Ehrhardt.

"Then, Herr Impatient, then you get a big surprise."

Derek reached the auditorium where the dance was to be held. Several people were running around, getting the auditorium ready. He avoided the dance organizers and went to the custodian's office. Understaffed, they had only one custodian to clean up the entire place. The middle-aged man was very surprised when Derek locked the door and strangled him.

He put the body in a corner, and undressed him for his uniform. The room was barely more than a large closet, with shelves and cleaning supplies along one wall. Derek quickly dressed in the uniform, putting his own clothes in the backpack with the book. Derek would wait for Cody.

There was a knock at the door, "Hi. Oh, where's Dan?" said a blond woman in her twenties.

He answered smoothly, "Poor guy started throwing up. I'm the sub. What can I do ya for?"

"I just wanted to remind Dan, um, you," she said, "that cleanup should start around ten or ten thirty, okay?"

"Okey dokey," said Derek, "I'll be here if any kids puke from the spiked punch bowl."

"My god, we know they'll try!" she said, walking away. Derek looked at her backside as she left, but lost interest and went over his plan again.

His brother would be very surprised by what Derek had planned. He walked the hallway in uniform, and checked out the dance room where he was to meet Cody. *Perfect.* He smiled at his own cleverness, and went back to unwrap the spell book. He had a few things to do before Cody arrived.

* * *

John circled the grounds, and did not spot the brothers. But they would be there; if not already, then soon enough. He'd finally heard from Lucas, and confirmed with all the others, so the plan was set. It ended tonight, one way or another.

He picked up the kids one by one, but Cody left a note that he'd meet them there. David didn't like that at all, but he didn't want to make the others more nervous than they already were.

John told them, "Remember, you are all more powerful when you are together. That's what they ultimately fear."

"You make us sound like the Power Rangers," said Katie.

John replied, "I'm not sure I get that reference. Is that from a movie?"

"Never mind," said Katie. "You keep saying that, 'stronger together,' but we still can't hear each other's thoughts. And I can only do big stuff when I'm in danger."

"Everything will change soon." *Hopefully soon,* John thought.

Lucas said, "John and I will be just across the street, watching, ready to come and finish this."

David said, "Be ready for anything."

* * *

Cody walked into the hallway, avoiding the arriving chaperones. Being in sports, he knew his way around most of the buildings on campus. He saw Derek standing in front of the dance room, surprised he was in a janitor uniform.

"6:28. Cutting it close, young sir." said Derek.

Cody noticed Derek had a backpack. *That's not part of the uniform,* he thought.

"Pardon the attire. Easiest way to get the keys." Derek opened the door to the dance room and turned the lights on.

It was a multi-purpose room. The rectangle space would rotate activities daily: some days, mats would be laid out and it was a wresting room, some days it was used for rehearsals for student actors, when it was cleared out it was used for dance. Lit with banks of fluorescent lights above, floor to ceiling mirrors lined one wall. In front of the mirrors were ballet bars. The nickname 'dance room' had stuck.

The door closed behind them. Derek said, "So, what are we really doing..."

Cody slashed the long kitchen knife upward at Derek, who jumped back a moment too slow. It cut one of the shoulder straps to his backpack all the way through.

"Damn, boy. Well I guess that answered my question," said Derek, avoiding a quick slice from Cody. He swung his blade closer.

Derek didn't seem worried, even though he was backing away. Cody jabbed and Derek stepped to one side, using Cody's momentum, he shoved him toward the mirror. His wrist hit a ballet bar. The knife flew from Cody's hand and skidded across the polished wood floor.

Derek knew Cody would go for the knife, so he tripped him and Cody went down with hands splayed. He stepped on Cody's hand.

"Argghh." Cody yelled.

Derek laughed. "This was your big plan?"

Cody's hand felt like it was glued to the floor. Derek stepped harder.

Cody yelled, "I'll kill you! For my father!"

"You've got daddy issues, Cody. I get it," said Derek. "No one knew he was your dad, but him. He lied to all of us."

Cody's anger flared and the fluorescent bulbs above all burst at once. Cody kept his face toward the floor. Derek hunched over and covered himself the best he could. His foot slipped off Cody's hand.

"My god, you've got a weird power. Aahhhrg!" Derek grabbed for his pocket, pulling out his cell phone. It was smoking in his hand. He dropped the worthless phone and rubbed his leg. "That hurt!"

Cody stood, rubbed his hand. He went for the knife on the floor, but Derek ran over the shattered glass to Cody and grabbed him by back of the shirt. "Time to go."

He tried to get free, but Derek rammed him into another dance bar. Derek held up his hand and started speaking in a different set of languages. "Speculo Kinyit La Porte. Speculo Kinyit La Porte. Speculo Kinyit La Porte."

Cody thought he was casting a spell on him, but realized too late where they were going. He tried to grab a ballet bar, but Derek pushed Cody over the bar and through the mirror.

They both arrived in Elder Zamma's room. Derek stood up and brushed himself off, dropping the backpack on the floor. Cody tried to rush for the mirror, but Derek stood in the way and push him back down on the floor. "Sit down, Cody."

Elder Zamma stared at the boy. "Ah, Cody. Is he the first for the consuming?"

Derek bowed deeper than usual, "That was the plan. He said he was going to join us, but he lied. Pulled a knife on me. Which was adorable, and strangely ironic, if he knew what was going to happen next."

Zamma came closer, "You're using too many words again. And the others?"

"In just under twenty minutes, they will all be dead," explained Derek. "A true death, even if I have to use Pentoss' sword on all of them."

"I see. Consuming one will be something, I suppose" said the elder.

"Also, I brought you a present." Derek said as he lifted his backpack onto the table. Cody tried to run for the mirror again, but Derek caught him in the stomach with his fist. Cody doubled over and Derek pushed him onto a chair in a dusty corner, "Sit down, Destroyer of Cell Phones."

Derek unzipped his bag, and drew out the book wrapped in rich, red cloth.

"Finally," Zamma took the book, unwrapped it and set it on his podium. He opened the metal binding and flung open the pages. "You have no idea how important this book is. You've done well, Sazzo. You will be rewarded."

"Thank you, elder." Derek turned to Cody, "You know Cody, this is a very powerful man. His mastery is vast. The elders are few now, but they rule with a fist of steel. Wait, what's stronger than steel? Umm, adamantium? No that's not a real metal... Anyway, you get my point."

Cody said, "Just kill me, so I don't have to listen to another speech."

"Hear that Elder Zamma? A smart ass, even when facing death. I admire that. Well played, sir. So, where was I? Okay, so the elders rule with a steel fist, etcetera. They are in charge, and they give us assignments."

Zamma tried to ignore Derek's prattling, pouring through the book for the consuming spell, "You're making a speech again, Sazzo. Is this going somewhere? You have more people to kill."

"Exactly!" exclaimed Derek. "If I give someone a true death, they never move on. The ancient warrior dies along with their body. But something else happens. Can you guess what?"

Cody stared, "It causes bad guys to make long speeches?"

Derek laughed, moving around the room. The quip got Zamma's attention and he turned to the boy, "Too bad you have to die, boy. That was actually amusing."

"It was. Funny at my expense, sure. But I live to serve," said Derek. "No, it's about the River. All knowledge, power, everything flows from the River, returns to the River. But if you use a relic, the powers of the person you kill doesn't go back to the River, no. It becomes yours. I'll bet Pentoss, John, whatever, didn't tell you that. It takes time to wield these new powers. You have to learn to master it, kind of like you're doing now with that weird shock power you have."

"There's a spell missing," said Zamma, flipping through pages.

Derek seemed shocked, "What? Are you sure?"

"Yes. It's been taken out very carefully, with a sharp blade."

"Great," Derek said. "Those Sect jerks probably did it. You'd think they would respect the stuff they steal."

Cody eyed the mirror again. Derek saw him. "No, no. Wait, Cody. This is the best part. The powers don't come automatically, you see. At the same time, you need a relic *and* the right spell to take these powers."

Something occurred to Zamma. He hurriedly turned to the back cover of the book. The metal binding was present, but there was a large piece missing. A very important piece.

Derek shouted "Potestatum Niri!" and leapt at his elder.

The elder turned to attack, but Derek pushed the relic knife deep into the elder's chest. Derek kept speaking the spell, "Potestatum Niri! Potestatum Niri!" sliding the knife in and out of his elder.

It was too late to fight back. Derek finished the spell and carefully folded the page he'd cut out of the book. He used a cloth from his janitor's uniform to wipe the blood from his hands. Elder Zamma fell backwards on the floor, dead. A fine green mist left his body and swirled around Derek.

Derek smiled. He was already removing the blood-soaked janitor's uniform. He continued drinking in the green power, "You'd better run back to your friends now, boy. I'll be there soon..."

Cody was already sprinting for the mirror, hoping whatever talent he had didn't fail him now. He leapt through the mirror and came out into the dance room, forgetting there were bars at the height of his stomach. Cody hit one and flipped onto the dance floor, crunching in the fine fluorescent glass. He was on his feet quickly, brushing glass off his hands and clothes. He ran for the others as fast as he could.

* * *

Outside, Ariana looked at her phone. "It's nearly seven. Where are Cody and Lucas?"

"Where are the brothers?" asked Zacke.

"I am here," Ehrhardt said as he walked up, "But several of you are missing, so now you all die."

Cody ran out of the side door. His face was pale and sweaty, "I'm here. There's..."

Ehrhardt said, "Still one short. Time to die." He leaned down to touch the ground.

"Touch the earth and I'll pull your arms off." The voice came from behind Ehrhardt. Lucas stood there, but everyone could see he was more than Lucas. His face and body looked the same, but everyone could tell he had changed. The ancient warrior stood before them, fully activated.

Cody yelled, "Guys! We gotta go. Derek killed this elder guy. He says he got all his power."

"What?" asked John.

David whispered, "It's not possible."

"You lie! Sazzo would never kill an elder," shouted Ehrhardt.

Another strange voice surprised them all. "Hey. Folks. You can't be here." It was a security guard hired for the homecoming dance. His blue outfit was marked "Ocean Security."

John said, "It's alright. We were just..."

Before John could finish, the double doors at the back of the auditorium burst off their hinges and flew outward. One door hit the security guard, knocking him to the ground, unconscious.

Derek, who looked the same, was much more. He nearly glided toward them, and the smile on his face froze Ariana's blood. Even to Ehrhardt, his voice sounded strange.

Derek announced, "I bet you're wondering why I asked you all here tonight..." he laughed. "I've always wanted to use that line. Caron, could you please kill them all? I'm still getting used to all the power. Zamma was even stronger than I thought."

Ehrhardt stared, "Brother, what have you done?"

"Don't get all 'emo,'" said Derek, "you hated Zamma as much as I did. Now we're finally free."

Ehrhardt hesitated.

Ariana stared at Derek. "Guys, why does he look like that?"

"Like what?" asked Katie.

"You know how I can see your shields' colors?" said Ariana, "He's almost glowing. Like radioactive."

John looked from Derek, back to Ariana. His relic sword was drawn.

"No earthquake?" Derek said, "Alright brother, let's see what I just inherited."

Ariana and Cody saw something coming at them when Derek put his arms out, but they all felt the wave as it sailed past them. The tree closest to them shattered, its thick trunk exploding into splinters. The top of the tree fell, and barely missed the group as it toppled.

Derek laughed again, "That was awesome! Zamma was a bad ass."

The blast had knocked them all off their feet. They slowly got back up, but they were frozen with fear. Zacke looked to John and Lucas, but even they seemed unable to move. He scanned wildly and spotted the hill at the entrance to their town. He got an idea. A crazy idea.

Zacke shook his head, trying to push out the fear. He asked "Katie, can you make a shield like a full circle around all of us? Like a bubble?"

"I guess, but it won't help us against that," Katie pointed at Derek. He smiled back at her as he walked closer.

"Just do it. I'll do the rest," Zacke stepped away from the group.

Derek looked more puzzled than worried, amused by their next move. Ehrhardt still stared at his brother in disbelief.

"Get inside the shield!" shouted Zacke.

Katie asked, "What about you?"

Zacke replied, "I'm staying outside of it. Now, Katie!"

They all stepped close to Katie and she threw up her shield all around them, concentrating on making a sphere.

Zacke had never tried anything like this. The wash of shame that always accompanied his deep hidden talent was overtaken by the urgency of the moment. *I must do this.*

He grabbed the shield, from what felt like the bottom, lifting it like it was a huge ball. A warmth overcame every muscle, and he lifted all of them. The earth and grass the six people were standing on was trapped inside the bubble-like shield.

Slowly, Zacke shouldered the weight.

Then, he left the earth.

Zacke took flight, like gravity no longer existed. The six were secured inside the shield, and lifted into the air. He strained like never before, and a fierce yell escaped him as he took flight, expending more energy than he ever thought he had. Accelerating into the night, it became easier as they went higher, feeling just like the first flying dreams Zacke ever had.

After only a few minutes, Derek and Ehrhardt couldn't see them. The brothers stood silent, gaping at the sky.

"I wasn't expecting that," said Derek.

"He can fly?" said Ehrhardt, "I've never heard of an ancient that could fly."

"He's one of the new births," said Derek. "This could change everything."

"What do you mean?"

Derek showed his brother the dagger he'd used on Zamma. "This is a relic. With a spell I just learned, when I kill him with this, I get his powers."

"Where did you get that?" asked Ehrhardt.

"It was part of the metal binding on the back of the book. Zamma wanted it for the spells, but he'd momentarily forgotten the other reason it was important."

Ehrhardt still seemed confused.

Derek explained. "This relic knife was built into the binding."

"What do we do now?"

Derek noted the direction they were headed, up the hill to the entrance of the city. He saw a red blinking light in the distance; like a light that's used on tall objects so aircraft won't hit them.

Derek smiled, "I think I know where they're going."

CHAPTER THIRTY ONE
ACADEMY

Zacke set them down on the edge of the campus, just inside the grounds of the police and fire academy. As he set down the shield sphere, Katie let it fade away. They all fell to the ground. The mound of earth that was lifted with them inside the sphere crumbled under their feet. Zacke and Katie both breathed heavily as they all laid on the ground.

Lucas was the first to speak, "Okay, you can *fly*?"

Zacke was still out of breath. The immense strain of using the talent he'd rarely indulged, made every muscle ache. Between breaths he managed, "I don't like to use it. I'm not proud of it."

"You're not proud you can fly?" said Ariana. "Are you kidding me?"

"It's caused..." breath. "...trouble." breath. "My mom. Well, she went crazy when she found out." Zacke's heavy breathing gave way to crying. He didn't know if it was the adrenaline, the stain of using his main talent for so long, or the relief of confession. He sobbed, "She became a religious nut. Found a church with crazy beliefs, like cult stuff. Left our family when dad wouldn't believe her. She called me..." he sobbed, "she thinks I'm a demon."

"Oh my... your mother called you that?" asked Katie.

David said, "I'm so sorry Zacke."

"You should never feel ashamed of your talents," said John.

John comforted him. Zacke sobbed for a few minutes, exhausted. "Sorry."

"It's alright." John said, "But trouble is still coming. They will find us, and probably soon. Sazzo acquiring an elder's talents is very bad news."

Zacke wiped his face, shook off the tears. David helped him stand.

"But Derek can still die, right?" asked Cody.

John nodded. "Yes, he's still a man, just a very powerful one. It won't be easy to destroy him."

"How about fire?" Zacke pointed to the seven-story fire tower that dominated the campus.

"That's why you brought us here?" asked David.

"Yes," said Zacke, finally catching his breath. "If we can get them both anywhere inside that tower, I can turn on flames from the control panel."

"Fire will definitely kill their bodies. It will be tricky to get both brothers in there. You know how to work the controls?" asked John.

Zacke nodded. "Pretty much. I'm an Explorer here. We got trained today."

"Is there security?" asked David.

"They use two student trainees to walk the grounds until the regular security guy gets here at ten," Zacke explained. "We'll have to deal with them somehow."

John said, "David and I will do that. I assume there are cameras. You all might be recognized."

"No time to make masks." Katie blurted.

Ariana smiled. "Katie, only you could make superhero jokes at a time like this."

Katie shrugged.

John looked around at the environment, making quick plans in his head. "We'll make sure any guards are restrained without being hurt. I saw another area flying in that looked interesting. I'll make a backup plan if we have to separate the brothers."

"Good, then I'll get the tower going," said Zacke.

Katie asked, "How do we get them into the tower?"

"I've got some ideas." Zacke smiled.

* * *

The brothers had parked the car blocks away from the dance, but they hadn't counted on the heavy traffic around the event, students arriving and being dropped off. Police had been called after the exploding doors had been reported. An ambulance was there, presumably for the guard hit by the flying door. A yellow tape caution perimeter was set around the shattered tree. The brothers weren't worried about the authorities, since they had withdrawn and got to their car quickly. The enemy now, was traffic.

Derek said, "This is going to take forever."

Ehrhardt said, "How could you do it? He was our *elder*. This is unforgivable."

"Relax," answered Derek, "Zamma was a miserable old sow who was hiding in his little room. He deserved to lose his powers."

"And the others?" asked Ehrhardt. "The other elders will not abide this. They will send everyone after us, maybe come for us themselves."

"Since when are you afraid of anyone, brother?"

Ehrhardt answered, "Since you broke the oldest law we have."

Derek said, "If you hadn't noticed, we're the bad guys. Revel in that. Rules don't apply to us."

"It is not that simple." Ehrhardt shook his head. "We are the ones that keep order, control. It's not bad to want control, but even we must abide by some structure. The Amartus has always wanted this peace, love and happiness garbage, while fighting battles with us. They are hypocrites. We deserve to rule. But we must stay in the shadows."

"Our elders keep saying that. Why hide? We should be announcing our power to the world. This could be our world, brother, in the open. You want order? How about I rule and you keep the order. We could be gods on earth, like we are meant to be."

Ehrhardt stared at his brother, "Zamma's power has made you mad. I had no idea you felt this way. I knew you were unhappy, so was I. But this? None of this will end well."

"Well, first things first. After we get out of this RIDICULOUS TRAFFIC," Derek shouted in frustration, "We will head up the hill to that academy, kill them all. Then from the hill, you can wipe out the town."

"Why destroy the town now?" Ehrhardt threw up his hands.

"This sleepy little place had a station and a breakout of five potential Amartus, including new births, one of which can *fly!* We need to make sure nothing ever grows here again. We destroy this city and seed it with salt."

Ehrhardt thought of all the killing he'd done in this life; the heavy burden he would pay in the next one. But his brother had made sure the night would only get harder. He saw a break in the traffic, pulled illegally into the bike lane, and finally sped toward the edge of town.

* * *

On the academy grounds, Billy was the first one to see the unauthorized person on the monitor.

"I'll call it in," said Joey, the other student guard on duty.

Billy disagreed. "No. We can handle this. Too bad the armory is locked up, but we have these." He indicated his belt, club and pepper spray canister. "There's only one of them. Don't you want to test our training?"

Joey shook his head. "We should call it in. You know we aren't authorized to use this stuff."

"Stop acting like a big fat vagina," said Billy. "Let's go."

Joey threw up his hands and surrendered to Billy's will.

Billy looked at the monitor again. "Wait. I know him." He smiled cruelly. "This night just got a lot more fun."

There were doors at either side of the small room that contained the main control panel and monitors. Joey went out the left door. Billy was just reaching for his radio when he saw Joey taken by a man in a black shirt. Another man with a sword strapped to his back came for him. Forgetting his courage, Billy ran out the right door.

Billy realized the mistake of not grabbing the radio as he fled. There was more than one guy after all, and they had taken over the control room. *Who are these guys? Why take over a deserted training center? Why is Lucasfilm with them?*

Lucas and Zacke were standing around the corner of another building. They were out of camera coverage when they saw the young guard run by them. "One got away," said Zacke.

"I'll get him," said Lucas. He ran after the boy and caught up to him around the next building. "Stop!"

Billy turned around and faced Lucas with pepper spray in hand, but relaxed when he recognized him. "Oh, it's just you. Who are your friends, Lucasfilm?"

"Of course it would be you," said Lucas. "Billy, you need to leave. It's not safe."

Billy laughed and replaced the pepper spray on his belt. He drew his club, "I don't even need this, but it will make it more fun." Billy came closer.

"You really don't want to do this," Lucas resisted the urge to simply let the warrior rise within him. He knew he could take Billy in a fair fight, ancient or not. *I just need to be careful not to kill him. Remain in control. Okay, maybe I'll let myself break one arm...*

From behind Lucas, a blue light appeared. It slowly got brighter and took shape. It formed two archways, with a square space in between. They were not of solid form, only blue glowing outlines of a shape. From the empty center, a man and woman appeared with weapons in their hands.

Lucas saw Billy's face change, and knew that Billy realized this was no pretend magic trick. Lucas spun around.

"And who are you, boy?" asked the male. He was dressed in black. Athletic shoes. The weapon in his hand was a curved blade, a katana.

Lucas's ancient awoke, and they spoke with one voice, "No one you want to mess with, little man."

The female was also dressed in black, a short sword in hand. "That's not very nice. We're here for the elder-killer."

"Go back through your little hole," said Lucas, his ancient's voice strengthening his own, "this is our fight."

"You sound activated, despite your scrawny frame," the female said as she and her companion went in opposite directions and tried to flank Lucas. "Who are you really, little guy?"

"I'd be happy to show you," said Lucas. "Let the boy behind me go. He's a little monster, but he's not involved with this. Then we can have our dance."

The male said, "Sorry, no witnesses, no survivors."

"Then you'll need more than two," said Lucas.

"We don't even need our elder. She's about to walk through that gate, by the way."

His inner warrior sighed. Lucas realized, *Now I have to protect this little shit.* He turned to Billy and said, "Last chance to run."

"Hell, no!" Billy had been in shock for a few seconds, but now he raised his club. "I'll take all three of you down."

Lucas shook his head and thought about releasing the blood rage. He decided he could take these two without it. A smile came to his lips as both opponents attacked.

The two attackers were so fast that Billy couldn't follow them. But Lucas was faster. He ducked under the curved blade and came up, slamming his head under the man's chin. The man's head snapped back and Lucas twisted the man's wrist, relieving him of his blade, flipping him on his back.

His opponent was surprised, and laid on the concrete. The woman disengaged, went for Billy instead.

Billy came down with his club, but the woman cut it in two with her short blade. Billy froze, but Lucas was already on his way. He rammed into the woman just before her short sword came down on Billy's skull. The blow made the slice miss and she and her sword slammed into the wall.

Lucas yelled, "Should've run!"

She was back on her feet, and the man joined her. They fanned out again and the man went for Billy. Lucas knew he had to get Billy to safety. He was slowing down the fight. He dropped his newly acquired blade, and grabbed Billy by the waist. He spun around, and at the same time threw Billy like he was a plastic mannequin.

Billy went flying twelve feet in the air. He came down and landed on the roof of the one story building next to them.

The man dove for his blade, grabbed it, and sliced at Lucas. Lucas ducked and leapt into the man before he could swing again. Lucas punched the man's wrist, and heard bones crack. The man screamed, and Lucas caught the blade. In one continual motion, he brought the blade back down, slicing along the man's forearm.

Lucas stepped away and kicked the man in the gut. He went sprawling back.

The woman was already charging Lucas. He sunk to his haunches and her swinging blade went over his head. With one hand, he punched her shin. A loud crack resounded. With his other hand, he caught her ankle with his blade, the gash very deep. She wailed and fell to the pavement.

Before Lucas could put an end to them with his blade, the gate glowed a brighter blue and a middle-aged woman walked out. She had short grey hair, and was dressed in a dark suit. The blue lines reflected off her mirror-finished black flats.

Lucas squinted his eyes. "Elder Ordway."

The elder cocked her head to one side, and saw the condition of the two warriors. She sighed. "The Viking, right? Been a long time. I thought you got a true death. What an unfortunately small body you got this time."

Lucas stood. "You need to hire better fighters. Just about to kill these two."

Elder Ordway looked at them on the ground, "So I see." Her eyes flared blue and both warriors were pulled back into the gate as though sucked into a void. From their screams, it sounded like a painful journey.

Lucas said, "We have no issue with you, Elder Ordway. We both want the brothers dead. Help us and then we can part ways."

She seemed to consider it for a fraction of a second, "No." The elder's eyes glowed blue again.

"What the hell is happening?" Billy said from the roof.

Lucas shouted, "Get off that roof, and run!"

Billy finally got the hint. He saw the middle-aged woman's eyes turn blue. He ran for the other side of the roof. Billy made it to the ladder. Overhead, Lucas sailed into the air and over the rooftop.

CHAPTER THIRTY TWO
THE TOWER

Ariana, Katie and Cody reached the tower. They couldn't see any way up, no exterior staircase, so they tried the first door they came to. The plain door was locked. There was a rope hanging on the exterior wall, but they went around the corner, to the next side of the square building. This time, the door opened. The interior lights were all off in the concrete building, and the smell of smoke permeated.

Only by faint safety light, they saw that there was an open concrete stairwell leading up. They started to climb. There were openings like windows at regular intervals, at each landing. There was no glass, just a rectangle concrete opening. They stopped at the first one and looked out.

"Is that Lucas?" said Ariana.

They all looked out and saw him flying through the air.

"Yeah, it is." said Katie.

The outdoor campus was lit by lampposts at regular intervals, illuminating the series of one-story buildings below them. They watched Lucas land on one roof, jump to the next building, and deftly land on the third, narrowly avoiding the large equipment sitting on the flat roof. He almost didn't make the last building, but he tucked his head in and rolled onto the roof. The shoulder roll completed, he continued rolling until he was on his feet and running again, all in one swift motion. He ran toward the tower, flipped off the roof and hit the pavement like he was a trained acrobat.

"Did any of you know he could do that?" asked Cody.

"No. How did he get airborne in the first place?" asked Katie.

As she asked, a well-dressed middle-aged woman came into view. She casually looked around the unfamiliar academy.

Ariana asked, "Who is that?"

Cody said, "I think she might be an elder. She looks as nasty as the one I saw."

As though the woman heard Cody, she looked at them.

Ariana let out an involuntary squeak. "Yeah, she's glowing just like Derek."

"One German monster and two elders to fight?" asked Katie.

Ariana shook her head, "I hope Zacke's plan can handle another bad guy."

"Bad girl? Bad lady...?" Cody looked at the new elder through the opening. The elder looked back.

"Let's get higher," said Katie.

They kept climbing. Lucas arrived, trying the locked door first. He went around and found the way in. He raced up the stairs to join them. The elder casually strolled toward the tower.

As the three climbed and rounded each landing, they peered out the opening. The elder was still in no hurry.

Ariana said, "I think I'd be less worried if she was running."

Lucas caught up to them on the fourth landing. He'd let the warrior dive deep within him, saving him for later.

The elder was nearly to the tower entrance.

Lucas said, "She's not kidding around. I hope Derek and that elder will kill each other, before we have to deal with her."

"That'd be nice. Because I am freaking out right now," Katie added.

Ariana said, "We all are."

"Looks like the brothers made it to the party." Cody pointed to the parking lot in the distance. They had just parked.

* * *

In the control room, Zacke pointed to the brothers on the security camera, aimed at the parking lot, "There they come. Should we just let the new elder take care of them? That's what she's here for, right, to punish the brothers?"

"Yes. But anywhere an elder goes, trouble follows," said John.

David added, "Elders don't like witnesses, either. Secrecy is their favorite weapon. We're in much more danger now."

John pointed to a camera, "What is that area?"

"Concrete training tunnels. They can be flooded for different types of training." explained Zacke.

David asked, "What about those grates above them?"

"Can be lifted for evacuation, underground rescue scenarios, other stuff."

John nodded. "Okay. We'll split them up. David and I will take care of big brother. You get ready to hit the controls when the other brother is in the tower."

"Got it," said Zacke.

David and John left the building. They headed to where the brothers and the elder would intersect.

* * *

The brothers both saw the middle-aged woman. The elder stopped when she saw the two.

As she changed course, Ehrhardt whispered, "I told you. We are both dead."

Derek spoke as though he was meeting an old friend, "Elder Ordway!" He and Ehrhardt bowed to the elder. "What brings you out on this fine night?"

"To punish law breakers." the elder said, a blue glint in her eye.

"Wait, please," said Derek. "Before you get all judgey, you need to know something. We found the stolen Vitaeizicon. Elder Zamma told me that he was going to use a certain spell to kill both you and Elder Sorrento. He planned to take your powers."

"That spell is a myth, and your lies are clear as glass," her eyes flared blue, but Derek took out an envelope.

"This is the spell. A gift," Derek handed the envelope over.

The elder's eyes returned to normal, and she opened the envelope. Ordway read the spell that Derek had cut from the book earlier, then folded it, placing it safely in her coat pocket. "You think I won't kill you for breaking the ancient law and taking this spell?"

"You might," said Derek, "but I know you are the most honorable elder we've had in centuries. I propose a deal."

Ordway commanded, "Speak."

"We become your right and left hand. I have proven my loyalty by destroying the man who plotted against you..."

Ordway interrupted, "By breaking the law."

"Yes, I broke a law! But you are the maker of laws. There are only three of you left now. Then you kill Sorrento, and we go after the last elder. With that spell, you will get their powers and rule as the single elder, as it was in the beginning. You will also have us by your side, with a right hand that is as powerful as an elder, loyal only to you."

Ehrhardt was distracted. They all looked over to the next building. John was casually leaning on a wall, motioning for Ehrhardt to come over.

Ehrhardt fumed at the bravado, "Little brother. Can I go kill him now?"

"Sure," Derek said, "we can handle the rest. Do we have a deal, Elder Ordway?"

Silence hung in the night. John cleared his throat for attention, to annoy Ehrhardt further. It worked. Ehrhardt seethed.

The elder ignored the scene and looked only at Derek, "Deal. If your boldness doesn't get you killed tonight."

Derek said, "Go. Have fun, brother."

The elder and Derek casually walked to the tower. Ehrhardt followed John, who smiled and ran away as the German pulled his silencer-equipped pistol.

John led Ehrhardt around a series of buildings. Ehrhardt never had a clear shot, so he simply followed, looking forward to a kill he could do up close. He always kept multiple weapons hidden on his person, just in case an opportunity for fun presented itself.

John entered a concrete tunnel. Ehrhardt noticed the metal grates above the tunnel. He followed John into a maze of concrete passages, all with metal grates above, the only inlet of light. There were a few metal ladders at regular intervals. Ehrhardt assumed the tunnels were for police or fire training. *Perhaps urban hostage scenarios,* he thought.

He found John in a large, square section, a few steps lower than the rest of the tunnels. The shadows through the metal grates, cast John's face in a strange light. Ehrhardt assumed it was a trap, but by the look of it, a poor one.

Ehrhardt went down on one knee and retrieved a long knife strapped to his leg. "I want to do this up close."

John said across the room, "Come on over, and we can finish this. You and me."

Ehrhardt walked slowly to his opponent's side of the room, "My knife is no relic, so I must take your blade and give you a true death."

John shook his head, "You were never that good up close, Caron. You always liked your arrows, crossbows, guns. Cowards need distance."

"I've trained hard. Been a while since we tangled," Ehrhardt paused. "Hard to believe we were ever friends."

"Many lifetimes ago," said John, and drew the relic sword from the sheath. "This one will be your last."

They walked toward the middle of the room, when water started to trickle in and fill the sunken space.

Ehrhardt laughed. "This is your trick? I can kill you wet or dry."

They engaged, Ehrhardt attacking first. The German rushed forward and slashed. John dodged, but did not attack. The water was a few inches, and slowed their footwork. John kept dodging, backed away, used his longer blade to keep distance. He blocked every slash and thrust of Ehrhardt's knife.

Ehrhardt stopped, backed up. He bent down to get his second knife from the other leg. He stood and looked at John. "You're not trying very hard."

John smiled in response. Ehrhardt charged with a yell, slashing faster than John had expected. The yell bounced around the concrete room as John parried his sword to avoid both blades.

Ehrhardt feigned a lunge at John, but pulled back at the last second. He kicked John's knee and heard a sickening crack. John screamed in pain, but didn't go down. He hopped on his good leg as he countered the next attack.

Ehrhardt rushed in a volley of slashes. They were powerful, and John had to fight to stay upright. His fast sword parried the attacks, but just barely.

The powerful slashing attacks were wearing out Ehrhardt's shoulders. His attacks came slower, easier to knock away with John's sword, even on one leg.

The water was up to their shins now, slowing them both. Then the water stopped. John retreated, hopping toward a wall.

"Is this your big move?" Ehrhardt breathed hard, his arms sore. "Slow me down with water? Wear me out?"

The grate above Ehrhardt was lifted up and away.

"No. This is." John leapt onto the wall mounted ladder, safely out of the water.

David appeared above.

"Now!" John yelled.

David said, "Witness this," as white lightning erupted from the sky and shot down into Caron, standing in over a foot of water.

The electric shock made Ehrhardt gyrate for a few seconds. John stayed on his ladder and shielded his eyes from the bright, dancing light. After a moment, Ehrhardt lay face down in the pool, dead. The lightning faded.

David looked at his tormenter's body. John was slowed by his injured knee, but climbed up the ladder and stood next to David.

"I could have given him a true death with this." John put his sword back in the sheath.

David stared down at Ehrhardt's body, knowing that he might have to face him again in another life, "It had to be me."

John sighed. "Unfortunately, he was the easy one."

* * *

"No!" Derek shouted, a flash of his brother came; lying in a concrete room filled with water.

Derek blinked wildly, hot anger flashing. Elder Ordway clamped her hand down on Derek's shoulder. "Stop."

"They killed my brother!" Derek raged.

"You have experienced his death many times before. Focus. With these new powers, you are unstable. Your emotions will make it harder to control them."

"I'll try." Derek had no intentions of taking orders from another elder. But he would bide his time until he could kill her. He focused on getting to the vexing teens.

Ordway changed the subject. "Why is there a tower like this, here of all places?"

"Fire and police training of some sort. I haven't had time to soak up all the local flavor."

They were on the second-floor landing inside the fire tower, heading upwards. Ordway said, "Well, it will be simple enough to throw them off the roof. Seems a bit too easy."

Derek looked around, "It does, doesn't it?" The elder was right. There would be time to mourn later. He thought of his brother. *Well, there's always a next time, brother. Sleep well.*

He noticed the strange series of pipes all around. Each level was a collection of rooms. Some were bare concrete rooms; others were fully furnished. This one looked like a hotel room, that one arranged like a family living room.

The elder guessed, "These rooms must be for urban assault training? Hostage maneuvers?"

"From the smell of it, fire training as well." It was dark, except for the safety lights. When they reached the fourth floor, the stairway ended, and they had to walk among the rooms to find the stairway on the other side of the building. They would soon reach the troublesome teens.

* * *

"Come on, come on," said Zacke. His fingers were on the computerized controls. He'd programmed the whole fourth floor to fill with fire. At least, he thought he did. He chided himself for not paying more attention in the training session. He hoped John was right, that fire would do the trick.

On the camera, they were rounding the stairs up to the third floor, when Billy burst in, "Zacke?"

"Not now, Billy."

Billy said, "You're with them? Step away from the panel, Zacke."

"Billy, you have no idea what's going on."

"I know you're betraying your brothers in the Explorers."

"If I don't do this," said Zacke, his hands still on the controls, "everyone in our town is going to die."

Billy reached for his club, but remembered it was in pieces on the campus grounds.

The cameras showed Derek and the elder on the fourth floor, in the perfect spot. Zacke was about to press the button, when the door behind Billy opened. Zacke turned his head. As he did, Billy released his pepper spray.

Zacke fell from his chair, screaming. David and John had opened the door, and now subdued Billy. David used Billy's own zip ties to bind his hands.

Remembering his training, Zacke tried not to rub his eyes. They had told them what it felt like, and some of the older officers had been pepper sprayed so they could describe it. Zacke could barely think. The pain was excruciating. He yelled out again.

John grabbed a bottle of water and poured it over Zacke's eyes. It helped a little. Zacke tried not to scream again.

David gagged and subdued Billy in the small cleaning closet with the other boy, then went to the control panel. He had no idea how to manage the controls, it might as well have been in a different language. He glanced at the cameras and saw that the elder and Derek were on the fourth level, only three levels away from the roof, where the others were waiting.

"We have to get up there!" yelled David.

"I know. Zacke, I know it hurts but can you tell me how to work this?"

Zacke tried to open his eyes, but he couldn't. Tears poured down his face. "God, it hurts."

David guided Zacke to the small bathroom and helped him furiously wash out his eyes. Zacke knew the effects of pepper spray could last hours. He hoped he hadn't got a full blast.

John said, "I'll never make it with my knee, up all those stairs. Here," he handed David his blade, "help them. Go save your son."

David left without hesitation, but as soon as he was running for the tower, he was racked with doubt. The years of enslavement had weakened him. Hopefully his resolve would compensate for that. He would do anything to save his son.

John stared at the complex control board and glanced up at the cameras. The elder and her new friend Derek had reached level five. John hoped he could at least slow them down. He recalled Zacke saying the roof of the tower was safe, so he couldn't injure the kids by accidentally starting a fire up top. He would just have to wing it.

John looked over the controls for the number five and started pressing buttons.

* * *

In the tower, some lights came on. The elder remarked again how strange the tower was, with the random room configurations. She seemed fascinated by everything. The last two levels they climbed had offset stair wells, forcing them to zig-zag across the entire floor to find the next stairwell. They were still in the center of level five when fire erupted from the pipes.

Instantly, the room was engulfed in flames. They saw the only exit and ran for it quickly, narrowly escaping the flames. When they hit the next room, the smoke followed them.

Coughing through the heavy smoke, they stumbled to the next room, as flames shot from the ceiling pipes above them.

"This way!" screamed Derek, seeing another exit sign.

They escaped to the next room and found the stairwell. They paused to catch their breath, coughing and sputtering.

Derek looked out the window-like opening and saw David running toward the tower, the relic sword in his hand. Derek pushed out his hands and a large section of the concrete wall exploded outward.

* * *

Down below, David neared the tower, when a huge section of concrete exploded, raining down in front of him.

David shielded his eyes from the concrete dust, narrowly avoiding a large chuck. He shook his head and cleared his vision. The door he'd been running for was now completely blocked by concrete. He went around the building, but the other door was locked tight. David looked up and realized there was no way for him to reach the top.

* * *

On the monitor, John saw David's problem and kept pressing buttons on the next three levels. But David had the only relic, and he was now unable to reach the others. He needed some way to get to the top before Derek and the elder reached the others.

He went to Zacke, who still couldn't see. He explained the bold new plan.

Zacke said, "That's crazy. I can't..."

"Yes, you can. We have to, or they win, and everyone dies."

Zacke blinked furiously, but it still hurt to open his eyes. "Okay, okay. Let's do it."

* * *

Derek and the elder had reached the sixth level of hell. Fire swirled all around them from random commands John had given the system.

"Enough of this!" shouted Ordway, and Derek felt the air vibrate. Water exploded all around them. Derek was knocked to the ground and doused. He was pushed by the rush of water toward a wall. He noticed with alarm that there were large rectangle holes at the bottom of the walls, presumably to let water drain out.

The water drained away, and Derek stopped just before his leg caught in the water relief hole.

Some of the fire jets still tried to spit flames, but the drench of water overloaded the systems. Derek was stunned. He stood on soggy legs.

"You will be capable of such things, and more," said Ordway, "once you've mastered your new powers."

The elder helped Derek to his feet and they continued to the roof.

When they arrived, Cody, Katie, and Ariana were standing far apart from one another at the far side of the roof. Derek gave them a quizzical look. Cody yelled, "Now!"

Katie threw her shields. This time, they all saw the colors as they flew. She made them into self-contained balls and hurled them at Derek and the elder as fast as she could. But they seemed to veer off, harmlessly going around them.

"That was adorable." laughed Derek.

Ariana tried to freeze them. She focused, her hands in front of her, but the elder swept her hand, and they kept walking. It was as though the elder had raised her own invisible shield.

Digging deep, Ariana imagined their stomachs turning inside out. Derek got a strange look on his face, grabbing his stomach automatically, but the elder stepped in front of him. Ariana felt like someone had thrown cold water into her mind.

Cody had hoped the girls could at least buy time. He knew his talents were useless on the roof, only concrete. No electronics, no mirrors. From behind Derek, a wild cry came from Lucas. He rushed them. Ordway spun around. Her eyes flashed blue. Lucas was airborne again, spiraling toward his friends. He hit the concrete roof just in front of Cody.

Derek smiled, "That's all you got? Wow. Sad. The fire on the way up was a nice touch, but we both have the powers of elders. You know, I really hoped I could convince at least one of you to join the winning team, but nope. Now you all die right here. I should probably thank you. The fire gave me a good idea. Let's have some more fire, shall we?"

Ordway stared, "Do you always talk this much?"

Derek ignored her and closed his eyes. "I've always wanted to conjure one of these things. Azdaja Trylle Mihi. Azdaja Trylle Mihi. Azdaja Trylle Mihi." The elder smiled, apparently guessing what was coming. The four teens looked around, but saw nothing appear.

Then the tower shook.

The teens ran to each other. They abandoned their plan to stay separate. They had decided fanning out would keep them safer, four targets instead of one. Now, fear brought them together. They realized no one was going to help them. They were on top of a seven-story fire tower on the edge of town. Derek and the Elder blocked the only stairway. There was no way down.

Their only tricks had failed. Cody thought furiously, but nothing came. Katie tried to will her ancient warrior to wake up, do something, but all she felt was fear. Lucas knew brute strength was useless against this powerful magic. Ariana looked around, hoping for someone to rescue them, thinking, *help, help, help.*

The tower shook again. It was rhythmic, like footsteps. Then, an enormous head rose over the edge, opposite from where the teens were standing, looming between the elder and Derek. Next, two giant claws gripped the edges of the roof. The dragon unfurled its leathery wings on either side. It dwarfed the tower.

The dragon's scales were black. As it raised itself up, it resembled a giant shadow against the starry sky. Cody's mind raced to make sense of the monster. He'd always imagined swimming next to a blue whale, the biggest animal on earth, over one hundred feet long. The dragon seemed far bigger.

The teens were frozen to the spot. Hearts raced, breath quickened, and none of them knew what to do. The dragon looked at the teens, and then pointed its head to the sky and spit fire straight up to show its power. The flames reached fifty feet in the air.

Elder Ordway said, "Very impressive."

"Thank you, Elder Ordway. I try."

"Can you control it, or merely conjure?" asked the elder.

"Oh yes, I can control it. I could conjure long before this night. But this new power fuels my imagination." He turned to the dragon behind him. "Dragon? Yes, hello there. Would you please take these children for a little ride? Then return here. Then, you may eat them. Thank you."

The dragon obeyed. Before anyone could react, the beast had grabbed all four. Lucas, Katie in one talon, Cody and Ariana in the other. All of them screamed as it went up into the night. The dragon flew high, flapping its wings, shooting straight up. It felt like they were shooting up in a rocket, the earth moving away from them in a blur.

This was no safe roller coaster. They held tight to the talons. The dragon stopped suddenly. Their stomachs lurched at the change in velocity. It hovered, flapping its wings just as the moon appeared through the swift moving clouds.

They could see the entire coastline for miles, the moon reflected on the thrashing waves. Then they saw something coming toward them. The dragon saw it too, and let out a blast of flames right at Zacke and John.

John yelled, "Left. Now!"

Zacke obliged and the flames missed.

John was tied to Zacke's chest, a rope under their arms.

"We're coming closer," John shouted, "Katie, put a shield around all of us when we're close enough."

"You're coming *toward* the dragon?" shouted Ariana.

"Won't he disappear in a few minutes?" asked Lucas.

John said, "Not with Derek's new power. He may be able to keep the dragon around long enough to eat us all."

"Great." said Cody.

"Here we come," said John, "Zacke, twenty feet straight ahead."

The dragon was tracking John and Zacke, getting ready to spit flames at them.

John whispered directions to Zacke and they swooped under the beast, right between the two talons. "The strongest shield you've ever done. Now, Katie!"

Katie tried, and a crystal-clear shield appeared as an orb around them. It sliced through the dragon's talons and the beast roared. A gush of dragon's blood covered them as the talons released their grip inside the giant sphere. All of them were secure inside their new bubble. Katie concentrated on her shield. Zacke held them aloft like they were in a bloody snow globe.

The dragon screeched an otherworldly sound, as it flapped its wings to get way from the pain. Zacke's hands were on the inside walls of the orb-shield and couldn't get out of the way when the flames hit them. Thankfully, Katie's shield held. They barely felt the heat. The dragon sprayed fire in all directions, wildly. It then aimed fire down at its own legs, heating the fleshy stumps.

It's cauterizing its own wounds, thought John.

Within a minute, the beast stopped screaming and faded back to wherever it had come. The talons disappeared inside the orb and Ariana looked down and saw the blood had faded too.

"Anyone still taste dragon blood?" asked Cody, a gag reflex kicking in.

"We better land somewhere soon," said Katie, "I can't hold this forever."

Ariana said, "Somewhere safe, please."

"I'm afraid not, guys," said John. "We have to go back to the tower."

"What, why? They'll kill us!" said Cody.

"Two reasons. We have to end Sazzo," John pointed down, "and we have to help your dad, Cody."

"What? Where is...?" Then Cody looked at the tower and saw his dad climbing over the edge of the roof, up a rappel line used for training. David was behind the elder and Derek, who were looking at the spectacle in the sky. Cody had noticed the metal rings all over the tower, and the one rappel rope. His dad had bravely climbed the tower to destroy his tormentor.

"We can't. We're not ready," said Ariana. "John, we can't do it."

"Yes, you are," said John. "Zacke, take us down."

John instructed Zacke which direction to fly, his vision still compromised from the pepper spray.

"David was right," John said, "One thing we can do that they can't, is link together."

Katie asked, "Are we Power Rangers again?"

"You said that would kill us all," Zacke said.

"Yes, but we have someone special. We have a hub that can link us all." John looked into Ariana's eyes, "You are the hub. I should have seen it before when you could see Katie's shields. How you became other people's thoughts, instead of hearing them. All of you, open your minds, think of each other. All five of you can act as one."

"I don't understand," said Ariana.

"When you were on the roof, I heard you call for help in your mind. You are the lynchpin to this breakout. With your strength, you can link us all together. Imagine each mind, concentrate on each person, and then take them all into your mind and link us together."

As they floated closer to the tower, Ariana shut out the fear and closed her eyes. She thought of each of her new friends one by one, trying to flow into their minds.

Nothing happened.

Then, she thought of her own mind's silver jewelry box. She opened it. Ariana imagined a chain. Then other images popped into her mind...

A metal sphere
A small metal suitcase
A treasure chest
A closed door
A metal cabinet

Ariana imagined the chain running through all of them, linking them together.

Then, she flung them all wide open.

CHAPTER THIRTY THREE
FIGHT

David ran at Derek and Ordway. Their backs were still turned to him, watching their opponents float toward the tower.

David slashed downward. The elder pushed Derek with her power. He was thrown to the floor of the roof. At the same time, she bent low, and raised her hand, lifting David like a rag doll ten feet upward, and flung him. He smashed down on the far side of the flat concrete roof.

David hit with a thud. The relic sword clanged off the edge of the roof, lost. The others landed near David. Katie's shield faded as they touched down.

Derek got back on his feet. He and the elder calmly walked toward them.

Cody got David to his feet, and they all gathered on the far side of the roof, as the elder and Derek came closer. John instructed, "Everyone, close your eyes."

It was crazy to close your eyes when people were about to kill you, but they did. As hard as it was to concentrate, they all felt an immediate calm overtake them.

Ariana was in their minds, and they all felt a strange connection. The sensation was new, but somehow comforting.

Their minds cleared, and they all perceived something swell inside them. Everyone felt like more than themselves. In their minds, it wasn't voices they heard, but the essence of each of them was now one. It was like their cores were linked.

Seeing their eyes closed, the elder lost her cool demeanor, feeling an ancient dread rise in the pit of her stomach. She quickened the pace, "Attack! They're linking."

Derek's arrogance evaporated, and he and the elder ran at them.

The Amartus group opened their eyes and energy exploded within them. They all felt the talents of the others, as though they'd had them their entire lives, for many lives.

John smiled. He turned to face the two enemies, knowing this was the first real chance of beating them. Elder Ordway was fast. Her eyes flared blue.

David flew off his feet, over the edge, and off the tower.

"No!" shouted Cody. Lightning erupted from the sky, straight for the Elder. Cody felt David's talent erupting inside him. Ordway deflected the bolts, but just barely.

"Go get him!" shouted Zacke to Cody.

"What?" yelled Cody, then he felt Zacke's talent inside him. Cody launched into the sky. He dove for David, fearing his father had not felt the surge of new talents; he may not have realized he could save himself.

The others took flight to the dismay of the two enemies. Energy of all types flashed back and forth. Fire, water, lightning, shields turned into balls of energy. Derek and Ordway were on the roof, blocking and ducking, as the five of them: Zacke, John, Katie, Lucas, and Ariana buzzed around them, like angry hornets with supernatural talents.

Derek was fighting Ariana. He realized that he was simultaneously fighting all of them. His focus on her let Zacke swoop in from behind and take him into the air by his left arm. Derek growled with rage.

Katie did the same thing with the surprised elder, lifting her up by a leg and taking flight. Ordway hit her head on the concrete as she was taken upside down. A gash appeared, and she was too dizzy to throw magic for a few seconds.

Zacke flung Derek into open air.

Derek was caught by Ariana, and then flung again. They didn't need to speak to each other. In their minds, they all knew the two enemies had to be kept off balance. Their enemy couldn't be allowed to focus their powers on any individual.

They threw them up, then one by one they swooped by and punched Derek and the elder. Then they were flipped again, only to be hit with another barrage of punches.

After being flung from John's grip, Elder Ordway's head had cleared and she'd had enough. Before she could be punched again, she opened a square blue gate in front of her and vanished. The blue lines of the gate winked from existence.

As Derek tumbled back to Ariana, he saw the elder disappear, and shouted, "Coward!"

Ariana caught, then flung Derek back to John. Derek focused. He managed to get his relic knife out, the very knife he'd used on his own Elder. When he was close enough, he sliced John's arm.

John caught Derek, made a grunt of pain and knocked the knife out of his hand. It fell to the tower roof. He threw Derek to Zacke.

"John, are you okay?" asked Lucas.

"I'll be fine. Let's end this," said John.

Then David's voice rang out, "Over here!"

Zacke smiled. Derek tried to twist his body to see who it was, but Zacke took his arm and spun in a circle, then launched Derek like a Frisbee.

Derek tumbled around and around and finally hit something that stopped him for good. There was a terrible pain in his stomach, and he was surprised to be face to face with David, who floated next to his son Cody. The terrible pain, he saw, was the relic sword. It went all the way through, and stuck out his back.

Derek tried to look down, and managed, "Witness... is that...?"

"The relic sword, yes. My name is David. Goodbye forever."

Derek's face twisted in fury as dozens of lifetimes came to an end. David tipped the sword down, and the body slid off the blade.

The ancient foe tumbled to the ground a hundred feet below, landing next to the base of the tower.

They all landed on the fire tower roof. As the adrenaline faded, the first waves of shock sank in. They sat on the roof in a rough circle. A few shook like it was cold, others cried freely. The emotional and physical fight took its toll on all of them.

The group heard sirens far in the distance, knowing they were headed their way. They had little time to come up with a story.

After a quick, decisive discussion, one version of events was agreed upon. John repeated it aloud so they could let it sink into their minds, "You were kidnapped before the dance. You fought back in the car, and were almost out of town when the two men lost control and had to pull over. You all jumped out, and ran for the tower. The two men subdued the two student guards. Zacke broke away from the group while the others ran up the tower. He tried to stop the men with the fire systems, but was unsuccessful. On his way to help them at the tower, one man chased him into the flood tunnels and had his fatal accident. Just deny seeing elder Ordway at all. There are no cameras on the roof, so no one could prove anything that happened up here. Zacke, you're sure Lucas' ground fight happened in a camera blind-spot?"

"Pretty sure," said Zacke. "We got lucky there."

John continued, "Then you all made it to the roof and tried to subdue the second man, who accidentally fell from the tower. An autopsy might find the sword wound, but from that fall, probably not. One of the boy guards didn't see us subdue him. The other one who pepper sprayed Zacke, will be a problem."

"I'll take care of Billy." Lucas said with steel in his voice.

"The story is flimsy. You all need to tell the same version. It will be five against Billy's version," said John.

David knew what John was going to say next.

"The only thing that we can't explain is David and I. We had to be caught on camera somewhere. If we don't disappear, the questions will be too hard to answer."

David finished the thought, "If we vanish, the authorities are more likely to believe your story."

"No! There's... there's got to be another way. Dad, I just found you," said Cody.

David hugged his son. "I know. But we must leave, Cody. The story is shaky enough. I'll come back. I promise."

"So will I," said John. "But quietly, when all of you have made your decisions about whether to continue the fight."

Lucas asked, "What about your wound? Doesn't that mean you won't move on to the next body?"

John nodded, "Yes. It means this is my last body. I'll age like everyone else. If I don't get myself killed, that is. Then all the lives I've lived will come to an end."

"That's sad," said Ariana.

"Not really," said John. "I've lived enough. Memories going back... well, too long. I have a lot left to do in this life. It will be nice to know it will end, eventually."

The sirens had reached the campus perimeter and people were headed their way.

John said, "The link is fading, but David and I should be able to get off this tower and away well enough. We will see each other again."

Emotional goodbyes were said. John and David flew off.

The police questions were endless. They knew there would be trouble with Billy, the only one who saw strange things happen. It was highly unlikely that anyone would believe him. The police did seem to eventually believe the five of them. They were all seen as victims.

School wouldn't start until Monday. That gave them Sunday to tell their stories to family and friends. It felt strange to disconnect with each other, like they'd always been so intimately linked. But they would always be bound by their shared experiences.

There would be a lot to decide for the five new friends.

* * *

Sunday morning, Lucas went to see Billy.

Billy's mother answered the door, "Lucas, isn't it? It's so nice to see you. Want to come inside? Billy's in his room. What a crazy week. I still think Billy is confused. I'm so sorry to hear what happened to you. Kidnapping? Men with guns? It's all over the internet. You're a local celebrity."

Lucas tried to act casual, like he wasn't on enemy territory. He smiled at Billy's mom. "Thanks. Yeah, it was scary up there. Is that his room?"

"Oh, sorry. Yes, have fun." she motioned to Billy's room and thought to herself that Lucas looked a lot older than his fifteen years. She walked into her garden wondering why Billy and Lucas hadn't been closer friends.

Lucas thought about Billy's mom. *Does she not know that I was one of Billy's victims?* She probably had no idea what Billy was like to the outside world.

Lucas' parents had wanted to talk with Billy's parents, especially after the suicide attempt. Lucas wouldn't let them. He didn't want to give his bully the satisfaction of saying he had whined to his parents.

He thought about just opening the bedroom door, but that's something Billy might do. He knocked.

"Come in," said Billy.

Lucas opened the door to Billy's room. The bully he'd hated for so long, the monster of his childhood, had a bedroom that looked much like his own room. Star Wars poster, a band poster featuring musicians that he listened to. They might have been friends. Billy had chosen a different path.

Ear buds in, Billy laid back on his bed, laptop open. He glanced up, saw Lucas. Lucas closed the door firmly, and stood there as Billy slipped off his ear buds. Billy rose slowly from his bed. His posture wasn't the swaggering bully, but he wasn't scared either.

"They're calling me a liar."

"I know," said Lucas.

"You and your little friends are the liars, Lucasfi..." the look in Lucas's eyes stopped Billy. He continued, "They're probably going to kick me out of the Explorers if I keep telling the truth."

Lucas said, "What you say is up to you."

"You're not here to change my mind?"

"No." Lucas said, "I'm here to say I forgive you."

Billy blinked in surprise, then his face reddened, "What? What the fu...?"

Lucas stepped up to Billy, still a few inches shorter, but Billy flinched anyway.

Lucas clarified, "I forgive you because I can't hold onto this anger anymore. I'm done with it."

"You? Angry at me?" Billy tried to smirk, but found he couldn't. He was sweating. "Why, because I hurt your feelings? Because you got pushed around a little? Man up."

He almost told him that he'd tried to kill himself, in part, because all the years of fear. But he didn't.

Billy had not earned the right to know that.

Lucas smiled, feeling the relief of forgiveness. "I'm calling a permanent truce," he said, and extended his hand to Billy.

He looked at the hand, back to Lucas, "We'll see about that." Billy took Lucas' hand.

Billy's face changed when Lucas squeezed. Billy didn't cry out, but slowly shrank until he was sitting on his bed again. Lucas stopped the pressure to his hand just before he broke a bone. He didn't stoop down to Billy, just stood tall.

Lucas hadn't let go of his former bully's hand, "Billy, it wasn't a request. I'm putting you out of business. Stop being a dick. If you ever give a funny look to *anyone* at school, I will come for you in the night. They will never find your body."

Shock mixed with fear covered Billy's face. Lucas kept firm pressure on the hand.

"Do you understand?" asked Lucas calmly.

"Yes," Billy said through gritted teeth.

"Say it."

Billy closed his eyes. "I understand."

"Good."

Lucas released Billy's hand, knowing it would be sore for days. He didn't look back to his former bully. He just left.

Outside, the sun hit his face and he felt years of wasted hate fall from him.

There would be many trials ahead, but he had four other people who understood him like no one else ever could.

Whatever they faced, they would do it together.

AUTHOR NOTE

Some people ask why I didn't use a real city in California. Many of the landmarks I write about are very much like real places, but the names and details have been changed. I didn't want to be tied down to all the physics of real life – how many miles away was that beach? how big was that Spanish Mission Church? What's the actual population of that town?

This is a love letter to a special place, but my version of it. I embellished heavily and didn't want the tap on the shoulder, "Umm, Mr. Sewall, the camera system doesn't work that way." It works that way in my story. It's a fantasy. Hopefully a fun, awesome, exciting fantasy. I think it's okay to make real places fantastical.

If you liked, or even better, loved this book please leave a review on Amazon.com or Goodreads.com (or anywhere else you can tell the world how amazing the book was). If you hate my stories, you can always yell and throw things at me at mjsewall.com

Thanks for taking the ride.

M J Sewall,
October 2016

THANKS
AND
ACKNOWLEDGEMENTS

To everyone that helped me with this weird little story, thank you. But especially:

My wonderful editors, Mindy T. Conde and Natalie McDermott. You continue to amaze.

Aidan McCalister, Alyssa Shultz, Anna Chastain, Brian Dillard, Carol Weible, Chelsea McKinney, Danielle O'Brien, Ellen Hecht, Emma Chastain, Fiona Jayde, Hillary Frye, Irene Getchel, Janet Wallace, Jason Flint, Jenna Elizabeth Johnson, Jennifer Honey Moore, Lea Shultz, Mandy Griffith, Michele Casteel, Nellie Sewall, Preston Frye, Robert Lee, Rose Torres, Ryne Torres

AUTHOR BIOGRAPHY

M J Sewall lives on the spectacular Central California Coast. Spoiled, soft in the middle and not as smart as some people think, he generally keeps to himself. He can be seen at locally eateries and book stores. Not a joiner in general, he avoids most gatherings of people; especially if they are talking politics.

Always eager to talk about story in all forms, feel free to contact the author anytime.

Especially if you like his books.

For more information, please visit mjsewall.com

M.J. Sewall's page in Next Chapter Publishing
https://www.nextchapter.pub/authors/mj-sewall-fantasy-author-california

Forever Warriors
ISBN: 978-4-86745-468-8

Published by
Next Chapter
1-60-20 Minami-Otsuka
170-0005 Toshima-Ku, Tokyo
+818035793528
30th April 2021

Lightning Source UK Ltd.
Milton Keynes UK
UKHW012207110521
383564UK00001B/81

9 784867 454688